# JACOB THE LIAR

# JUREK BECKER

# JACOB THE LIAR

Translated and with a Preface
by Melvin Kornfeld

New York and London

A HELEN AND KURT WOLFF BOOK

HARCOURT BRACE JOVANOVICH

Library of Congress Cataloging in Publication Data

Becker, Jurek, 1937–
  Jacob the liar.

  Translation of Jakob der Lügner.
  "A Helen and Kurt Wolff book."
  I.  Title.
PZ4.B3952Jac3  [PZ2662.E294]    833'.9'14    75–19184
ISBN  0–15–145975–4

First edition
B C D E

# PREFACE

A Yiddish proverb defines a naïve person as someone who expects logic from history. That expectation, however, provides the mentality of so much Yiddish literature: the belief in the triumph of justice, divine purpose, and reason. Only thus can all the suffering and destruction be made comprehensible and, perhaps, bearable. If the reality should prove otherwise, if the actual course of events does not permit a logical forbearance and an affirmation of logic, then it would be necessary to change logic so that history would better reflect that hope for divine purpose and reason.

Sholem Aleichem's story *Dreyfus in Kasrilevka* exemplifies the implacable belief of an entire community in justice, even when newspaper reports indicate the contrary. Eventually, the community's insistence that the newspaper lies when it reports Dreyfus was found guilty is vindicated. Dreyfus is freed. The narrator asks, "Who was right?" The narrator is simultaneously both mocking such a naïve stance and agreeing with the naïve principle of abstract justice. The tension between the two gives the story its humor.

The Yiddish storyteller Sholem Aleichem has found a worthy descendant in Jurek Becker. Born in Lodz, Poland, in 1937, Becker survived the German occupation and concentration camps and grew up a German in the German Democratic Republic. His first novel, *Jakob der Lügner,* was published there in 1969 and may be termed what has now become known as "holocaust literature," a documentation of reminiscence by survivors of life under German occupation between 1939 and 1945. That literature up to now seems not to have captured what Becker has done in German, that quintessential dilemma of Yiddish-speaking Jews.

Becker's nameless narrator, a survivor of an entire *shtetl* sent off to the extermination camp, has eschewed strident tones and conveys his story through understatement and irony. Lament and accusation are avoided. The horror is often conveyed parenthetically. Neither aggressive nor angry, the novel is astonishingly gentle, while Becker's composure has nothing in common with lukewarm reconciliation.

Sholem Aleichem's narrators repeat events to the other *shtetl* members, thereby making the experience of having lived through those events more bearable by sharing them. Becker's narrator no longer has a community of Jews to tell his tale to. He has survived within a culture foreign to his pre-war life. It is Germans to whom he talks himself out. He mixes up events and invents details in telling of his lost community. His survival is all the more difficult because the community solidarity is lacking along with the logic of his survival.

Becker, like Sholem Aleichem, makes use of two narratives, the past story itself and its present telling or unburdening by the narrator. The effect is one of reliving the fate of his community while providing for himself some overview and distance from those events. Becker's narrator, recognizing the impossibility of understanding his survival, admits "my caprice has no limits." He can permit his imagination but not his reality to spin off happy endings for his community. The tension between his necessarily naïve belief in logic and the realization that the belief is and was naïve leads to the irony in the novel, as it does in the stories of Sholem Aleichem.

In order to survive, Sholem Aleichem's characters accept compromise. Such compromise does not exist for

Becker's characters, since choice is taken from them. While a good-natured humor flows from a situation of compromise in the former, the humor in the latter hovers on the edge of despair. Jacob's lie, because it is life-giving, is in constant need of replenishment in order to make it viable. That search provides the basis for most of the novel's desperate humor. Jacob, having once raised the Jews' hope, can no longer play a neutral role. Either he actively continues and embellishes his lie, in which case he risks raising false hopes and wretched disillusionment, or he abrogates his life-giving role and accepts the Jews' anger and despair. He decides finally to get rid of the Jews. That is, he tries to have nothing to do with them—unsuccessfully.

The possibility for meaningful action is extremely meager in the ghetto setting here described. Only in the fairy tales from Jacob's childhood do possibilities exist for salvation. In a like manner does the narrator, through his narration, establish the possibility of finding meaning for himself and for his lost *shtetl*.

Melvin Kornfeld

## WRITTEN IN PENCIL
## IN THE SEALED RAILWAY CAR

here in this carload
i am eve
with abel my son
if you see my other son
cain son of man
tell him i

—Dan Pagis
(translated from the Hebrew by Stephen Mitchell)
*Present Tense,* Summer 1974, p. 54.

In serene souls there is no wit. Wit indicates a disturbed equilibrium. It is the result of a disturbance and at the same time the means of regaining balance. . . . The situation of the dissolution of all relationships, despair, or spiritual death, is the most frightfully witty of all.
    —Novalis

# JACOB THE LIAR

# I can still hear them saying: A tree,

what's so special about that? At best, a trunk, leaves, roots, insects in the bark, and a respectably shaped top. So what? I hear them saying, Don't you have anything better to think about, to cheer up your expression—like that of a hungry goat who sees a nice, juicy bunch of grass? Or do you mean, maybe, a special tree, a particular one that, for all I know, possibly gave its name to a battle like the Battle of Stony Pine? Is that the kind you mean? Or was someone special hanged on it? Wrong? Not even hanged?

All right, it's probably senseless, but if you think it's so much fun, let's play this silly game a bit longer, just as you wish. Do you mean maybe that gentle sound that people call "rustling," when the wind discovers your tree; when, so to speak, it "turns over a new leaf"? Or the amount of commercial lumber in such a log? Or do you mean the well-known shade it provides? Why if it's a question of shade, then, strangely, everybody thinks of trees, although houses or blast furnaces provide far greater shade. Do you mean its shade?

All wrong, I'd say then, you can stop guessing. You'll never guess. I mean none of that, although its heating value should not be underestimated. I mean quite simply a tree. I've got my reasons for it. First of all, in my life trees have played a certain role that maybe I'm overestimating. But I find it so. At the age of nine, I fell from a tree, an apple tree, and broke my left hand. Everything mended more or less, but there are a few difficult move-

3

ments since then that I haven't been able to do with the fingers of my left hand. I mention that because it was taken for granted I was to become a violinist. But that's not important. First my mother wanted it, then my father, too, and then finally all three of us. But no violinist.

A few years later—I was about seventeen—I was lying with a girl for the first time in my life. Under a tree. This time it was a beech tree, a good fifteen meters high. The girl's name was Esther—no, I think, Moira. Anyway, it was a beech and a wild boar interrupted us. Maybe, there were even several—we didn't have time to turn around. And a few years later my wife Chana was shot to death under a tree. I can't say what kind of a tree it was. I wasn't there. They merely told me and I forgot to ask about the tree.

And now the second reason why my eyes light up whenever I think of this tree—probably, or certainly, the more important of the two reasons. In this ghetto, you see, trees are forbidden. (Regulation #31: "It is strictly forbidden to maintain ornamental and produce plants of any sort in the ghetto area. The same for trees. Should any wild plants be overlooked in setting up the ghetto, they are to be immediately removed. Violations will be . . .").

Hardtloff devised that; the devil knows why. Probably because of the birds. In addition, a thousand other things are forbidden. Rings and similar valuables, pets, being on the street after eight o'clock. It wouldn't make sense to name them all. I can imagine what would happen to anyone seen on the street after eight, with a ring on his finger, walking his dog. But no, I can't imagine that at all. I don't think at all of rings, dogs, or the time. I think only of this tree and my eyes light up. I can understand everything. I mean, theoretically, I can conceive of it. You are Jews, you are less than dirt. What do you need rings for? And what do you have to be around on the street after eight for?

4

We plan this and that with you and want to do it thus and so. I can appreciate that. I cry over it. I'd kill them all, if I could. I would wring Hardtloff's neck with my left hand whose fingers can't do any difficult movements any more. But I do think about it. Why do they forbid us the trees?

I've tried a thousand times already to forget this damned story, always in vain. Either it wasn't the right people to whom I wanted to tell it, or I've made some mistakes. I've mixed up a whole lot. I've confused the names. Or, as I said, it wasn't the right people. Every time I've had a few drinks, it's there. I can't help it. I shouldn't drink so much. Each time, I think, these will be the right people and I think I've got everything quite straight. Nothing more can happen to me in telling it.

When you look at him, Jacob doesn't remind you in any way of a tree. There really are such men of whom it can be said, that fellow is like a tree: big, strong, mighty. Such people you might even like to lean against for a few minutes each day. Jacob is much smaller. He resembles such a fellow up to his shoulders—at best. He's afraid, like all of us. He's really no different from Kirschbaum, or Frankfurter, or me, or Kowalski. The only difference between him and all of us is that without him this goddamned story couldn't have happened. But here, too, there may be a difference of opinion.

Well . . . it's evening. Don't ask me the exact time. Only the Germans know that. We have no watches. It's been dark now for a while. In a few windows the lights are on. That'll have to do. Jacob is in a hurry. He doesn't have much time left. It's been dark for quite some time. And suddenly, he doesn't have any time left at all. Not even half a second, because all around him things suddenly light up. It happens right in the middle of Kurländischendamm, at the edge of the ghetto, where the women's fashion shops used to be. There's the sentry five meters above Jacob, on a wooden tower behind barbed wire strung diagonally across the avenue. He says nothing at first. He just fixes the searchlight on Jacob in the middle of the avenue and waits. On the left corner is the former shop of Mariutan, an emigrant from Rumania, who had since had to return there to tend to the interests of his native land at the war front. On the right is the former shop of Tintenfass, a local Jew, who is now in Brooklyn, New York, still sewing made-to-order dresses. And meanwhile, Jacob Heym, alone with his fear, is standing on the cobbled street, too old for such a test of his nerves. He snatches his cap from his head, can't make out anything in the light, and knows only that somewhere in this brightness are two eyes of a soldier that discovered him. Jacob quickly thinks of his most obvious oversights and none occur to him. His identity card is with him; he hasn't been absent from work; the star on his chest is exactly on the prescribed spot. Once again he examines it; the one on his back he sewed on just two days ago. If the man doesn't shoot right away, Jacob can answer all the questions to his satisfaction.

"Am I wrong, or is it forbidden to be on the street after eight?" says the soldier finally. One of the nice kind, his voice doesn't even sound angry, but rather gentle. You might even wish to chat a bit, if it weren't so serious.

"It's forbidden," says Jacob.

"And what time is it now?"

"I don't know."

"But you should know," says the soldier.

Jacob could now reply "That's true"; or he could ask "How?"; or "How late is it?"; or he could be silent and wait. He decides on that since that seems the most expedient.

"Well, do you know what that house over there is?" asks

the soldier, after he had decided his partner wasn't the proper man to keep a conversation going. Jacob knows. He hadn't seen where the soldier's head indicated or where his finger pointed. He sees only the glaring searchlight. Behind it are many houses, but at this moment it can mean only one.

"The police station," says Jacob.

"Well, you go right inside. You report to the officer on duty and tell him that you've been on the street after eight and ask for the proper punishment."

The station house. Jacob doesn't know very much about this house. He knows that some sort of a German administration is there. At least, that's what people say. What is administered there—nothing is known about that. He knows that the revenue office used to be there, that there are two exits: one in front and one leading into the ghetto. And he especially knows that a Jew's chances of coming out alive from this house are very slight. Up to today, no such case is known.

"Anything wrong?" asks the soldier.

"No."

Jacob turns around and goes. The searchlight accompanies him, drawing his attention to the uneven spots in the paving, letting the shadow become longer and longer, reaching the heavy iron door with the little round peephole, and getting bigger there, even though Jacob still has many steps to go.

"And what are you going to ask for?" asks the soldier.

Jacob stops, turns around patiently, and answers: "For the proper punishment."

He doesn't shout. Only uncontrolled or disrespectful people shout. Neither does he reply too quietly, otherwise the man in the light would not understand him clearly at that distance. He makes the effort to get just the right tone. It must be noted that he knows what to ask for. It's simply necessary to ask him. Jacob opens the door, quickly closing it again between himself and the searchlight, and looks at the long, empty corridor. He used to come here often. Just to the left of the door there used to be a little table behind which sat a petty official—Herr Kominek—for as long as Jacob could remember, who always asked all those entering, "Can we help you?"

"I'd like to pay my semi-annual taxes, Herr Kominek," Jacob used to say. Kominek would act as if he had never seen Jacob, although from October to the end of April he frequented Jacob's café almost every week and ate potato pancakes there. "Occupation?" Kominek would ask. "Small business," Jacob used to say. He didn't in the least show his irritation. Kominek used to eat at least four pancakes every time, and sometimes even brought his wife along.

"Name?" Kominek asked then.

"Heym. Jacob Heym."

"Initials F to K, room sixteen."

But whenever Kominek came to his café, he didn't order pancakes, but said, "Same as always." Because he was a regular customer.

At the spot where the table formerly stood there is no longer any table; but there where its legs used to be, four indentations can still be seen on the floor. The chair, however, didn't leave any marks, probably because it didn't stand constantly in the same spot as did the table.

Jacob leans against the door to rest a bit. The last few minutes weren't easy—but no matter. The smell in this house is different, somehow better. The stink of ammonia that was formerly noticeable in the corridor has disappeared. Somehow it smells more civil. A bit of leather in the air, an odor of women, coffee, and a breath of perfume. At the very end of the corridor a door is opened. A woman in a green dress comes out, walks a few steps—

8

she has nicely shaped legs—and goes into another room. Two doors are open. She can be heard laughing. She comes out of the room again and goes back. The doors are closed again. The corridor is once more empty. Jacob is still leaning on the iron door. He wants to go out. Maybe the searchlight isn't waiting for him any more. Maybe it has searched out something new. But maybe it's still waiting. It is hardly likely that it's no longer waiting. The soldier's last question sounded so final.

Jacob enters the vestibule. On the door only numbers are written, not who is sitting behind them. The officer on duty probably has the room of the former director of revenue. But that's not certain and it's not a good idea to knock on the wrong door. What do you want—information? Did you hear that? He wants some information. We're planning this and that with him and he just comes in and wants information.

Behind Number 15—formerly Small Business, initials A to E—Jacob hears sounds. He puts his ear to the door, tries to hear, can't understand anything, only single words that don't make sense. But even if the wood were thinner, he still wouldn't get much out of it, since no one is talking to anyone in charge. Suddenly the door opens. Just his luck, room fifteen! But fortunately the doors here open out, so that the person who comes out doesn't see Jacob, since the door hides him. And, fortunately, the person leaves the door open. He'll come right back. When you think you're alone you leave the door open. And Jacob has his cover. Inside a radio is playing, there's some static. Surely one of their "People's Radios," but no music. Since he has been in the ghetto Jacob hasn't heard any music. None of us has. Only when someone sang. The announcer is reporting unimportant things from headquarters. Somebody has been promoted posthumously to lieutenant colonel. Then something about guaranteed public assistance

9

for all. And then this report which has just come in: "In a sharp, defensive battle, our heroic fighting men succeeded in bringing the Bolshevik attack to a halt twenty kilometers from Bezanika. In the course of hostilities, our side. . . ." Then this person is in his room again, closes the door, and the wood is too thick. Jacob stands still; he has heard a lot. Bezanika isn't very far, not a stone's throw to be sure, but not so terribly far either. He hasn't ever been there, but has heard something or other about Bezanika. It's a very small town and if you take the train through Mielo-worno southeasterly through the market town of Pry, where his grandfather (on his mother's side) had a drugstore, and transfer to Kostavka, then you'll get to Bezanika somewhere along the way. Maybe a good four hundred kilometers, maybe even five hundred, not more, hopefully. So, they're there now! A "goner" heard the good news and is happy. He would even be happier, but for the circumstances: the officer on duty is waiting for him and Jacob must continue.

The next step is the most difficult. Jacob tries, but in vain. His sleeve is caught in the door crack. The person who came back into the room has caught him without the slightest malicious intent. He simply closed the door behind him and Jacob was caught. Carefully he tugs. The door is well made; it fits exactly. No superfluous gaps! Not even a sheet of paper could slip through. Jacob could cut off that piece of sleeve. His knife is at home with his teeth, half of which are missing. Useless. He hits upon the thought of taking off his jacket. Simply take it off and leave it caught there! What does he need a jacket for now?

Already he has slipped out of one sleeve, when it occurs to him that he does need his jacket. Not for next winter, if he's still here. No fear of the next frost. The jacket will be needed for the officer on duty, if he can be located. Yes, for the officer on duty—who, to be sure, can bear the sight of a Jew without a jacket—Jacob's shirt is clean and almost devoid of patches—but hardly the sight of a Jew without a star on his chest and back (Regulation #1). Last summer the stars were on his shirt; traces of the stitches could still be seen. But no longer—now they are on his jacket. So he puts his jacket on again, trusts to his stars, and tugs harder. A few millimeters, but not enough.

The situation is, as they say, desperate. He pulls with all his might. Something rips. That makes a noise and the door opens. Jacob falls down. Above him is an astonished man in civilian dress. He laughs, then once again becomes serious. What is Jacob doing here? Jacob gets up and chooses his words very carefully. It wasn't that he was on the street after eight—no—the sentry who stopped him had said that it was already eight and that he should report here to the officer on duty.

"And now you're eavesdropping here?"

"I wasn't eavesdropping. I've never been here and didn't know which room to go to. So I was just about to knock here." The man stops his questioning. He nods toward the end of the corridor. Jacob walks on ahead of him, until the man says, "Here." It's not the revenue director's room. Jacob looks at the man, then knocks. The man leaves; but from inside, no answer. "Go in," says the man and disappears into his room just as Jacob presses the latch.

In the room of the officer on duty he remains standing at the door. Since discovered by the searchlight, he hasn't put his cap back on his head. The officer on duty is quite a young man, at most thirty years old. He has dark brown, almost black, wavy hair. He's in his shirt sleeves. His rank is not noticeable since his jacket is hanging on a hook on the wall, its shoulder emblems hidden. His leather belt and revolver are hanging over his jacket. That's somehow illogical, for they should be under his jacket. The belt is usually removed first and then the jacket. But there it is—

hanging on top. The officer is lying on a black leather sofa and sleeping. Jacob believes he's sleeping deeply. He's heard many people sleeping and has an ear for it. He's not snoring but breathing deeply and evenly. Jacob has to somehow let him know he's here. Usually you clear your throat, but that won't do. That's done when visiting good friends. That is, when visiting a very good friend, you don't clear your throat either. You simply say, "Get up, Solomon, I'm here," or you just tap him on the shoulder. But clearing the throat is still improper. It's about halfway between here and Solomon.

Jacob is about to knock on the door, but drops his hand. On the desk he sees a clock, its back to him. He has to know what time it is. Nothing is so important to know now. The clock shows 7:36. He walks quietly back to the door. They've played a joke on you. Not them but that one behind the searchlight. He played a joke on you. And you fell for it.

Jacob still has twenty-four minutes and, to be fair about it, really twenty-four minutes plus the time he has been here. He still doesn't knock. He recognizes the black leather sofa the officer is sleeping on. He had sat on it himself. It belonged to Rettig, the broker, one of the richest men in town. In the fall of '35 Jacob borrowed money from him, at twenty-percent interest, when the whole summer had been so cool that ice cream would hardly sell. His income was worse than ever; not even his famous raspberry ice cream had sold. Jacob was forced to begin with his pancakes as early as August, but didn't have the cash for the potatoes and had to borrow. And it was on this sofa he sat in February '36 when he repaid Rettig the loan. It stood in his anteroom. Jacob sat for an hour on it and waited for Rettig. He had even thought about the waste. Two coats or three jackets—easily—could have been made from the leather. In the anteroom yet!

The officer on duty turns over on his side, smacks his lips a few times. A lighter slides out of his trousers pocket and falls to the floor. Jacob must wake him now, by all means. It wouldn't be good if he woke up without Jacob waking him. He knocks inside on the door. The officer says, "Yes?" stirs, and sleeps on. Jacob knocks again. How can you sleep so soundly? He knocks hard. The officer sits up before he's really awake, rubs his eyes, and asks, "What time is it?"

"It's several minutes after seven-thirty," says Jacob.

Finished rubbing his eyes, the officer now sees Jacob, rubs his eyes once more, and doesn't know whether to be angry or laugh. Nothing like that has ever happened to him. Nobody'll believe him. He stands up, takes his belt off the hook, puts on his jacket and his belt. He sits down behind the desk and leans back, stretching out both arms.

"To what do I owe this pleasure?"

Jacob is about to answer. He can't. His mouth is so dry. So that's what the officer on duty looks like.

"No false modesty now," says the officer, "out with it. What's the hurry?"

A little saliva gathers in his mouth. A friendly person. Maybe he's new here. Maybe he doesn't even know the bad reputation of the house. For a moment it occurs to Jacob that he miscalculated the distance. Maybe Bezanika isn't so far after all. Probably not even three hundred kilometers, even appreciably less. Perhaps the clever man is afraid and is taking precautions for the future. There must be a rational explanation for everything. But then it occurs to him that the report just reached the announcer. The officer was sleeping and could not have heard it yet. On the other hand, it may be advantageous that he didn't hear the news since it was reported that the Russians were stopped, their advance successfully stopped. Maybe he's thinking that they're getting closer and closer. Jacob thinks too long. The officer is getting impatient and that's not good, for wrinkles are forming on his brow.

"Don't you talk to Germans?"

Of course, Jacob talks to Germans. Why wouldn't he talk to Germans? For heaven's sake, that impression mustn't be given. We're all reasonable people and certainly can talk to one another.

"The sentry in the tower at Kurländische told me to report to you. He said that I was on the street after eight."

The officer looks at the clock standing on the desk in front of him, pushes his sleeve back, and looks at his wrist watch.

"And he didn't say anything else?"

"He said also, I should ask for the proper punishment."

That answer can't do any harm, Jacob thinks. It sounds obedient, captivatingly honest. Anyone with that degree of candor could expect righteous treatment especially since the offense he's been accused of wasn't even committed. Any clock can attest to that.

"What's your name?"

"Heym, Jacob Heym."

The officer on duty takes pencil and paper, writes something, not only the name. He writes more, looks at the clock again—it's getting later and later—writes more, almost half a page, then puts the paper aside. He opens a little box, takes out a cigarette, and searches in his trousers pocket. Jacob goes to the black leather sofa, stoops, picks up the lighter from the floor, and lays it on the desk in front of the officer.

"Thanks."

Jacob goes back to the door. He saw now the clock on the desk indicated past 7:45. The officer lights the cigarette and takes a deep drag. His fingers play with the lighter; he clicks it a few times, letting it snap shut.

"Do you live far from here?" he asks.

"Not even ten minutes."

"Go home."

Is that believable? How many has he already told that to? And have they come out alive? What will he do with his revolver when Jacob turns around? What is out there in the corridor? What will the sentry do when he sees that Jacob evaded his proper punishment? Why should Jacob Heym in particular—this small, unimportant, trembling Jacob Heym with tears in his eyes—be the first Jew to tell what the inside of the police headquarters looks like? As they say, six new Days of Creation are necessary and the chaos has become even greater than it was then.

"Well, out you go. Scram!" says the officer.

The corridor is empty once more. You can almost be sure of that, if you should consider that among the more minor sources of danger. But the door leading to the outside. Did it really make noise before when it was opened? Did it open quietly or did it squeak or creak or scratch? Go notice everything! Impossible! If one only knew before that it would be important later. But what good is "important"? Really! It's completely unimportant whether it opens quietly or not. If it doesn't squeak, you'll open it. And if it does, then maybe Jacob should stay here—at ten minutes to eight?

The latch is carefully depressed. Pity that there is no other word for "carefully." At best, "very carefully" or "infinitely carefully"—all just as far from what is meant. Maybe you can say, open the door quietly. If he hears you, it could cost you your life which has suddenly become so meaningful. He is opening it. And then Jacob is standing outside. How cold it is suddenly. The big square is out in front of you. You feel like crossing it. The searchlight has grown tired of waiting; it's having fun somewhere else; inactive; possibly resting for new adventures. Just keep close to the wall, Jacob. Fine. When you reach the corner of the house, then clench your teeth, and twenty meters straight across the square. If it notices something, it has to weave to and fro and find you, but then the corner is there. A miserable twenty meters.

It's almost exactly twenty meters. I've measured the area: exactly nineteen meters and sixty-seven centimeters. I've been there; the house is still standing, completely undamaged. Only the sentry tower is gone. But I had them show me the exact spot in the middle of Kurländischendamm. Then I paced off the distance. I can estimate a meter quite well. But it wasn't accurate enough for me. I bought a measuring tape, went there again, and measured. The children stared and took me for a big shot. The adults looked on astonished and considered me cracked. A policeman even appeared, asked me for my identity card and what I was measuring there. At any rate, it's exactly nineteen meters and sixty-seven centimeters, that's definite.

The house is at the end. Jacob gets ready for the sprint. Several minutes to eight and twenty meters to be covered. It's as good as certain—and yet . . . Would it be better to be a mouse? A mouse is so unseemly, little, and quiet. And you? According to the regulations you're a louse, a bug. We're all bugs, ridiculously big, despised bugs through a whim of our Creator. And when did a bug ever wish to exchange places with a mouse? Jacob decides not to run. He prefers to slink. That way you have greater control of the sounds. If the searchlight swings into motion you can still hurry up. Halfway across he hears the sentry's voice—don't worry—not directed to him. The sentry says, "Yes, sir." Then he says "yes, sir" once more, and then once again. The only explanation is that he's telephoning. Maybe another sentry, who is also bored, called him up. But he wouldn't say "yes, sir" to him constantly. Out of the question. His superior, giving him orders? Really unimportant. But let's assume the most favorable circumstance: the officer on duty is on the line. What's the matter with you? Have you gone mad? Trying to frighten a poor, innocent Jew so! ("Yes, sir.") Didn't you notice that the man was quite beside himself, that his legs trembled from fear? Don't let it happen to me again, you hear! ("Yes, sir.") At the fourth "yes, sir," he reaches the corner. Let him talk on till he's blue in the face, for Jacob is less than ten minutes away from home.

Jacob shares his room with Josef Piwowa and Nathan Rosenblatt. They only got to know one another here in this room. None can stand the others very much. The crowded conditions and the hunger make for friction. But, for the sake of justice, it must be said that even their first "hello" had been quite formal.

Rosenblatt had died a good year before Jacob's happy homecoming. He had gobbled up a cat that was careless enough to disregard the warning signs on the barbed wire, and one day it lay there in the yard—starved. Rosenblatt was the first to find it and, as mentioned, had gobbled it up. He died from that. Piwowa died only three months ago. His departure from this world had been accompanied by mysterious circumstances. It is known only that he had been shot to death by a supervisor in the shoe factory where he worked. He had become impudent, made remarks that even in normal times are better left unsaid to a supervisor, and consequently, in anger, the man killed him. One theory has it that Piwowa didn't know how to control his temper. He had always been hotheaded and so it had to come to such an end. Others claim that tempers and emotions explained nothing. They say it was rather a question of a quite common, although very cleverly arranged, suicide. Either way, Piwowa had been dead for three months and Rosenblatt for a year at least. Last winter his bed was consumed up the chimney. Piwowa's bed—piece by piece —is still waiting in Jacob's cellar for future cold days.

Fresh replacements of roommates have not arrived yet. The supplies are used up. Whether or not all cats and supervisors are cursed or blessed, in any event, those three didn't like one another.

Rosenblatt, at least, is quiet when he's home. He sits on his bed with his eyes closed and prays. He's the last to go to bed and the first one up, because his debates with God consume great amounts of time. Even after his death he hasn't given up this habit, but at least he's quiet, sitting there silently with his eyes closed, and, at most, chancing a glance now and then.

Piwowa is quarrelsome. He was the last to be billeted but acts as if he were the first one there. Rearranges everything, insists on lying with his feet facing the window. The bread rations have to be hidden from him. To tell the truth, Piwowa worked in the forest previously—as a poacher. His father had been a poacher, too, but Piwowa was an even better one. He was childless.

Well, Jacob comes home. The day was exhausting. He experienced, lived through, survived, trembled, and heard a lot. Brothers, rejoice! Go crazy with joy! The Russians are twenty kilometers from Bezanika, if you know what that means! Open your eyes, Nathan Rosenblatt! Stop quarreling, Piwowa! The Russians are on the way! Don't you understand? Twenty kilometers from Bezanika! However, Rosenblatt is still praying, Piwowa still lying with his feet toward the window. Let them lie there and quarrel and pray and be dead! Jacob is home and may the Russians hurry up!

Let's chat a bit now. Let's chat a bit, as is fitting for a proper story. Grant me this little joy. Without a bit of gossip everything is so wretchedly sad. Just a few words about doubtful memories. A few words about our fleeting life; we'll bake a quick cake with modest ingredients, eat a little piece of it, and push the plate aside again before our appetite turns to something else.

I'm alive, no question about it. I'm alive and no one can compel me to drink and remember trees and Jacob and everything concerning that. On the contrary, I get a small sum so that I can even live it up a little. They tell me you only live once, my friend. Wherever I look there's variety: new, cheerful problems with a little misfortune thrown in. Women still interest me, as do the replanted forests and well-tended graves that on every occasion are so full of fresh flowers; it looks almost wasteful. I don't want to be immodest. Piwowa, whom I had never met, was immodest. Wild game and bread rations had to be hidden from him— but I'm not Piwowa.

Chana, my quarrelsome wife, once said to me, "You're wrong"—almost every sentence to me began that way—"a person is modest when he's happy with what he has a right to. Not with less."

From that point of view, I must be very happy and sometimes even feel blessed. People are friendly and obliging and make an effort to look patient. I can't complain.

Sometimes I say that was the whole story, thank you for having listened. You don't have to prove anything to me.

"I have no intention to. But you must know that I'm twenty-nine. . . ."

"You needn't prove anything at all to me," I repeat.

"Oh, yes I do. When the war was over, I was just . . ."

"Kiss my ass," I say, get up, and leave. Five steps later, I get angry at myself because I was so uncouth, so needlessly insulting, since he meant nothing by that. But I don't turn around. I just walk on. I pay the waiter my check and in leaving look back over my shoulder to the table and notice that he is sitting there, puzzled as to what got into me. I close the door behind me and don't wish to explain it to him.

19

Or I'm lying in bed with Elvira. To explain: I'm forty-six, born in '21. I'm lying in bed with Elvira. We work in a factory. She has the fairest skin I've ever seen. I think we'll get married some day. We're still breathing heavily. We've never yet spoken about it, when she asks me suddenly, "Say, is it really true that you . . ."

The devil knows who told her. I hear the sympathy in her voice and get crazy. I go to the bathroom, sit down in the tub, and begin to sing, so that I won't do what I know —after five steps—I'll feel sorry about. When I return after a half hour, she asks me astonished, what was wrong so suddenly. I say, "Nothing," give her a kiss, turn out the light, and try to fall asleep.

The entire city is in rural surroundings. The area is splendid. The parks are well cared for. Every tree brings forth memories and I make liberal use of them. But when any tree looks me in the eyes, to see whether they light up, then I must disappoint it, for it's not that one.

Jacob tells it to Misha. It isn't that he went to the freight station with the intention of telling just anyone about it; nor is it any less likely that he planned to tell no one about it. He simply went to the railroad station without intentions. He knew it would be difficult to keep the news to himself—hardly possible. Nonetheless, it was a question of the best of the best possible alternatives. Good news exists in order to be passed along. On the other hand, you know how it is. The informant is responsible for all the consequences. In time the information becomes misinformation. Nothing you can do about it. At the opposite end of the city they'll say that the first Russians have already been spotted: three youths and one who looked like a Tatar. The old women will swear to it as well as the anxious fathers. Someone will say that he knows about it from that one and that one knows about it from another and somebody along the way knows that it comes from Jacob. From Jacob Heym? Inquiries will be made about him. Everything concerning this most important of all matters must be checked out precisely. An honorable, reliable person, makes a good impression; he is said to have owned a modest restaurant somewhere here once. It seems as if they could rejoice.

Then days will pass—if God thinks it necessary—weeks! Three hundred kilometers or five hundred are quite a distance and the looks that Jacob will get no longer will be so friendly from now on. On the other side of the street there will be muttering. The old women will sin in wishing evil upon him. The ice cream he sold will by and by have always been the worst in the entire town, even his famous raspberry ice cream, and his potato pancakes never quite kosher. All that is possible.

Jacob and Misha are hauling crates onto a freight car.

Or let's take another possibility. Heym claims to have heard that the Russians are advancing and are already four hundred kilometers from the town. Where does he claim to have heard that? That's just it—at police headquarters. At police headquarters? A horrified look might ensue. A slow nod of the head might answer, a nod that confirms the suspicion. One wouldn't have believed that of him, not Heym, never. But you can really be fooled about a person. Thus the ghetto might be enriched by a presumed informer.

At any rate, Jacob arrived at the railroad station without firm intentions. It would be nice if they already knew it without him. If they had greeted him with the news—that would have been best. He would have rejoiced with them. He wouldn't have revealed that three people already knew about it: Rosenblatt, himself, and Piwowa. He would have kept quiet, rejoiced with them, and at the most, asked hours later from whom the news came. But as soon as

Jacob arrived at the work area he saw that they didn't yet know. By their backs he saw it. Such a stroke of luck didn't occur, nor could it be expected. Two such strokes of luck in so short a time happen at best to Rockefeller on Sunday.

They're carrying crates onto a freight car. In the hauling department Jacob is not a particularly desirable partner. No one fights over him. Pancake frying develops giants only with great difficulty and the crates are heavy. The railroad station is filled with such people whom no one fights over. The giants must be searched out with a magnifying glass. That is, the giants are sought after, but they are not negotiable. They prefer to work together. Now don't tell me about camaraderie and similar nonsense. Whoever talks about that doesn't understand anything about this place, nothing at all! I myself do not belong to the giants. I cursed and hated them like the plague whenever I had to work with a lad like me. But if I had been one of them, I would have acted exactly like them—no way different!

Jacob and Misha are carrying a crate to the freight car.

Misha is a lanky lad of twenty-five with light blue eyes —quite a rarity among us. He boxed once for Hakoah, only three fights, two of which he lost, and his other opponent was disqualified because of a low blow. He was a middleweight. He was really rather a light heavyweight, but his trainer advised him to take off a few pounds since the competition in the light heavyweight class was too stiff. Misha followed his advice, but it didn't help much. Even in the middleweight class he didn't do too well, as his three fights prove. He had even played with the thought of putting on enough weight to reach the heavyweight class. In the area of 170 pounds this ghetto situation came up, and since then he has been losing weight steadily. Nonetheless, he is still relatively strong. By rights he should have deserved a better partner than Jacob. Many are of the opinion that his amiability will some day cost him his head. But no one will tell him that, since he might some day be of use to themselves.

"Don't stare off into space. Pay attention. You'll cause both of us to trip," says Jacob. He's angry because the crate is so heavy, despite Misha, and he's especially annoyed for he knows that Misha will be the first one he'll tell it to. He just doesn't yet know how he'll start.

They put the crate down on the opening of the freight car. Misha seems distracted. They walk back to the pile to get a new one. Jacob tries to catch Misha's attention. Misha is driving him crazy with his distracted glances. The station looks the same as ever.

"That car there," says Misha.

"Which car?"

"On the next to the last track. The one without a roof." Misha is whispering, although the nearest sentry is standing at least twenty meters away and isn't even looking at them.

"So what?" asks Jacob.

"In that car there are potatoes."

While loading the next crate Jacob grumbles the entire time: so there are potatoes there; what's so special about that; potatoes aren't interesting until you have them, or eat them raw, or make pancakes out of them, but not when they're lying in some freight car or other, at a station like this one; potatoes in that car there are the most boring thing in the world. And even if there were marinated herring, or roasted geese, or millions of pots of *cholent;* Jacob talks and talks; Misha's thoughts must be directed elsewhere and he has to be involved in other conversation.

But Misha pays him no mind. The guards will have to be changed in a moment. They always make a small ceremony out of it with their snapping to attention, sounding off, and presenting of arms. That's the only moment it could be attempted. Jacob's objections are not to be taken seriously. Of course, it's a risk. Right! Even a big risk and so what? Nobody claimed the potatoes were as good as eaten. Every opportunity is a risk must be explained to a business man yet! If there were no risk, there wouldn't be any opportunity. Then it would be a sure thing. Sure things are rare in life. Risk and chance of success are two sides of the same coin.

Jacob knows he doesn't have much time. This lad is in a state in which you can't talk in a rational manner with him. And then he sees the relief guard marching up in a column. Now he must tell it to him.

"Do you know where Bezanika is?"

"Just a moment," says Misha excitedly.

"Do you know where Bezanika is?"

"No," says Misha and his eyes accompany the column up to its last several meters.

"Bezanika is about four hundred kilometers from us . . ."

"Aha."

"The Russians are twenty kilometers from Bezanika!"

Misha succeeds for a moment in freeing his glances from the marching soldiers. His uncommon eyes smile at Jacob. That's really very nice of Heym and he says: "That's nice of you, Jacob."

Jacob almost has an apoplectic stroke. Brought to the point of paying no heed to all the rules of care and precaution (which haven't been set up out of thin air), he has chosen a blue-eyed young idiot. And what does this smart aleck do? He doesn't believe you. You can't simply go away. You can't let him just stand there in his stupidity, telling him to go to hell and then leave. You have to stay with him, saving your rage for a later time. You can't even envision which time. You must plead for his good will as if your own life depended on it. You must prove your credibility, although that shouldn't be necessary for you, but only for him. And you must get that all over with right away, before they're standing in front of each other, slapping their rifles against their shoulders, reporting that there were no special occurrences.

"Aren't you happy?" asks Jacob.

Misha smiles kindly at him. "Fine," he says in a voice that sounds a bit sad, but which also contains a certain recognition of Jacob's charming endeavor. But then Misha has more important things to watch. The column is coming closer, approaching the little stone house where the railroad workers and the sentries have their quarters. Now they've passed it.

Misha is trembling from excitement and Jacob is trying to have his words go faster than the soldiers. He relates his story in an abridged version. Why didn't he begin it sooner? He tells about the man with the searchlight, about the corridor in the station house, about the door that opened outward and hid him. The news that came from the room, the word-for-word formulation that he repeated to himself at night a thousand times, nothing added and nothing left out. He omits his short-term imprisonment in the door crack. Only the essentials. Also nothing about the man who brought him to the officer on duty who must have been a kindly soul and thus a weak link in the otherwise logical chain of events. He looked at the clock like a kindly soul and then told Jacob to go home—like a kindly soul.

And then Jacob sees with horror that nothing will hold Misha back now except certainty. The soldiers are now standing in front of each other. The enemy must be attacked when he least expects it, when his attention is the most minimal. Misha crouched, ready to sprint. Certainty and Russians are far away. Jacob's last resort is to grab him, holding on to his leg. They both fall down. Jacob sees the hatred in Misha's eyes. He's ruined his chance, at least he tries to. Misha frees himself; nothing else can stop him. He shoves Jacob aside.

"I have a radio!" says Jacob.

It wasn't the sentries who fired. Up to now, they haven't seen anything. They are busy with their changing-of-the-guard game. Jacob fired and hit the bull's eye. A lucky shot from the hip, without having aimed properly. And yet he hit the mark. Misha remains sitting—motionless. The Russians are four hundred kilometers away from us, near some Bezanika or other, and Jacob has a radio. They're sitting on the ground and looking at each other as if there never were a freight car with potatoes and no one were ever waiting for the changing of the guard. All of a sudden tomorrow is another day. To be sure, it's still true that the prospect for success and risk are two sides of the very same coin, but you have to be crazy if you overlook the fact that between the two there must somehow be a healthy relationship.

They remain sitting a bit longer. Misha is smiling happily with his goyish eyes, as Jacob sees them. Jacob gets up. You can't sit forever. He is even more furious than before. He has been forced to utter irresponsible statements. That unsuspecting idiot there with his ridiculous distrust has made him invent them, simply because he suddenly got a yen for potatoes. He'll tell him the truth yet—not right away, but today certainly, no matter whether this car is still here tomorrow or not. Within the hour, at most in an hour, maybe even sooner, he'll tell him the truth. Let him be happy, carefree for a few more minutes, though he doesn't deserve it. He soon won't be able to live any more without that joy. Then Jacob will tell him the truth, and then he'll have to believe the story of the police station. Ultimately that won't change anything about the Russians. He'll have to believe it.

"Pull yourself together and get up. And above all hold your tongue. You know what a radio in the ghetto means. Nobody must find out about it."

Misha couldn't care less about what a radio in the ghetto meant. Even if a thousand regulations proscribed it under pain of death, then let them. Is all that still important when tomorrow is suddenly another day?

"Ach, Jacob . . ."

The leader of guards sees a lanky lad sitting around idly on the ground, someone just sitting there who hasn't even collapsed, just leaning back on his hands, staring into the sky. He pulls his jacket tight, that little fellow does, and sets off.

"Look out," Jacob calls, nodding his head in the direction from which the danger is striding with dignity toward them.

Misha is once again alert, back to earth. He gets up, knowing what will happen in a moment, but can't help his joyful expression. He sets out for the pile of crates, is about to turn one on its end, when the leader slams him from the side. Misha turns around to him. The leader is a head shorter than he, and it takes some doing to reach up and strike him. It almost looks a bit comical, not the kind of thing for German newsreels, but rather like a joke from the silent films when the little cop Charlie tries to kayo the giant with the bushy eyebrows. He's really exerting himself, and the big lad doesn't even notice it. Everybody knows that Misha could pick him up and tear him apart—if he wanted to. The leader beats him a bit longer. His hands must be hurting. He's shouting some sort of nonsense that no one is interested in and doesn't let up until a thin stream of blood runs from the corner of Misha's mouth. Then he straightens his jacket again, notes belatedly that he lost his hat in all the excitement, picks it up, puts it on his head, goes back to his men, and orders the just-relieved guard to follow him.

Misha wipes the blood from his mouth with his sleeve, winks at Jacob, and reaches for a crate.

"Let's go," he says.

They pick up the crate. While they are carrying it, Jacob's anger becomes so intense that he nearly opens his mouth. He's not superstitious and there is no Higher Power. But inexplicably, maybe just because it was a bit funny, Misha deserved the beating, he thinks.

"Ach, Jacob . . ."

We know what will happen. We have our own modest experience of how stories manage to turn out. We have a little imagination and therefore we know what will happen. Misha will not be able to keep quiet about it. Promise here, promise there—it won't be because of ill will that he'll break his promise or even attempt to keep it. It won't be out of malice that Jacob will get into difficulty, but simply out of happiness and nothing else. Stop taking your own lives, you'll need them again—soon! Stop your despairing, the days of our grief are numbered! Exert all your energies toward survival; you are experienced in that. You know all the thousand tricks by which Death can be cheated. You've done it up till now! Just survive the last four hundred kilometers, then survival stops and life begins.

These are the reasons that Misha will not be able to hold his tongue. They'll ask him how he knows and he'll tell them. Nothing unusual about that. Soon, even the children in the ghetto will know the big secret—of course, in the strictest confidence. They'll find out when their parents in their joy forget to whisper. The people will come up to Jacob, to this radio-owner, Heym, and want to know what's new. And they'll come with looks in their eyes such as Jacob has never seen before. And just what is he to tell them?

Half a day has passed. The large crates are stacked in the freight cars. Now come the smaller ones, the kind one man can carry by himself. Jacob has lost sight of Misha. That is, not completely. They do see each other every few minutes, but always at a distance of a few meters, only in passing, their backs under a load or on the way to a new load. The opportunity for conversation hasn't yet come up. You can't simply take him aside and say, look here, the situation is such and such. Every time they meet, Misha winks to him, or smiles, or makes a face, or nods secretly. Either with or without a crate, it hardly matters to him. Each time something confidential, as if to say, both of us know what's what. Once Jacob even forgets and winks back, but immediately remembers: that would be going too far, that would ruin the opportunity of setting things straight. But it's not in his power. Each time his annoyance becomes weaker: why, the lad is right to be happy. Why shouldn't he rejoice after all that has happened?

The sky is blue as if chosen for this special occasion. The sentry at the wooden barracks is sitting on a few bricks, has taken off his rifle, put it down beside him, and is leaning his head against the wall. Keeping his eyes shut, he is sunning himself. He's smiling. You could almost feel sorry for him.

Jacob strolls past and looks him over. He walks very slowly, studying the sentry's face and closed eyes, his smile, his big Adam's apple, and the fat gold signet ring on his little finger. Jacob walks on and discovers, as he told me, that he himself had changed. His senses are suddenly much more alive; as if overnight he begins to observe things closely. His indifferent despair didn't survive the excitement of the previous night. No trace of his stupor. As if now he has to take exact note of everything in order to be able to report about it afterward. Afterward.

Jacob invents an innocent little prank. On his way to the frieght car or on his way back to the crates, he walks quite close past the dozing sentry, almost stepping over his outstretched legs—so close that for a moment each time he blocks the sun from him. Of course, the sentry doesn't notice it. Doesn't even open his eyes, although he's not sleeping. Moves his head barely once or twitches his mouth involuntarily, it seems to Jacob. Or does nothing at all. But at every passing, the sentry misses out on a little sun. Jacob pursues his little prank so long that he works through a whole stack of crates. The sentry is no longer lying in his path. He would have to make a detour. For that the prank is too insignificant and the risk too great. Jacob sees with satisfaction that a few little clouds are carrying on his practical joke. Then it's noon.

Out of the stone house comes a man in a railroad worker's uniform. The same person since we've been working here. He has a lame leg that, at every step, makes a sound like that of a pebble falling into water. A wooden leg. We call him "The Whistle"—not at all derisively, since we know nothing about his human or professional qualities. The only thing we have against him is that he happens to be a German, which on careful consideration, to be sure, should be no grounds for a bad opinion. However, our troubles at times make us so unfair. As soon as he comes out of the house, he takes out of his breast pocket a whistle attached to his buttonhole with a black cord, and blows it with considerable intensity as a signal that it's now noontime. This is the only sound we've ever heard from him, apart from the splashing of his wooden leg. Thus we call him "The Whistle." Maybe he is a deaf mute.

We line up, very orderly and without the least bit of shoving. They've taught us that under the threat of no food. It must appear as if we had no appetite at all at that moment—that food again! No sooner do you get down to real work when there's an interruption by one of the many meals. We line up without haste. You look around and align yourself until everyone is standing on an imaginary straight line. With arm extended you check your distance from the one in front of you, correcting yourself by a few centimeters—all of this to give the appearance that you're among cultured people. You take your spoon from your trousers pocket, in your left hand at the seam of your left trousers leg. Then the wheelbarrow comes around the corner of the barracks, the stack of tin bowls next to the two steaming, green army kettles. The barrow stops at the head of this voracious line. The first man steps forward and opens the kettle, burning his fingers in the process every time, and starts apportioning. "The Whistle" stands there silently with his eyes glued, seeing that everything comes off properly.

On this clear day I am the ladler. I don't know about anything. I always find things out last. I woke up in a bad mood. I'm furious. I'm annoyed at this additional work. My burned fingers are hurting. I'm the last one to eat. I'm clanging the soup ladle into their bowls. They take them away with them. I discover nothing unusual in anyone's face, but neither am I paying particular attention. I don't even see when I'm giving soup to only the bowls.

Jacob has gotten his, as they say, and is looking around for Misha who was in line way ahead of him. Noon would be such a favorable chance to exchange a few undisturbed words together, a small correction that wouldn't alter any of the essential facts of the case. Misha is nowhere to be found. The area is big and one can get lost with his bowl. The break is too short for a thorough search. Jacob sits down on a crate and is eating his hot soup. After all, he's only human. His thoughts are far away from his bowl: what will happen and how much longer and what then. He is oblivious to the sunshine and, besides, no one is blocking it. Then Kowalski appears.

Kowalski appears.

"This spot is free, isn't it?" asks Kowalski.

He sits down beside Jacob and starts to spoon up his soup. Kowalski is great! He considers himself cunning and sophisticated. But his face can't hide anything. It prattles.

If you know him even a little bit, you know exactly what he's thinking, even before he has opened his mouth. His words are always simply the confirmation for long fostered suspicions, if you know him even a little bit. At the station everyone knows Kowalski a little bit. And Jacob knows him since they had gone to school together. Here they've lost contact with one another, in these dark times. The reason for that is simple enough. Neither of them is a giant. A crate doesn't become lighter when the one on the other end is an old friend. To such a pass have circumstances brought things. Nor are there otherwise any opportunities. You either associate or don't associate with someone. They hardly have. And now Kowalski appears with his bowl, says, "This spot is free, isn't it?" sits down beside Jacob, and is eating.

Kowalski was Jacob's most frequent customer. Not his best, his most frequent. Every day around seven the café bell rang. None other than Kowalski arrived, sat down at his seat, and ate pancakes until you could get dizzy watching. Never less than four or five and usually topped off with a drop or two. In secret—since Jacob had no liquor license. Any proprietor would have been enraptured with such a customer. Not Jacob. For Kowalski never paid. Not a cent. Not even once. Ex-school chums was not the reason for Jacob's generosity. What kind of a reason would that be for generosity! In a stupid moment during an evening of drinking they came to an agreement. Kowalski's barbershop was only a few houses away and they met almost every day anyway. The agreement seemed advantageous to both of them: for you no cost at my place and for me no cost at your place. They both regretted it later. An agreement is an agreement and, after all is said and done, one man alone can not bankrupt another. But they both tried to. At first, pancakes were Kowalski's favorite dish—that was undoubtedly the reason for his proposition—but that soon changed.

In time he got sick and tired of them. He ate all four of them only because Jacob served them to him out of habit—without saying a word. Meanwhile, the drop or two afterward became much more important to him.

On the other end, at first Jacob suffered from the undeniable fact that while pancakes can be consumed daily, you didn't need a daily haircut. After some thought he hit upon shaving. He gave up even the sparsely growing hair on his chin, although in bad conscience. He was best off in the summers. Fortunately for him, Kowalski's stomach couldn't tolerate ice cream. Thus he was at a temporary advantage in their agreement. However, his ambition disappeared in time. Other worries were really more important. He let his beard grow again and the situation slowly cooled, only to flare up now and again.

But that's an old story. Kowalski is sitting beside him, spooning up his soup, silent for a long while. On his skinny cheeks is a single, repressed question with red dots. Jacob stares fixedly into his empty bowl thinking, maybe it's a coincidence. There are odd coincidences. "How are you?" would sound idiotic, he thinks. He finishes licking his spoon carefully and puts it in his pocket. There's no reason to stand up yet; the noon break will last a few more minutes. The last ones in line are just getting their food. He lays his bowl aside, puts his hands behind him, and leaning back, closes his eyes, his head up—for several minutes a sentry, enjoying the sun.

Kowalski stops eating. With eyes closed, Jacob hears that Kowalski's bowl isn't empty yet. There's been no scratching on the bottom. Thus Jacob knows that Kowalski is looking at him. It won't take long now. Merely the proper start.

"Anything new?" asks Kowalski casually.

When Jacob looks up at him, he's eating once again, his next thoughts still on his cheeks, with his innocent eyes in the midst of his soup. It sounds as if you came into his barbershop, sat down on the only chair in front of the only mirror while he's shaking the black hairs of the previous customer from the cape, ties it around you—much too tight, like always. "Anything new?" Mundek's son won his first court case. It looks like he's on his way to success. But that's old news. Hübscher revealed all that yesterday already. But what you don't yet know is that Kwart's wife left him. Nobody knows where she went. But really! No reasonable person can get along with Kwart. It all sounds so familiar that Jacob wanted to say, "Don't cut it so short in the back as you did the last time."

"So what's new?" Kowalski asks, while his eyes are about to drown in his soup.

"News?" says Jacob. "How come you ask me of all people?"

Kowalski, with his cunning face that can't hide a thing, looks Jacob straight in the eye with a gentle reproach, with sympathy for Jacob's caution, and with an indication that his caution in this particular case is out of place.

"Jacob! . . . Aren't we old friends?"

"What's that have to do with it?" says Jacob. He's not sure whether he'll succeed credibly in playing dumb. Kowalski has known him, after all, for a very long time. And he may think that actually it's rather unimportant whether or not he succeeds. If Kowalski knows something, he won't let go. If Kowalski knows anything, he could even be a dragon. He is capable of wringing your heart out.

Kowalski moves somewhat closer. Letting his spoon float in the soup, he grabs Jacob's arm with his other hand. He won't get away from him.

"Well, O.K., let's talk frankly." His voice drops to a volume used in speaking of secrets. He whispers, "Is it true about the Russians?"

Jacob becomes startled at the tone. Not at the whispering. People whisper on all possible occasions—that's not frightening. He is startled at the seriousness. He realizes that it won't be easy—not a laughing matter. He's startled at the trembling in Kowalski's voice. There is an expectation which won't tolerate a joke being made of it. Here certainty is demanded. Here a man is asking who wants to have only this single question answered. It's necessary, only this one question—nothing else, forever. And yet Jacob makes one last useless attempt: "About what Russians?"

"About what Russians! Must you torment me so, Jacob? Have I ever done you wrong? Remember, Jacob, remember, who is sitting beside you! The whole world knows he has a radio and to me, his one and only friend, he doesn't want to tell anything!"

"The whole world knows it?"

Kowalski backs off. "Not exactly the whole world, but this one and that one probably do. Did someone tell me or am I clairvoyant?"

In Jacob's head one annoyance suppresses the other. Kowalski is overshadowed by Misha. This latter prattler is putting him in an impossible position. It is suddenly no longer necessary to take Misha aside and set him straight—completely superfluous. The fire is out of control now. Who knows how many would now have to be taken aside? And even if one took the trouble with each and every one of them, even if one would attempt with the patience of a saint to explain to each and everybody the stupid way in which the glorious news reached their ears in the ghetto, what else would they conclude, but not to believe him? Even amidst all the appreciation and understanding for his situation. Or can one seriously believe that Kowalski could afford to have himself put off with a story full of hitches?

"Well, what's the story?"

"It's true about the Russians," says Jacob. "And now leave me alone."

"They're twenty kilometers from Bezanika?"

Jacob rolls his eyes and says, "Yes."

He stands up. That's how they spoil your joy. And to think that you should have the same reason for it that the rest of them had! It would have been so much better if Kowalski had been the one discovered by the sentry in the Kurländischendamm—or someone else. What was he doing there anyway last evening? All the good people are in their beds and he has to spook around the streets when it's getting dark. Because the ceiling is falling on his head. Because Piwowa and Rosenblatt are once more unbearable. Because a stroll after a day's work has such a rare flavor of normal times. A walk in a town familiar to you since you were in a baby carriage propped up with pillows. The houses tell you almost forgotten trifles. There you once fell, spraining your left ankle. On the corner you once finally told Gideon the truth to his face. In this yard there was a fire in the middle of winter. Such an ardent flavor of normal times had he promised himself. He didn't feel it for long. And now this.

"Will you at least keep it quiet?"

"You know me," says Kowalski. He wants to be left in peace, first of all because the break is short, and he is sufficiently preoccupied with himself as well as with what happens suddenly.

Jacob picks up his bowl from the ground and leaves, taking with him the image of Kowalski's face slightly inclined, his eyes fixed upon a distant point invisible to anyone else. He hears Kowalski's lips whisper lovingly, "The Russians. . . ." Then he's at the wheelbarrow. He piles his bowl on the others and looks at Kowalski again, who in the meantime is fishing his spoon out of the soup. The whistle blows. Even Kowalski hears it. A pile of bowls is quickly formed. It seems to Jacob as if everyone were looking at him strangely, differently even from yesterday, as if there were a secret in their glances. Perhaps it's an illusion—undoubtedly so. They can't all know it so soon. But some were probably in the know.

I would like—it's not yet too late—to explain a few things about my information, before any suspicions arise. My most important informant is Jacob. Most of what I heard from him will be found here somewhere. I can vouch for that. But I say "most"—not "everything"—advisedly. And this time it's not because of my bad memory. Still, I'm telling the story, not he. Jacob is dead. Besides, I'm not telling his story, but rather a story.

He told it to me. But I'm talking to you. That's a big difference, because I was there. He tried to explain to me how one thing led to another and how he couldn't do anything else. But I want to explain that he was a hero. No three sentences ever came out of his mouth that he didn't mention his fear. But I want to talk about his courage. About those trees, for example, those trees that don't exist and which I'm looking for, about which I don't want to think and must. My eyes get misty over it. He knew nothing about that. That is completely my own affair. I can't recall everything now, but there are some things he knew nothing about. Whereupon he probably would have asked me how I knew about them. But I think they simply belong here. I would gladly tell him why I think so. I owe him that. I think he would agree.

Certain details I learned from Misha, but then there is a big gap for which simply no witnesses are available. I say to myself it must have been approximately thus and so. Or I say to myself, it would be best if it had been thus and so, and then I tell it and act as if it fits. And it really does fit. It's not my fault that the witnesses who would be able to verify it are no longer available.

Plausibility is not the decisive factor for me. It is implausible that I, of all people, am still alive. It's much more important that I think it could or should have happened thus and so. And that has nothing at all to do with plausibility—for that, too, I can vouch.

It wasn't Misha's worst brainstorm—striking up a conversation with Rosa during the distribution of food stamps: having gathered his courage to ask her whether they didn't have to walk a bit in the same direction. Fortunately, she agreed to. At first it was only her face that caused him to speak up. How many girls have been accosted only because of their shining eyes? But, later, one thing led to another and today, about one year later, he loves her completely as she is. Their first steps were embarrassingly reserved. His head felt as if hollowed out. From her he didn't receive even the slightest encouragement, not even a cheerful glance. Bashfully, she looked straight ahead and apparently waited for something important to happen. But nothing happened, nothing, until they were at her front door. Her mother was standing at the window, concerned that her only daughter was away so long. Rosa said good-by quickly, with eyes lowered. But she must have happened to hear when and at what exact spot he would wait for her the next day.

In any event, she kept the date. That was a load off Misha's mind. He reached into his pocket and gave her his first gift. It was a small book of poems and songs. He knew them all by heart already. It happened to be the only book he owned. He had really intended to give her an onion, if possible, one with a bluish skin. Right from the start he took this Rosa matter very seriously, too seriously. In such a short space of time, despite all efforts, he wasn't able to succeed in getting a single onion. At first, as inexperienced girls frequently do, she politely hesitated a little whether to accept a gift at all; but then, of course, she finally pocketed the book and told him she was very happy about it. Only then did he formally introduce himself. Yesterday in all the excitement they hadn't got around to it. And now he heard her name for the first time: Rosa Frankfurter.

"Frankfurter?" he asked. "Do you happen to be related to the famous actor?"

That was, as was later easily verified through programs of the municipal theater, somewhat of an exaggeration. Frankfurter the actor never got beyond middling roles. However, Misha didn't mean it ironically. He had never seen Frankfurter; he had only once been to the theater and had only heard or read about him. Nor had Rosa taken it as irony. Blushing, she admitted that such was, in fact, the case, that the actor Frankfurter was her father. They then chatted a little about the theater, about which he knew next to nothing. However, he skillfully succeeded in changing the conversation gradually to boxing, about which she then knew nothing. Thus, they had a splendid time. And on this very same evening she had no objection to Misha's first kiss upon her silken hair.

When Misha arrives Felix Frankfurter is seated at the table playing checkers with his daughter. He's a big man, tall and haggard. Misha described his appearance to me with much loving care. A once robust bulk had creased Frankfurter's skin. All this is especially underscored by the clothes he is wearing, which originate from much better times. Photos show that years ago man and skin had formed a well-balanced harmony, according to a thick album full of pictures that Frankfurter had heaped on Misha at his very first visit. He could by no means tolerate the unflattering impression he knew he made. Around his neck is draped a scarf, sporty and artistic, one end in front and one on his back. In his mouth a pipe, a meerschaum, that had long forgotten the taste of tobacco.

He's sitting at the table with his daughter. For Rosa it's a hopeless match. Frau Frankfurter is sitting next to them paying no attention to the game. She's sewing her husband's shirt, making it smaller, and dreaming possibly of a happy fate. As Misha appears, Rosa has just become annoyed that the game with her father is so boring, because he is taking so much time with every move. He tried to explain to her that it's better to win one game in two hours than to lose five.

"But why are you still racking your brains?" she asked. "You're winning in any case."

"I'm not winning in any case," he said, "but because I ponder my moves."

She nodded, annoyed. There was no question now of any fun in the game. It was only out of deference that she didn't overturn the board. And because Misha wasn't there yet. But then there's a knock. She runs quickly to the door and opens it and Misha comes in. They greet each other. Frankfurter challenges Misha to a game. Misha sits down. Rosa clears away the checkers and the board before Misha can take over her lost game. He often takes her place, looks for a solution, but finally has to give up and ask for a return match. Frankfurter assents. Both of them sit there musing then. And suddenly it gets so late that Misha has to leave before Rosa has had any time alone with him.

"You played a game today?" Misha asks. "Who won?"

"Who else?" says Rosa, and it sounds like a reproach.

Frankfurter puffs on his meerschaum pipe, happy as one can be, and winks to Misha. "She plays faster than she thinks. But I bet you've noticed that yourself by now in other situations. Right?"

Misha pays no attention to the remark. Today he doesn't come empty-handed. He's simply biding his time how to break the news effectively, since Frankfurter likes nothing better than a story with a point to it. Whenever he speaks about the theater, where—if he's to be believed—the craziest things happened, he does not miss the slightest opportunity to relate things to himself. Someone fell, or made himself ridiculous, or ruined the performance, or didn't understand why others laugh. If it weren't so, Frankfurter thinks, it wouldn't even need to be told.

"Just what can you offer a guest these days?" says Frankfurter to his silent wife. And then to Misha, "What can you offer a guest besides your daughter?"

He smiles, his remark successful; then he puffs again on his pipe. Anyone can puff on an empty pipe—child's play—but not like Frankfurter. He affects an enjoyment, the gratifying body of smoke. If you don't look closely, you might be tempted to wave the smoke away.

For a few thoughts long there is silence. In a moment Frankfurter will tell an anecdote, one of his type stories, at the end of which he will react with such delight that he will slap his thigh. Like the one, for example, that William Tell at the opening performance doffed his hat to the hat on the pole on a stupid bet. Or the one about the actor Strelezki —said to have been a divine Othello otherwise—who dropped his false teeth just when he was bent over Desdemona choking her to death. Rosa is putting her fingers on Misha's hands; her mother is making the shirt even smaller; Frankfurter is rubbing his knee. Maybe he won't be in the mood today, and furthermore, Misha has brought such good news. He's merely pondering, like over a move at checkers, on the best way of telling it.

"By the way, have you heard the latest?" Rosa suddenly asks him. Misha, startled, looks from one to the other. He ceases his searching and wonders why Frau Frankfurter doesn't even glance up from the shirt. They already know it and till now he didn't notice that they know it. He wonders why everything in the room still looks the same as it did at his last visit. He wonders why everything happens so quickly. He hadn't heard it from Jacob until this morning. Now the Frankfurters know it via how many others. But, most strangely, Rosa hasn't mentioned it until now. Surely she hadn't forgotten and just now thought of it! Hardly. Something doesn't make sense. Perhaps they have their reasons for not believing it.

"You already know about it?"

"They talked about it earlier at work," Rosa says.

"And you're not even happy?"

"Happy?" says Frankfurter. (He really does say it elegantly!) "Should we be happy? What for, kid, huh? Once upon a time they really could have been happy, called together all their relatives and made merry, but today there are a few small details that have changed. I consider the situation a crying shame, my boy, even a terrible misfortune for the folks, and you're asking why I'm not happy?"

Misha realizes right away that they're talking about something entirely different—the only explanation for the mood. If not, then Frankfurter has lost his reason. Then he doesn't know any more what he's saying.

"It will be hard bringing up that child," says Frau Frankfurter between two stitches.

The first solid clue. New surprise in Misha's eyes. They're talking about some child or other. Of course, news can't travel that fast. Obviously, two crazy people have brought a child into this world (without having heard of the news). In normal ghetto times, of course, a subject for conversation. But since yesterday, times are not normal. Now another wind is blowing. Now we can tell you things so that you'd forget child and man, wife and eating and drinking. Since yesterday, tomorrow is another day.

Now Rosa is astonished. First she's astonished and then she smiles at Misha's look. "Oh, you don't know it, but that's the way he is. He can't stand it when others know more than he. He always plays the know-it-all and yet he doesn't know anything. In another district a baby was born, in Vitebsk Street. Actually, there were twins, but one died right after birth. Last night. When all this is over, they want officially to name him Abraham."

"When all this is over," says Frankfurter. He lays his pipe on the table, stands up, walks through the room with bowed head, hands on his back. His disapproving looks meet Misha who isn't even sneering. They make light of everything. Rosa, too. They may be too young to understand. They talk about future times like about a weekend that will surely come, like going with your entire family and a basket full of food into the park whether it is raining or not. "When all this is over, the baby won't be living any more, and the parents won't be living any more. We all won't be living any more. Then it will be all over."

Frankfurter has arrived, his stroll at an end, and he sits down again.

"I find David prettier," says Frau Frankfurter quietly. "Dovidl . . . If you remember, that was the name of Annette's son. Abraham sounds so old, not at all like a baby. Only children's names are important. Later, when they're grown, it isn't so important any more."

Rosa likes Jan or Roman better and thinks people ought finally to be free of traditional names. When it is no longer necessary to wear the star, then other names, too. Frankfurter shakes his head over the women's prattle while Misha wishes suddenly that he had come just now into the house with the fresh news. Because when he starts telling it, they'll be just as puzzled as he was. Why didn't he tell it right off? He could not have forgotten it. He's sitting already and sitting while their conversation is getting increasingly gloomier. Either he says nothing until tomorrow and acts as if it were the latest news or he makes up a story that explains why he saved it till now instead of telling it right away when he opened the door. He decides on today, with a

43

bit more emphasis for Frankfurter. He stands up, acts affected; he himself doesn't know whether he's acting or for real. He looks at Frankfurter, who is already wondering about the long warm-up, and asks him in the proper manner for his daughter's hand.

Rosa discovers something on her fingernail which occupies her completely, something so important that she blushes and begins to glow. They hadn't spoken about it at all, but it's really quite fitting. Frau Frankfurter hunches deeper over the shirt, which is still a long way from being small enough. The collar is causing the greatest difficulty because of her meticulousness that it fit properly. Misha is enjoying his brainstorm—successful or not. Frankfurter is bewildered, but will manage to say something. He is about to answer. A polite question deserves an answer, even if the question is wrongheaded. As it seems now, it will lead to the revelation of the big news and that, in turn, will open a way to the explanation as to why Misha asked just now. That is Misha's plan conceived in the utmost haste and really not so bad. Felix Frankfurter will open a way. It's his turn. Everyone is waiting for a reply.

Well, Frankfurter's complete astonishment, disbelief in his eyes; he just took a puff on his pipe and forgot to blow out the smoke again. The father, who wouldn't give his only daughter to anyone but Misha and loves him already like his own son, the man of sober reality whom no one can fool, is simply dumbfounded.

"He has gone crazy," he whispers. "Our distress has unhinged him. It's these goddamned times, when quite normal wishes sound monstrous. Why don't you say something!"

But Frau Frankfurter says nothing, lets a few tears fall silently on the shirt. What can she say? All important questions have been decided only by her husband up till now.

Frankfurter starts walking again, inwardly agitated, and

Misha looks full of hope, as if the only answer could be, "Take her and be happy."

"We're in the ghetto, Misha. Do you know that? We can't do what we want, because they will do with us what they want. Should I ask you where you intend to live? Should I tell you what sort of a dowry Rosa will receive from me? That will surely interest you. Or should I give you a few tips on achieving a happy marriage and then go to the rabbi and ask him when the *chassene* is most convenient for him? . . . You go ahead and rack your brains where you'll hide when they come to get you."

Misha is confidently silent. After all, that was not really an answer.

"Now imagine that! His ship has sunk. He is stranded in the middle of the ocean. No one in sight to help him, and he is making up his mind whether he'd rather go to a concert or to an opera."

His arms sink. Frankfurter has said everything there was to say, including even a pleasant allegory at the end. You can't be more explicit than that.

But an impression on Misha he didn't make. On the contrary, everything went as he would wish. No help in sight; Misha waited for such a statement. You'll soon know what it's like. It certainly makes sense to talk about the future. Misha is no idiot. Of course, he knows how serious it is. Of course, he knows that you can't marry until—and that's just the point—until the Russians come.

Misha said to me, "Then I simply told them (literally: 'simply'), that the Russians were twenty kilometers from Bezanika. You understand, it wasn't just an announcement; it was also a reason now. I thought they would begin to shout with joy, since something like that doesn't happen every day. But Rosa didn't fall upon my neck. That didn't occur to her at all. She just looked frightened at the old man who looked at me. For a long time he didn't say a word, but just looked at me so that I became restless. At first I thought they needed perhaps time to understand it, the way the old man looked at me. But then I realized that it wasn't time they needed, but certainty. I had felt the same way. I also thought that Jacob had just wanted to get my mind off the loading of the potato freight car. I continued believing it until he told me the whole truth of how he found out. Such news without the source is just not worth a thing, but just simply a rumor. I wanted to open my mouth and take away their doubt, but I decided to wait. Let them ask, I thought; when you force it out of someone, you'll feel better than if he tells it to you himself, all at once. And that's just how it happened."

Well, endless silence, the needle motionless in the middle of a stitch, Rosa holding her breath, Frankfurter's eyes —Misha standing there as if in the spotlight and the audience hanging on every word.

"Do you know what you are saying?" says Frankfurter. "You don't joke about such things!"

"You don't have to tell me," says Misha. "I found out from Heym."

"From Jacob Heym?"

"Yes."

"And he? How does he know?"

Misha smiles weakly, acts embarrassed, twitches his shoulders wretchedly, which you can well imagine, since a promise has been made. That he won't keep it is another matter. But the promise was nonetheless made, and you should at least be forced to break it, should do everything in your power so that you, too, couldn't have acted differently were you in his place.

"How does he know!"

"I promised him not to tell anyone," says Misha, already prepared to tell, but clearly not prepared enough—in any case not clearly enough for Frankfurter. It isn't time to pay attention to nuances in the voice. Frankfurter takes two, three quick steps forward and gives Misha a slap, in between a theatrical and a real one, but more toward the real because there is indignation in it—after all, we're not talking here just to kill time.

Misha is, of course, a bit intimidated. Surely that much coercion wasn't necessary. But he can't be offended since the coercion had to take some form. Neither can he sit down with a shocked expression, his arms folded on his chest, and wait for an apology. That would be long in coming. He can—and he does—dispel all doubts. It has come to that; his confidentiality disappears. No one will ask any more, "Why just now?"

"Jacob Heym has a radio."

Some more silence; a few glances exchanged; the shirt that is still too large touches the floor unheeded. You can believe it if your own son-in-law says it. Finally Rosa hugs him—he waited long enough for it. Over her shoulder he sees Frankfurter sitting down exhausted, clapping his hands to his wrinkled face. There won't be any conversation. There is nothing to say. Rosa tugs his ear to her mouth and whispers. He doesn't understand. The old man still has his hands on his face and Misha looks at her puzzled.

"Come on, let's go to your place," Rosa whispers again.

A splendid idea. She takes the words right out of Misha's mouth. Good ideas follow each other in quick succession today. They leave needlessly quietly. The door clicks shut. No one hears it. Outside it is already getting dangerously dark.

Frankfurter is then alone with his wife without witnesses. I know only how it ended. I know only the end result, nothing in between. But I can imagine it only this way or similarly.

His wife gets up eventually. She wipes away her tears—

not those of the marriage proposal—or she doesn't wipe them away. She goes to her husband quietly as if she didn't want to disturb him. She stands behind him, lays her hands on his shoulders, bends her face close to his—which is still covered with his hands—and waits. Nothing happens, not even when he drops his arms. He stares at the opposite wall and she nudges him gently. She looks for something in his eyes and can't find it.

"Felix," she could have said after a while, "aren't you happy? Bezanika is not so terribly far. If they have got so far, then they'll also get to us."

Or she could have said, "Just imagine, Felix, if only it is true! My head is spinning! Just imagine that! It won't be long and everything will be as before. You'll be able to play again, on a real stage. Our theater will surely be renovated. I'll pick you up after every performance and wait for you next to the billboard at the gateman's box. Just imagine that, Felix!"

He doesn't answer. She helps him up and he goes to the closet. Maybe he looks like a man who has made an important decision and doesn't want to lose any more time carrying it out.

Frankfurter opens the closet, takes out a cup, or a little box, with the key in it.

"What do you want in the cellar?" she asks.

He weighs the key in his hand as if there were something to think about. Whatever the point in time, the sooner the better. Nothing is more important now. Maybe he tells her right now what he intends to do, or perhaps lets her in on it right in the room. But that is improbable. Besides, it's completely unimportant when he tells it to her. Nothing will be changed by it. The key is already in his pocket. Let's say, then, that he locks the closet without a word, goes to the door, turns around there to her, and says only, "Come."

They go to the cellar.

In such a poor-folks' house, which previously you'd never think of entering, the wood steps are worn down. They creak like crazy, but he walks close to the wall on tiptoes. Concerned, she follows him quietly, also on tiptoes. She doesn't know why, but just because he does. Up to now she has always followed him without asking. She had often guessed what was to be done. It was not always good.

"Won't you tell me now what we're doing here?"

"Sshh."

They walk down the narrow cellar corridor. Here you can walk along normally. The next to the last section of the cellar on the right is theirs. Frankfurter unlocks the gate lock, opens the wire door with the incombustible iron frame, still extant. He goes in. She follows him hesitantly. He closes the transparent door behind her and there they are.

Frankfurter is a cautious man. He looks for a piece of sackcloth, or a sack with holes, which he then tears up; or if no sack is there, he takes his jacket off and hangs it on the door in any eventuality. I imagine him putting a finger to his lips for a moment, closing his eyes, and listening but hearing nothing. Then he begins rummaging in the little mountain that fills one corner of the room, a little mountain of useless things, a hill of memories.

At that time, when the news came, they sat for two days deciding what they were going to take along—except for what was prohibited, of course. The situation was very serious, no doubt about it. They didn't expect it to be a paradise, but no one knew exactly. Frau Frankfurter thought practically, too practically for him, only of bed linen, dishes, and clothing. But he would not part from much that she considered superfluous. Not from the drum upon which he had announced the arrival of the successor to the throne of Spain in a very successful production. And not from Rosa's ballet shoes when she was five years old and which are nearly new even today. And not from the album with the theater reviews carefully pasted in, where his name is mentioned and underlined in red. Give me one reason why I should part from that. Life is more than just stuffing yourself with food and sleeping. The problem of transportation? He had quickly purchased a handcart for an outrageous sum of money, since the price of handcarts rose enormously at that time. And now that little mountain fills one corner of the cellar.

He takes off piece after piece. His wife watches silently, even wildly curious as to what he is looking for. Perhaps, for a moment, he looks at the framed picture with all the members of the theater, in which he is standing close to the right side between Salzer and Strelezki, who wasn't yet so well known then. But that is not what he is looking for. If he did take a look at the picture, he laid it aside again and rummaged further into the mountain.

"This Jacob Heym is an idiot," he says.

"Why?"

"Why! Why! He heard the news—great!—but that is his business. Good news, very good news at that, but he should be happy and not make everyone crazy with it."

"I don't understand you, Felix," she says. "You are unjust to him. It's nice that we know about it. Everybody should know it."

"Women's logic!" says Frankfurter angrily. "Today you know it, tomorrow the neighbors know it, and the next day the whole ghetto talks about nothing else."

She might nod her head, amazed at his anger. Even so, that's no reason to reproach Heym in the least.

"And suddenly the Gestapo knows it," he says. "They have more ears than you think."

"But Felix," she interrupts, "do you seriously believe the Gestapo won't find out without us where the Russians are?"

"Who is talking about that? I mean, suddenly the Gestapo knows that there is a radio in the ghetto. And what will they do? They'll immediately turn every street upside down, one house after the other. They won't give up until they find the radio. And where will they find one?"

The mountain has been leveled. Frankfurter picks up a cardboard box, a white or brown one, in any case, a cardboard box in which there are grounds for a legal and valid death sentence. He takes off the top and shows his wife the radio.

Perhaps she cries out softly, perhaps she is horrified, but certainly frightened. She stares at the radio and him, and doesn't understand. "You took our radio along," she whispers and wrings her hands. "You took our radio along. They could have shot all of us for that. And I didn't know anything about it . . . I didn't know anything. . . ."

"What for?" he says. "Why should I have told you? I myself trembled enough, and you trembled enough, too, without a radio. There were days when I had forgotten it, completely forgotten it, even weeks. You have an old radio in the cellar and don't think about it any more. But as soon as I remembered, I started trembling and haven't ever been reminded of it as I have today. The worst part of it is that I never listened to it, not even once, not even in the beginning. It's not because I wanted to hide it from you. I just didn't dare. At times, I wanted to. Out of curiosity, I almost couldn't hold back. I took the key and I went to the cellar from time to time, as you know. You asked me what I was doing there, and I told you I wanted to look at pictures or read through the old critiques. But that was a lie. I wanted to listen to the radio. I went to the cellar, covered the door, but I didn't dare to. I sat down, looked at the pictures or read the critiques just as I had told you, but didn't dare turn it on. But now all that is over!"

"I didn't know anything," she whispers to herself.

"Now it's done with for good!" he says. "You were right then; it was a useless thing. I don't need it anymore. Nothing will be left of it—nothing that resembles a radio. Then they can come and search."

He takes the radio apart piece by piece, apparently the only radio that we have. Without much ado, he destroys it. The tubes are trampled to dust, an indestructable wire simply tied around a box, the wooden casing dismantled and stacked aside until several weeks later when it can be burned, since any smoking chimney is suspicious during this season. But that's not so tragic; wood is, after all, wood.

"Did you hear, too, that the Russians are almost in Bezanika?" Frau Frankfurter asks quietly.

He looks at her quite perplexed.

"I told you already that I've never heard of it," he might have answered her.

Misha goes to his room with Rosa and that's an entire story in itself. If it's a story about how someone has to be fooled in order to be a bit happy, then nothing else happens to Rosa. If it's a story of how bold cunning has to be used and fear of discovery plays a role and no slip up can, for heaven's sake, occur and your face must always remain serious and innocent—if all of that results in a useful story, then it is, in addition, a story of how Rosa goes to Misha's room.

In the middle of the room is a folding screen.

Fajngold is the name of the man who sleeps in the other bed. It's Isaak Fajngold's fault that such a to-do is made, even if he himself finds it ridiculous. Besides, he is worn out every evening. He is over sixty and completely white-haired. He has his own troubles, but go complain! At first, only the chest of drawers divided the room. For Misha that seemed sufficient and even more so for Fajngold. But for

Rosa it was not enough. She told Misha that while Fajngold was deaf and dumb, he wasn't blind, and the moon shone so cheerfully into the room, and the chest of drawers was, in any case, too narrow. Misha merrily took the sheet from the window and tacked it onto the ceiling over the chest. The moon could now shine in even more cheerfully, but not for Fajngold. The main thing was that Rosa was reassured.

Fajngold is as deaf and dumb as I or Kowalski or anyone else who knows what to do with his ears and tongue. But for Rosa, he is as deaf and dumb as a clam. Right from the start, Misha was certain that Rosa wouldn't take a step toward his bed since another bed was there with a stranger in it. The understanding landladies and secretive pensions with their bellhops who discreetely look the other way and ask no questions—they are situated in another city. He knew precisely that she would only say no under these conditions. She's not that kind of a girl—that goes without saying—and he himself isn't that kind of a man. But even if you take into account denial as the last of all possibilities, there was still much time for racking your brains—no one can blame him for that—and Misha did so quite a bit.

On a certain blessed evening he lay awake in bed and thought of Rosa; Fajngold was in the other bed not yet asleep; and Misha started to tell him about Rosa: who she is, what she's like, how she looks, and how he loves her and how she loves him. Fajngold merely sighed. Misha confessed to him his burning desire to bring Rosa over for a night.

"Fine," Fajngold answered without pursuing the matter further. "I have nothing against that. But now do let me get some sleep."

Misha didn't let him sleep. He explained to Fajngold that it was not a question of whether he, Fajngold, agreed or not. In addition, he hadn't told her anything about him —he hardly dared to and that if they didn't hit upon any ideas, hardly anything would come of the matter.

Fajngold put on the light and looked at him wide-eyed. "You can't ask me to hang round outside on the street. Did you forget the laws?"

But Misha didn't expect that. That idea never occurred to him. Nor had he forgotten the laws. He simply looked for a solution which, it seemed, was not to be found. Fajngold turned out the light again and soon fell asleep. It's not us who have to come up with a solution, but rather Misha—all by himself.

After an hour or two, Misha woke up Fajngold, stoically permitted himself to be cursed out, and then proposed his solution to him. As stated, Rosa will never come to him overnight if she finds out that another man shares the room, no matter whether you're twenty or a hundred years old. If he doesn't tell her, she'll come over and then discover Fajngold. She'll leave then and never forgive Misha. No matter how you twist and turn it, the only possibility is that Fajngold remain in the room, but yet as if he weren't there.

"Maybe I should hide?" asked Fajngold wearily. "Should I maybe lie down under the bed every night, or in the closet?"

"I'll tell her you're deaf and dumb," Misha announced.

Fajngold really didn't want to and tried with all his might to have his own way. But in the end Misha succeeded in convincing him of the urgency. At night very little can be seen anyway and, in addition, if she's convinced that nothing can be heard—well, then, the matter can be worked out. With very mixed feelings, Fajngold agreed to it, "if you really must," and since then he has been for Rosa deaf and dumb as a clam.

For Misha there was an additional worry, because he realized from several of Fajngold's allusions that they had been overheard. To be sure, Rosa didn't notice anything. Fajngold kept mum, but must have heard this and that—all of which was not meant for his ears. When you're in each other's arms, all kinds of words are expressed that are not meant for other ears, and Misha was very embarrassed. Subsequently, he studied Fajngold's sleep and lay awake purposely in order to pay close attention to the sound of his breath and snoring. No one ever heard himself sleeping nor can he imitate his own sleep. You can imitate how a person sleeps, but you can't know anything about your own sleep. And Misha knows how Fajngold's sleep sounds. He would be willing to bet on it, he says, that he knows precisely. In the infrequent nights that Rosa is with him, Misha lies next to her at first listening and not until he is completely certain that Fajngold is asleep behind the screen does he begin to caress and kiss her, while Rosa forgets her disappointment that he has kept her waiting so long.

Something horrible happened once in the middle of sleep. Apparently in a nightmare, Fajngold suddenly began talking: clearly audible, disconnected words, heedless of the fact that deaf-mutes are supposed to be deaf and dumb even in sleep. That woke Misha up; his heart almost stopped beating. He looked timidly over at Rosa who lay in the moonlight and slept and simply nodded her head from one side to the other. He couldn't shout, "Fajngold, shut up now!" He could only lie still and hope, and fortunately Fajngold stopped his dream before any damage was done. Dreams last only seconds, they say, and it never happened again.

So much for this little comedy—all in all, tricky ways that led Rosa into this room, even under this ceiling, not down a straight street, a left and a right around the corner. Misha made it possible; Fajngold was cooperative; and Rosa feels good here.

She's lying on her back—for all I know her hands under

her head, today as always, although that's a bit shameless because the bed has more than it can handle in a fellow like Misha. Thus, he has to resign himself to the edge. She's lying there, her eyes somewhere; the evening, more beautiful than all the others, is already over. They have already whispered everything in each other's ears. Although Fajngold is deaf and dumb, they always whisper. When two people are lying like Rosa and Misha, they would whisper even on deserted islands if something absolutely had to be said. The night is so far gone that the taciturn Fajngold has been long asleep behind the wall of closet and sheet. The hot day and the news must have truly exhausted him. He was only a short obstacle today. After only a few minutes Misha was satisfied with the sound that drifted over to him and could expend his entire attention on Rosa.

Rosa nudges Misha gently with her foot against his quite persistently until he is enough awake to ask her what's wrong.

"My parents will live with us, won't they?" she asks.

Her parents. Never had *they* got as far as this room. There had always been only that one night when the two of them happened to be lying together making love—only that night and no other. All of those to come had to await their turn, and it wasn't worth a lot of talk. But now that they're here, let's glance quickly upon what might possibly happen. Only a little eyeful through the hole in the curtain. Her parents are here as well as a presentiment of later —they cannot be cast aside. Rosa insists upon it.

"They won't live with us," says Misha at a moment when one should be sleeping.

"And why not? You have anything against them?"

Rosa raises her voice—now it concerns things that cannot be breathed into one's ear—so intransigently loud that maybe Fajngold could wake up. But she knows nothing of this danger.

"For heaven's sake, is that so important that you had to wake me in the middle of the night?"

"Yes," says Rosa.

O.K., he leans on his elbows. She can be proud that she finally drove away his sleep. He sighs, as if life were not difficult enough.

"O.K. I have nothing against them, not the slightest. In fact, I like them a lot. They won't live with us. Now, I want to sleep!"

With a flip he turns over on his other side. A little demonstration by moonlight that the first difference of opinion is there. Not yet a real argument, only a presentiment of daily cares. A few quiet minutes pass when Misha realizes Fajngold is awake.

"Mama could take care of the children," says Rosa.

"Grandmas only spoil children," says Misha.

"Nor can I cook."

"There are books."

Now she sighs; let's argue later, there is still so much time. Rosa has to lift her head a bit because he shoves his conciliatory arm underneath, adds a kiss for reconciliation, and then to sleep. But she can't simply close her eyes and run away. What she sees, she sees. How long we have waited for this sight! When they knock, when they stand in the doorway those Russians—hello, we're here, you're free—then it'll be too late. Then it'll be too late to start thinking; you've got to know by then what is to be done first and what second. But Misha wants to sleep and Rosa can't—so much disorder. At least some things should be put in order. The big things will be taken care of. There will surely be important people who will take care of that. Let's begin with our small personal matters; we'll have to take care of that ourselves. While thinking, Rosa starts to whisper: there should be a house where you would feel comfortable; it might be something besides a house if need be, but let's begin with that. Not too small, not too large, let's say five rooms, that's not asking too much. Don't start yelling. We can ask for that. We've been modest long enough. One room would be for you, one for me, and two for my parents. And, of course, a children's room where they can do what they want—stand on their heads and paint the walls. We'll sleep in my room, not a separate bedroom; that would be wasted space, a pity during the day. You have to think a little practically. Whenever guests come, we could sit in your room; a sofa could be put there; that's stylish—a somewhat long table in front of it, and three or four armchairs. But I won't tolerate too many guests—that you should know right away. Not because of the disorder they make—that's no big problem, but I'd prefer to be alone with you. Perhaps, when we're somewhat older. And as for the kitchen, no one is to give me any advice. It must be tiled; that's clean and beautiful; blue and white would be best of all. The Klosenbergs had such a kitchen—exactly one like theirs. You can't imagine a nicer one. The floor is tiled a bright green; on the wall are shelves for dishes, pots, and ladles; and a spice shelf must hang there for all kinds of spices. No one knows how many spices there are. Saffron, for example. Did you know what saffron is used for? Did you know that it makes cake and noodles yellow?

More I don't know. In this realm my informant Misha finally fell asleep amidst all the spices. Maybe Fajngold could have been able to tell me more about this particular night. Maybe he lay awake from the cellar to the attic, but I didn't ask him.

Then it is daylight again, finally daylight again. At the freight yard we are running to and fro with our crates. Only several years ago it would have been called a cheerful bustling. The guards are behaving quite normally. They're shouting or dozing or shoving as usual. They show no fear

58

or at least aren't yet familiar with it. Perhaps I'm wrong, but I imagine that I can remember this day quite well, although nothing extraordinary happened, not to me at least. Today, I think, I'm in a freight car, receiving the crates and stacking them so that as many as possible fit in, together with another man, Hershel Shtamm—which in itself is something special, because Hershel Shtamm has a brother. Not only that, he has a twin brother, Roman, and both usually always work, stand, and walk together. But not today. Hershel had a little accident on this very morning. He tripped while carrying crates. Roman couldn't manage the crate alone, and Hershel, together with the crate, fell to the ground. For that, Hershel got the usual beating, but that wasn't the worst of it. He sprained a foot in the fall and could hardly walk, and thus couldn't work any more with Roman—which explains why he is now with me in the freight car.

He is sweating like a waterfall. I've never seen anyone sweat so. He won't stop sweating until the Russians have captured this cursed ghetto—not one day sooner. Hershel Shtamm is pious. All his life he has been a servant in a synagogue. We call it a *shammas*—as pious as the rabbi himself. And there are the earlocks—the ornament of all orthodox Jews. Go ask Hershel if he is prepared to be divested of them. Not for anything, he will tell you. He will look at you as if you were crazy. How can you even suggest such a thing? But the earlocks are permitted to be displayed only within his own four walls. Only there. On the street and here at the railroad station you meet Germans who don't care much for them. Where do you think we're living that you can run around looking like that? There are even known cases where the nearest scissors was used. Amidst secret prayers and laughter till tears ran down your face, the matter was settled on the spot. Even worse cases are known.

Hershel drew the only possible conclusion. He hides his earlocks. He smuggles them through time. In summer as well as winter he wears a hat—hats are still allowed—a black fur hat with ear flaps that can be tied under the chin. In the sun it is horribly hot. It was the only one he could get, but superb for his purposes. We non-believers smiled only during the first warm week and made fun of him—so did his brother Roman. Then we lost interest. Hershel himself must know what he is doing.

We are stacking a crate at the top of the pile. He is wiping the sweat from his face when he asks me while we are loading the next one, what I think about the matter. It's clear to me what he is talking about. I tell him that I'm already crazy with joy and can think of nothing else. Everything I had before will once again belong to me, everything including my Chana who was shot to death. There will be trees again. In my parents' garden I envision myself sitting in the walnut tree, in the thin branches, so that my mother would pass out from fright, and at the very top I'd gorge myself with walnuts. Your fingers get so brown from the shells that the color doesn't disappear until weeks later. But Hershel doesn't seem very enthusiastic to me.

Jacob and Misha lay a crate on the edge of the freight car. What's the hurry? Jacob rushes back to the pile and Misha scurries right after him. Since yesterday Jacob is a lucky dog—one of the chosen ones. Everyone is scrambling around him, the giants as well as the dwarfs. Everyone wants to work with him, with the man who has a direct line to God. Misha was the first in line, the first one who set to work with him as soon as Jacob looked at a crate. And now he has been dogging him. The most equitable thing would be to raffle him off: thus and so many blanks and a first prize. Then everyone would have the same

**60**

chance of winning Jacob's proximity that had so suddenly become important. Only Jacob makes a disgruntled face—thanks a lot for such sudden good luck! Since morning he has been asked confidentially and full of hope five or ten times what's new on the radio, even from complete strangers. And five or ten times he didn't know what to answer and repeated only what he had said yesterday, Bezanika. Or he had put his finger to his lips and in a conspiratorial tone said "sshh," or said nothing and walked away angrily. And all this trouble was the fault of this tall simpleton who is now jogging along behind him naïvely, in undeserved pleasure of anticipation. No one could have predicted it. They are behaving like children. They are clamoring around like those looking for entertainment clamor around advertising posters. If a miracle doesn't occur, it will take at most a few hours until the guards notice something amiss. He would hope for such a crowd in normal times. Jacob's café is open every day except *Shabbas* throughout the entire year, and a radio is clearly visible behind the counter. Everybody can hear whatever he wants to. But then you stop coming in regularly and you have to be treated like a king, otherwise you leave and don't come back. And now you are treating me like a king and are not leaving, but keep coming back. He needs a bodyguard to keep you off.

Misha has no notion what angry thoughts his presence arouses, or that it is rage that is speeding up Jacob's steps. They carry a few crates. Misha thinks it will continue that way till noon. He neglects to pay attention to the unfriendly looks which greet him from time to time and increasingly more often. Finally the pot boils over; Jacob stops short hoping that Misha would go away, as far away as possible. But Misha stops also. His eyes question puzzlingly. He really knows nothing. So let him find out!

"Please, Misha," Jacob says tormented, "there are so

many nice people here. Why do you have to choose me to work with?"

"What's wrong so suddenly?"

"Suddenly? I can't stand your face any more!"

"My face?" Misha smiles stupidly. His face had never bothered anyone, least of all, Jacob. At most this or that remark about his sky-blue eyes if anyone had fault to find. And now, suddenly, such an almost slanderous eruption.

"Yes, your face! With your talkative mouth," Jacob adds, since Misha is so totally in the dark. Now Misha understands which way the wind is blowing. He is the weak link in the chain of secrecy. Jacob is right. Although that's no reason to make such a to-do about it. God knows, worse has happened. Misha shrugs his shoulders as if to say, well it simply happened, it can't be changed now! Before Jacob gets more upset, Misha goes away. Why should our business be revealed to the guards? Later on, tomorrow, will be time enough for a conciliatory word.

Misha goes over to the crates by himself and quickly finds another partner. After all, he didn't remain unwanted. His powerful arms are not yet forgotten. They are still respected, and if not Jacob, then at least Misha as a partner. Jacob, too, goes over to the pile of crates by himself and doesn't at all notice who reaches for a crate with him. His eyes are still glued to Misha who finally disappears without turning around, insulted or not. After a few steps Jacob notices that his new partner isn't holding the crate as firmly as Misha did—by no means like Misha. He looks at him and sees that the new man is Kowalski. He winces and knows that he has gone from the frying pan into the fire. Kowalski won't let him alone for long.

Kowalski doesn't say a word; that is, it isn't that he is exactly quiet. Instead, he is keeping himself under control. For as long as that may last, Jacob is grateful. But somehow it's making him nervous: Kowalski and silence. The red spots on his cheeks don't come from exertion. For three entire crates long there is no talking. If Kowalski thinks for a moment that he can outstare him, he's wrong. Jacob will never come out with it on his own. There's nothing to tell. It's just simply that his nerves are twitching. I'll outwit you yet, Jacob thinks. I'll trap you. An innocent conversation could make you forget the question that you are keeping to yourself for the time being. It's just a question of what to talk about before the whistle blows for lunch. Then, go try to find me!

"Do you know anything for loss of hair?" asks Jacob.

"What?"

"My comb is full of hair every morning. Can't anything be done about it?"

"Nothing," says Kowalski, and Jacob hears clearly that the subject doesn't interest him.

"There must be something that can be done. I recall that you massaged a customer with something in your shop. I think it was green."

"All fake," says Kowalski. "I've massaged many with it, but I could have just as well used water. Some insist upon having something. And it wasn't green, but yellow."

"There's nothing that helps?"

"I told you already."

So far . . . Silently they continue hauling. In Jacob the hope grows that he's wrong, that Kowalski doesn't want anything from him and that he took hold of the same crate simply because he happened to be right beside him, that the red spots could really be from exertion, or bedbug bites. You don't always hit upon the most obvious answer. Bad experience should not put all sincerity in doubt. Kowalski has his good points, too. A whole host of memories can attest to that. They were, after all, almost close friends. Jacob is already looking more kindly at the perspiring

Kowalski, with a secret apology in his look. Secret, since fortunately even the reproaches had remained secret. Every new crate brought silently to the freight car leads him away from the suspicion that was from all appearances directed at an innocent person.

And suddenly, not long before noon, Kowalski asks his insidious question. Humiliatingly, innocently, devoid of any preliminary he says, "Well?"

Nothing else. Jacob twitches. We know what is meant. In an instant all his rage is there again. Jacob feels deceived. The spots are the same ones as always. And Kowalski wasn't coincidentally nearby. He was waiting for him. He ambushed him. The whole day he was working toward this disgraceful "Well?" Not out of consideration was he silent up to that moment; Kowalski doesn't know what that is. He was silent because he saw that Jacob had had an argument with Misha and waited for just the right moment—cold and calculating as he is—for Jacob to be lulled into security.

Jacob twitches. The worst thing about this ghetto is that you can't simply turn around and leave. It isn't advisable to repeat this game every five minutes.

"Is there anything new?" asks Kowalski more clearly. He is not about to undertake long staring exchanges. If you don't understand my "Well?" then too bad.

"No," says Jacob.

"You don't mean to tell me seriously that in the war nothing happened in a whole day? A whole day and a whole night?"

They lay the crate down on the edge of the freight car, walk back to the pile, and Jacob takes a deep breath. Kowalski nods reassuringly to him. Jacob loses his control and begins to talk louder as you can imagine.

"For heaven's sake, won't you leave me alone! Didn't I tell you yesterday that they are twenty kilometers from Bezanika? Isn't that enough?"

Of course, it's not enough for Kowalski if the Russians are twenty kilometers from some Bezanika or other, and he is here. Why should that be enough? But he doesn't have time for logical bullseyes—not right now. He looks around, frightened, because Jacob wasn't particularly careful. A guard is standing there quite close by. They have to pass by him and he is staring now. His uniform doesn't look good on him. He is much too young for it. He has already been noticed a few times. He has a big mouth, but seldom beats you up.

"What are you shitheads arguing about?" he asks, just as they are about to pass by him. In any case, he didn't hear anything precise, only loud words, and these are quickly explained away.

"We are not arguing, sir," says Kowalski loudly. "I'm just a bit hard of hearing."

The guard has something to inspect and rocks on tiptoes, then he turns around and walks away. Kowalski goes for a new crate. The incident is not dignified by a single word.

"A whole day has passed, Jacob. Twenty-four long hours. They have advanced at least a few miserable kilometers, haven't they?"

"Yes, according to the most recent reports, three kilometers."

"And you are acting so indifferently? Every meter counts, I tell you, every single meter."

"What good is three kilometers?" says Jacob.

"You're great! For you, maybe, it's not much. You hear new things every day. But three kilometers is three kilometers!"

He came through it all. Kowalski will leave him alone today. He is once again silent, like Fajngold. He found out what he wanted to.

Jacob confesses that it wasn't so difficult. He came out with it all quite easily. He explained it to me at great length. It was an important moment for him, he said. The first lie, which perhaps wasn't one at all, or was so small, and Kowalski is happy. It's worth it. Hope mustn't die, or else they won't survive. He knows precisely that the Russians are advancing. He heard it with his own ears. And if there is a God in heaven, they have to reach us, too. And if there is no God, they have to reach us, too. And they have to find as many survivors as possible. It's worth it. And if we will all be dead, then it was an attempt. That's worth it. It's just that he must think up enough things. They will constantly ask him new questions. They will want to know details, not only kilometer figures. He must invent answers. I hope his mind cooperates. Not everyone can invent. Till now he has invented only once in his life —many years ago—a new potato pancake recipe with cream cheese and onions and caraway seeds. You can't compare the two.

"And besides, it's important that they are advancing in general," says Kowalski thoughtfully. "You understand, better slowly forward than quickly back. . . ."

We're getting to Lena quite late, irresponsibly so, for she is of some importance for all of this. It is she who really rounds it out, if that's the right expression for it. Jacob goes to see her every day, but we're just getting around to it.

Lena is eight years old, has long black hair and brown eyes, as is fitting. "A strikingly beautiful child," most people say. She can look at you in such a way that you want to share your last bit of food with her. But only Jacob does so. Sometimes he even gives her everything. That's because he never had any children himself.

Lena hasn't had parents for two years. They went away. They boarded the freight train and went away, leaving behind their only child alone. Lena's father was walking in the street, just about two years ago. Nobody called it to his attention that he was wearing the wrong jacket, the jacket without stars. It was the beginning of autumn. He was walking, thinking no harm. At the latest, they would have noticed it at work. But he didn't even get that far. Halfway there, he ran into a patrol. One attentive glance sufficed. Only Nuriel didn't know what to make of it.

"Are you married?" one of the two asked him.

"Yes," said Nuriel, and didn't suspect what they wanted from him with their strange question.

"Where does your wife work?"

Right then and there, Nuriel replied. Immediately they went with him and took his wife out of the factory. The moment she saw him with the two men she noticed the bare spots on Nuriel's chest and back. She looked at him horrified and Nuriel said to her, "I don't know either what's wrong."

"Your stars," she whispered.

Nuriel glanced down at himself. Not until then did he know that it was all over, or nearly so. A far lesser reason would have sufficed—read the ghetto regulations! They went home with Nuriel and his wife. On the way they told them what they were allowed to take along. Lena wasn't playing in front of the house nor was she in the vestibule. Her mother had impressed on her to leave the house as little as possible. But you don't really know what children will do all day while their parents are at work. A short, fervent prayer: may she be disobedient just this one time! Nor was she in the room. She couldn't be surprised and ask what was the matter, why papa and mama were coming home so early. And the men would have known that Nuriel had not only a wife. They packed their few things. The two men stood beside them and watched that everything went smoothly. Nuriel was like a sleepwalker until his wife poked him and told him to hurry up. Now he did

**67**

hurry up. He understood her command. At any moment Lena could walk into the room.

Going downstairs, through a window on the landing, he saw Lena playing in the yard (all that without witnesses, but maybe it was just that way and no other). She was balancing herself on the little wall between the two yards. Who knows how often he had forbidden her that, but that's how children are. A neighbor, who happened to have the night shift that week, met them on the stairs. She heard Nuriel's wife tell him not to keep looking out the window but rather to pay attention to the steps, or he would fall. Which he did. He didn't fall. They reached the street without any untoward incident, and since then Lena hasn't had any parents.

A short time later a new family was given the Nuriels' room. In those days there were constant replacements. A problem arose: what to do with Lena? No one could take her in permanently and not only because of space or ill will. It would take only an unexpected inspection: what's your relationship to this child? Everyone had expected for weeks that there would be an investigation of Lena. In scrutinizing the matter, it would have occurred to someone in authority that instead of three Nuriels only two had left in the transport. But nothing of the sort happened. In the end, a couple of women from the house cleaned up the little attic; the bed was taken up there, as well as a chest of drawers with her belongings that were still around. Lena is living on the top floor. Only a heating stove was nowhere obtainable. In the coldest nights, when even two blankets are not enough, Jacob, who never had any children of his own, risks it and takes her secretly into his own bed. It simply turned out that she belonged mostly to him. In two years she had time to wrap him around her finger. The time was sufficient.

Today it is not a cold night—let alone the coldest. Lena

will have to sleep alone. Hershel Shtamm perspired horribly all day. Jacob visits her. He visits her every evening. Lena is lying there with her eyes closed. Jacob knows for sure that she isn't sleeping and she knows for sure that he knows it. Every evening there is another trick. He takes a bag out of his pocket. In the bag is a carrot that he lays on the chest of drawers beside the bed. Then he plays his trick for today. He blows up the bag and bursts it with his hands. But Lena is already laughing while her eyes are still closed. Something has to happen immediately. Then there's the bang; Lena sits up, gives him his kiss that he has earned, and asserts that she feels much better. She intends to get out of bed tomorrow at last. Such whooping cough can't last forever. But Jacob alone can't make the decision. He puts his hand on her forehead searchingly.

"Do I still have fever?" asks Lena.

"At most a little bit, if my thermometer is working properly."

She takes the carrot, asks him what "fever" means, and starts to eat.

"I'll explain it to you another time," says Jacob. "Was the professor already here today?"

No, he wasn't here yet, but he said yesterday that things were getting better and Jacob mustn't keep putting her off for another time. He must still explain to her what "gasmasks," "contagious diseases," "balloons," "martial law," are, and something else she had forgotten. And "fever" has been added to the list.

Jacob lets her talk on. She already makes a quite cheerful impression. He is thinking a bit morosely of the three cigarettes that the carrot cost him. He must purchase the next one cheaper. In the end, everything dissolves into sheer conversation. Lena is a master of conversation. She must have been born with it.

"How's it going at work?" she asks.

"Everything is fine," says Jacob, "thanks for asking."

"Was it so hot today, too, at your place? Here it was awfully warm."

"Not bad."

"What did you do today? Did you ride again on the train?"

"Where did you get that idea?"

"Recently you rode to Rudpol and back. Don't you remember anymore?"

"Ah, yes. But not today. The train has been out of commission for a few days."

"What's wrong?"

"It lost a wheel, and there is no replacement."

"Pity. How is Misha doing? He hasn't been here for such a long time."

"He is very busy. Good that you remind me. He sends you his regards."

"Thanks," says Lena. "Give him my regards."

"Will do."

That could go on for hours, over twenty carrots. No matter what they discuss. There is talking until the door opens. Until Kirschbaum comes in.

If I hadn't from the start undertaken another task, I would tell the story of Kirschbaum. Maybe I'll do it yet some day. The temptation is great. Even though we met fleetingly two or three times, he didn't even know my name. To tell the truth, I know him only through Jacob's few words. He mentioned him almost in passing, but aroused my curiosity. On the whole, Kirschbaum doesn't play an important part in the story. Most importantly, he cured Lena. Years ago Kirschbaum was a celebrity, not like Rosa's father, but an honest-to-goodness celebrity certified by official stamp and signature and a thousand honors, head of a Cracow hospital, and sought-after heart

**70**

specialist. Lectures at universities all over the world, fluent in French, Spanish, and German. It is rumored that he even had an informal correspondence with Albert Schweitzer. Whoever wanted to be treated by him had to go through all kinds of red tape. He still bears the dignity of the respected man without personal airs. Even his suits were of the best British fabric, a bit worn at the elbows and knees with age, but still flawlessly tailored, always of dark colors in striking contrast to his snow-white hair.

Kirschbaum never gave a thought to his being a Jew. His father already had been a surgeon. Jewish origin? What's that? They compel you to be a Jew and you yourself have no idea what that means. Now surrounded by nothing but Jews, for the first time in his life, nothing but Jews. He racked his brains about them. He wanted to find out what it was that was similar about them—in vain. They have nothing recognizably in common with one another and him, for sure not.

For most he is somewhat of a strange animal. That makes him uncomfortable. Better friendliness than respect. He tries to be accommodating. In the process he appears clumsy since everyone expects something special from him. And he has no sense of humor by which things could be smoothed out.

He comes into the attic room and brings along a pot full of soup for Lena. His steps have a spring to them like a man of thirty. His tennis club had kept him young.

"Good evening to all of you," he says.

"Good evening, professor."

Jacob gets up from the bed and makes room for Kirschbaum, who wants first of all to examine her. She is already taking off her gown. The soup is still too hot. First comes the examination each time. Jacob goes to the window. It's open. A little attic window, and yet half the city can be seen. Maybe a sunset, the houses in grey and gold,

**71**

very peaceful. The Russians will come through all the streets. Not a single one will be left out. The cursed stars will come off the doors and leave bright spots behind like ugly pictures that have hung on the wall too long and quite deservedly wind up in the trash can. Finally, you'll have a little time like all the others for cheerful thoughts, as if Kowalski had told you a surprise: that somewhere down there the future is hidden; no more big adventures; let the young folks rush into them! The café, for sure, has to get a new coat of paint; perhaps a few new tables added; perhaps even a taproom license, which was a slim possibility in those days. In the storeroom, Lena's room could be set up—I hope no relatives suddenly show up and claim her; only her parents will get her, if they're still alive. Next year she'll start school. Ridiculous—a young lady of nine in the first grade. The first grade will be full of children who are too big. Maybe they'll think of something so that they won't lose so much time. Not a bad idea for her to learn something ahead of time, at least reading and a little arithmetic; why wasn't that thought of sooner—let her first get well.

"Now I can tell you," says Kirschbaum. "It looked bad for this young lady. But with nice young ladies something can be done in most cases. We have, in the main, cured the disease. Take a deep breath and hold it!"

Downstairs in the closet is an old book, a travel description on Africa or America. That could serve well to learn to read. It even has a few pictures. It must be made appealing to her, because if she doesn't want to, you can stand on your head. As soon as it is possible, I'll adopt her. Of course, first search for her parents without her finding out. Adoption is not so easy, a lot of formalities and officials and in your old age you have a child! The Germans have their part in it and the Russians have their part in it; who has the greater part? I'll tell her that all this telling of fairy tales is finished now, not constantly princes and witches and sorcerers and robbers. Reality is far different. You are old enough—this here is an "A." She will be sure to ask what that means, she will want to know what an "A" is used for; she is very practical-minded; at her age questions are half her life; hard times could come. As a child, she is already eight years old. As a father, I am hardly two.

Kirschbaum is holding his stethoscope on her chest and listening intently. Suddenly he looks amazed, stares at Lena, and asks: "Well then, what's that? Is something whistling in there?"

Lena looks at Jacob amused, and he continues. He didn't notice at all that he started, but now he continues. He won't ruin Kirschbaum's weak joke. Lena laughs at the stupid professor, who doesn't understand at all that the whistling is coming not from her chest but from Uncle Jacob.

You ask: How do great events foreshadow? Far and wide no foreshadowings. A few insignificant days pass— insignificant for the historian. No new regulations, no external events, nothing tangible, nothing that could be interpreted as change. Some claim to have noticed that the Germans became more cautious. Some say that just because absolutely nothing is happening, it is the calm before the storm. But I say the calm before the storm is false. Absolutely nothing is false. The storm is already there or at least part of it. The whispering in the rooms amidst anxiety, speculation, hope, and prayer. The great age of the prophets has begun. Whenever two people argue, they argue about plans: mine are better than yours. Everyone already knows of the inconceivable. Whoever doesn't yet know must be a hermit. Not everyone knows of the origin of the news—the ghetto is too large for that. But the Russians are in everyone's mind. Old debts start to play a role. They begin to be mentioned self-consciously. Daughters are transformed into fiancées. During the week before the New Year holiday marriages will take place. The people are completely crazy. The suicide figure drops to zero.

Whoever is shot to death now so close to the end has suddenly lost his future. For heaven's sake just don't give them any reason for Maidanek or Auschwitz—to the extent that reasons mean anything. Take care, Jews, the utmost care and no rash steps!

For a long time the populace has been divided into two camps—it's apparent that Jacob has not only friends—two camps without ideology but with weighty arguments, program, and the art of persuasion. One of them gets violently excited about news, what happened last night, how heavy are the losses on each side. No report is so insignificant that this or that might not be concluded from it.

And the others have heard enough—Frankfurter's camp. For them this radio is a source of constant danger. Jacob would be able to pacify them so easily. I hear their misgivings in the railroad station and on the way home and in the house. In your naïveté, they warn, your talk is putting your life and ours in jeopardy. The Germans are not deaf and blind. And the ghetto regulations are not proposals for proper etiquette. It is written there in black and white what it means to listen to the radio. It also indicated what happens to those who know that someone is listening and don't report it. Therefore, be quiet and wait quietly in your nook. When the Russians are here, they're here. Your loose talk won't speed them up. And above all stop talking about your miserable radio, a possible grounds for a thousand deaths! Better destroy it today than tomorrow!

That's the situation. Jacob's circle, then, consists not only of friends; but he doesn't notice it. Nor can he even find out. The curious, the hundred Kowalskis who crowd around him, will take good care not to tell him, since Jacob could have second thoughts and see things differently and then suddenly start to keep quiet. So they'd rather keep quiet themselves. As for the warners, they for sure won't tell him. They won't send him any admonishing delegation. That would be much too risky. They'll make a big detour around him, so that no one may attest to seeing them in his vicinity.

Hershel Shtamm with his earlocks, for example, is one of the others who don't want to see and hear anymore or be an accessory. In the railroad station, behind hands kept over our mouths whenever we interpret the latest Russian successes fresh from Jacob's mouth, Hershel walks a few steps away, but not so very far. I estimate to within hearing distance. It mustn't be a conversation in which he outwardly participates; that's his quickly evident worry. Hershel's eyes then glance nonchalantly over the tracks, or they meet one of us with a disapproving sharp glance. But it is not impossible that under his perspiring fur cap his ears perk up like those of a hare.

The power failure that makes Jacob's radio a dangerous dust collector for several days is chalked up by him to his personal credit. To be sure he does not say so in public. Hershel is not the kind of man who likes to brag. We know it from his twin brother Roman who spends every evening and every morning with him in the same room and every night in the same bed. Ultimately, he must know it. When we ask Hershel how he accomplished that feat—a blackout in several streets lasting for several days is no child's play—his face becomes gentle, almost a smile after such danger surmounted. But he remains completely silent about it. And then we ask, "How was it, Roman? How did he do it?"

Those minutes before going to bed, reports Roman, are

filled with prayers, quietly in a corner, not just since the radio, but an old habit. Roman waits patiently in bed until the shared blanket can be pulled over his head. He hasn't demanded for a long time that Hershel hurry up and finally come to bed. He has been taught that prayers and haste must not be lumped together. He pays no attention to the monotonous mumbling and singing. It wouldn't make sense. Roman doesn't understand a word of Hebrew. But for some time familiar sounds have been reaching his ears, too. Since Hershel has been sending concrete requests to the good Lord, not only the usual pious nonsense about protection and turning everyone somehow to good, he has been using more and more often the general, comprehensible language. Roman can now overhear fragmentarily what is moving and tormenting his brother. Nothing extraordinary. If you would pray yourself, you too would not have very much different to say. Evening after evening God receives stories of hunger, fear of deportation, and beatings by the guards, all of which can not possibly be happening with His approval. Let Him please see what at least is going on and, if possible quickly; it is urgent. And may He give an indication that Hershel has been heard. That indication has been a long time in coming. For Hershel, a splendidly endured test of steadfastness. Each following day had been thoroughly examined for God's active intervention—in vain. Until it did come, that ardently desired sign from above, suddenly, like all divine action, and so mighty that the skeptical word would perish even upon the lips of the most irreligious.

On that evening the radio was the topic of conversation, the worry that overshadowed everything else at the moment. Hershel is explaining to God in minute detail the unpredictable consequences if thoughtlessness and deficient caution cause the gossips to overlook a German ear, and immediately it'll happen. The gossips will be prosecuted according to the law, as well as the silent accomplices. And it will be maintained that we are all accomplices, that the news was shared by everyone. They'll be right too. Besides, it need not even be a German ear accidentally in the vicinity. There are also disguised German ears. Only You know how many spies are among us. Or else, someone will want to save his own hide and betray it on his own. There are scoundrels everywhere. You know, too, that without Your consent they would not exist on earth. Don't permit that great misfortune to happen to us so close to the end, when You have all these years kept Your protective hand over us and have prevented the worst. For Your own sake do not allow it! Let the Germans find out nothing about the radio. You know what they are capable of. Or even better, if I may suggest a proposal to You: destroy this cursed radio. That would be the happiest solution.

So stood matters, when suddenly the light bulb on the ceiling started to flicker. Hershel at first pays no attention to it. Then he looks up, his eyes widening. In a flash he is enlightened as to the meaning of all that. God heard him. The prayers were not in vain. He sends a sign at just the right time, the confirmation of receipt and at the same time a sign that could not be conceived more useful. That's what God is for! Without electricity the radio will be condemned to silence. The more ardently Hershel prays, the more the light flickers. "Don't let up!" Roman spurs him on. But he need not tell him that. Hershel knows the score. Advice from scoffers is not wanted, not when bliss beckons as reward. Devoutly he lets his influential connections play on until it is accomplished. The bulb finally gives out. The last word is spoken. Hershel rushes to the window, with searching glances at the other side of the street. No speck of light through a single curtain, not even from Jacob Heym's house. We've silenced you, my friend; there will be divine peace. Take your wretched box to the devil. You won't be able to use it anymore. And don't think for a moment that the power failure that you in your frivolity consider a loss will be corrected by tomorrow. Short circuits from the Highest Authority last for a while.

Proud and happy—to the extent that circumstances allow—Hershel lies down in bed after his accomplished task and calmly receives Roman's congratulations.

Concerned faces surround Jacob. What's to be done? We're left high and dry without the slightest notion as to what's happening in the world. This unbearable situation is in its third day. It's no longer an electric failure; it's an act of God. With all our troubles, this too had to happen! We had quickly become accustomed to the good news. You get addicted every morning to the few kilometers. There was something to hope for and discuss for the whole day. But now only a gloomy calm predominated. In the morning our first step led us to the light switch. Some even got up in the middle of the night. We flicked the switch and became aware of the fearful answer: that Jacob today once again was no wiser than we. Only the electricity will make him omniscient once again. Only the electricity which the dark powers have turned off. Not until the lamps are burning again in all the rooms will his light shine especially brightly. But when will that be?

The only one for whom this new cause for worry is no cause at all is Jacob. By way of exception, that stroke of fate did not affect him. His tie to the outside world had not been cut. What doesn't exist can't be cut. It's as meager as ever. It's just that he must simply admit it. The sheer insanity of being the vessel of good fortune—although a very modest good fortune—disguised as a power failure, should only continue until the first Russian faces take the guards by surprise at the edge of the city! At least he can breathe freer now. Jacob can again be one among many.

No one will compel him to know more than everybody. However, he must continue to dissemble. He must dissemble all the time. He must feign regret when there is no word, regret at the electric failure, no small matter given his feeling of relief. Friends, you've seen, I'm doing the best I can. As long as it was possible, I've delivered the latest and best news to you. Not a single day were you without a consoling report. How I would gladly continue to report until the ardently desired great hour, but as you yourself see, my hands are tied.

The next morning Kowalski was again the winner. He is hauling crates with Jacob. Except that this time it was no longer a race. Overnight Jacob became an ordinary, common worker, an older person with two weak hands, I imagine, whom no one fights over anymore. Kowalski wound up with Jacob probably out of old habit or old friendship. In any case, they're lugging together. It's been a long time since things have gone so smoothly between them. For Jacob the crates seem a wee bit lighter now that Kowalski and the others have stopped showering him with questions, but for Kowalski, I suspect, heavier now that answers are lacking. As you see, weight is no absolute measure. The last question was whether, God forbid! the light in Jacob's house had also failed. Jacob answered simply and truthfully yes. He was quite happy to be able to tell the bald truth after such a long time. From that moment things are as peaceful with him as with anyone else. It'll stay that way until the electricity is on again. Thus no one should be surprised at Jacob's composure.

When the whistle blows for soup, they sit down beside each other in the sun. Kowalski sighs and spoons and sighs, not from the soup which tastes neither better nor worse than on any other day. Recently Jacob has learned to fear the proximity of Kowalski. Kowalski was the most eager of the curious and didn't let him eat or sleep. He used Jacob only as a vehicle for his curiosity, without mercy. But today his proximity cannot frighten Jacob. Questions would be wasted words. The sun is shining. They are sitting together peacefully and quietly and eating and somewhere, in the distance, Stalin's soldiers are approaching with unknown speed.

"How much longer do you think that electric failure can last?" asks Kowalski.

"Twenty years, I hope," says Jacob.

Kowalski looks up hurt from his bowl. That's no answer between friends. Surely the last few days were not easy for Jacob, the only tie to the outside, whom no one would leave in peace. You've been assaulted and punctured, and it certainly was not completely without danger. But do you take offense in our circumstances at such a little bit of additional trouble? In your place, who would have acted differently? Look for him among us and you won't find him, and then you get as an answer to your modest question such ugly words.

"Why are you so spiteful?" asks Kowalski.

"You'll never get the answer to that one," says Jacob.

Kowalski shrugs his shoulders and eats on. Today you can't talk to Jacob. Maybe he's in a bad mood. Come to think of it, he had always been inexplicably quarrelsome on some days. Whenever you came into his unpleasant café in those days, and even if you came in in the best of moods and sat down at one of the many empty tables and asked Jacob quite normally how business was—just as everyone asks—it could happen that Jacob didn't answer normally that business was such and such—as can be expected from a grown man. Instead, he used to attack you with "Don't ask such stupid questions. Just take a look around!"

Not completely coincidentally do Kowalski and Jacob get company. Misha sits down beside them and brings along Schwoch, the junior partner of Lifschitz and Schwoch: Ink Pads, Wholesale and Retail. At first Jacob thinks they are sitting down merely because there is room here, sun, and an unwatched spot, until he discovers that they keep looking at each other, Misha encouragingly and Schwoch uncertainly. Then he knows that it is not a coincidence. Some unknown deal is being cooked up. He has learned to pay attention to the finest nuances. Misha's glances mean "Well, go ahead and tell it" and Schwoch's glances mean "No, you tell it." When the glances seem like they'll never stop, Jacob says, between spoonfuls, "I'm listening."

"We've got an idea, Jacob," says Schwoch.

So far, so good. For a decent idea there is always use. Good ideas are like air for breathing. Let's hear what you've thought of, then we'll see.

But Schwoch clams up after his shy attempt. He looks again to Misha and his eyes speak: "You tell the rest."

"This is the situation," says Misha. "We were thinking, if the electricity doesn't come to the radio, the radio will have to go to the electricity."

"Are you telling me riddles?" asks Jacob concerned, when there is nothing puzzling in Misha's words. They mean no more and no less than the fact that in some street in this ghetto lights are still working. In a moment, you'll hear in which one. Common sense can easily figure it out.

"In Kowalski's street there is electricity," says Schwoch.

That promising sentence stated as an explanation for Jacob hits Kowalski just as he is scraping out the remains of his bowl. His hand pauses rigidly. For a short moment he closes his eyes. His lips whisper something embittered, wishing Schwoch a stroke, and he moves aside. Not far, only a few symbolic centimeters. He has heard nothing. Let these madmen say whatever they please! The entire matter is none of his business.

Jacob noticed the little disclosure. A pity that he can't smile. Important matters must be decided before the break is over and before Misha's and Schwoch's scheme gets bandied about and considered a viable alternative. That they will run their heads against a brick wall with Kowalski is as clear as day to Jacob. No danger from that direction. Whoever has lived so many years within earshot of Kowalski knows what a hero does not look like. To trim your beard according to the latest fashion and to cut your hair so cleverly that people on the street look around at you— that he can, perhaps, do. But, under pain of death to listen to forbidden broadcasts and to circulate their contents— for that you'd have to get someone more stupid. By no means is the problem Kowalski. The concern is rather that someone else will be found. Kowalski's street is long. Another may come and say, "Give me that thing, we'll let it play and sing and proclaim heaven on earth."

They must be thoroughly dissuaded from their plan. If nothing will come of it—it must be intrinsically because of the plan, not because of Kowalski. He can come out of the affair only as an honorable man. Words must be found that will discredit the idea itself and prove its complete uselessness. Well then, proof is necessary. And where to obtain it in a hurry? Perhaps Kowalski will think of the right answer. In the final analysis he is Jacob's ally. They're in the same rocking boat. Kowalski, too, will flail away with all his might at Misha's and Schwoch's brainstorm. He will say anything except that he is too frightened. You need only push him to the wall and he'll talk. It is only to be hoped that the proper hypocrisy can be found in such a short time.

"Did you hear what they want of you?" says Jacob.

Kowalski turns his head to him, acting as if he had been lost in thought, and asks in complete innocence, "Of me?" And then he asks Schwoch, "What?"

"It's about the electricity," Schwoch explains patiently. "Someone could bring the radio to your place, couldn't he?"

Kowalski acts as if he heard a bad joke. "To me?"

"Yes."

"The radio?"

"Yes."

"Splendid!"

The idiots want to kill me, he'll think. They want to ruin me, as if I weren't loaded with enough other *tsooris*. They're talking about my annihilation, as if it were the most natural thing in the world.

"And you, Jacob? What do you say about it?"

"Why not?" says Jacob. "It's up to you. I'm agreed."

It only appears as if he were playing with fire. He knows precisely what Kowalski is like. Besides, if Kowalski were to mature into a hero on the spur of the moment, you could even reconsider the matter later on. But, as far as can be judged, that won't be necessary. Kowalski is a classic example of a pushover.

"Do you know what risks you, too, are taking?" asks Kowalski, boundlessly amazed at so much carelessness. "What do you mean, someone could bring the radio to me? Who is that 'someone'? I? You? He? Who is it? Would you carry the radio through the ghetto in broad daylight? Or, even better, at night maybe?"

He leans back horrified. It's almost funny what they propose to you. And they claim to be intelligent people!

"A procession they want to make! The patrols and guards will go to sleep during the entire thing and when we're done, we'll go wake them up and say, now you can go about your work. The radio is safe at Kowalski's."

Schwoch and Misha look at each other crestfallen. Stripped to its essentials, their plan no longer looks so splendid. Jacob also throws in a few expressive glances, serious and full of doubt. Kowalski's penetrating words appear to have made even him think twice.

"Besides, there is one more important point," says Kowalski. "That there is a radio in the ghetto is already known to many. But who knows that it's at Jacob's? Only we here

**83**

at the railroad station and, at most, his neighbors too. If everything has been all right till now, that is, if the Germans have no hint till now, then decent people must live in Jacob's house. But how do you know it is the same in my house? I live together with three men. Who can guarantee that there is no traitor or coward over me, or beside me, or below me? And that he would not react swiftly by running to the Gestapo and telling what he knows?"

A long pause. Kowalski's words are considered and weighed, and Schwoch says quietly, "Shit, he's right."

Misha shrugs his shoulders undecided. Jacob stands up and says, "If you think . . ."

"Don't be in such a dangerous hurry, fellows," says Kowalski. "The electric current will come on again. If not tomorrow, then the day after tomorrow. And then Jacob can still tell us soon enough how far they've advanced."

By the time the whistle blows again for work, the plan of Misha and Schwoch is dead and buried. It has been thoroughly discussed as is proper among intelligent beings. Its weak points have been exposed and it hasn't withstood the exposure. It would have been quite nice. It's a pity, but a clearheaded person would have opened our eyes. Schwoch and Misha put their empty bowls on the cart. They are almost the last to do so. The guard is already staring impatiently and threateningly.

Jacob and Kowalski are once again a lovely pair, both liberated from a worry that the matter would have come to pass.

"What brainstorms they have!" says Kowalski amused, more to himself than to Jacob, and with that brings that chapter to a close.

Lena is standing around lazily in the doorway and looking over to Rafael and Siegfried, who are sitting on the edge of the curb talking quietly—exaggeratedly quietly and cautiously for her. As soon as anyone passes, they stop and blink innocently into the sun. Lena perks up her ears in vain. Her reserve is quickly overcome and she strolls across the street to find out what those two chatterers are whispering about. She catches Siegfried asserting that there isn't much more time and Rafael's reply that they're saying at home, it could last at most only a few days more.

Then she is discovered. The two eye her indifferently and wait for the end of the interruption with immobile glances. But they could wait a long time. Lena doesn't move on. She remains standing where she is, smiling sweetly. Until Rafael finally stands up.

"Come on. What we have to discuss is not for her to hear," he says.

That's exactly Siegfried's opinion, too. He raises himself to his full height in front of Lena and can't suppress the remark that she would get a beating if only she weren't such a half-pint girl. Lena takes the threat without flinching, since the two boys take off and disappear, moreover, into their own vestibule. Lena waits a few more seconds. Jacob, who has strictly forbidden her to enter strange houses, is far away, and Lena pursues them. Sticking her head carefully in through the yard door, she manages to catch sight of Siegfried and Rafael entering the shed where the cabinetmaker Panno once used to maintain his workshop in more propitious times. It still stinks today of lime. The shed window no longer has any glass panes. Lena knows that even without investigation. She herself was present when Rafael smashed the last one at the very first throw. Well, the mysterious thoughts of the two boys will not remain hidden from her for long, not from her. On tiptoes she steals up to the dark window and quietly crouches on the ground. For all she cares they can continue.

"At best, we'll blow up the police station," she hears Siegfried's voice.

"And if they catch us?" asks Rafael.

"Don't crap yourself. The Russians will soon be here, as you've heard. Besides, they won't be able to catch us if we blow them up, since they'll all be dead. We just shouldn't let ourselves blow it ahead of time."

Siegfried had always been a loudmouth. Lena could bet on the spot that nothing would come of it.

"Will the commanding officer of the Russians give us something if we carry it off?" asks the greedy Rafael.

"What do you think! a medal, or a real pistol, or something to eat!"

"Or all of them?"

"Of course! Isn't that worthwhile? They mustn't find out about it at home."

For a few moments, silence. Of course, the two blockheads are imagining everything that the Russians will give them from their lavishly filled pockets as a reward for their heroic deeds.

Suddenly, Rafael says sadly: "Say, . . . it won't work."

"Why?"

"How will we get the dynamite? When I use up my two rounds of ammunition, it won't be enough."

"True. Don't you have any more?"

"No."

"Neither do we."

Lena laughs holding her hands to her mouth to keep from shrieking. Really, it's hard to believe how stupid two ten-year-old boys can be!

Rafael has a new idea. "Do you know what? Let's just lock them in!"

"Whom?"

"The Gestapos! We'll just lock the police station. At night they are all asleep and then we'll lock them in. The doors are at least this thick and they themselves put bars on the windows. They won't get out so quickly. And then when the Russkis are here, we'll have them all in one swoop!" Rafael can hardly catch his breath from excitement.

"We don't have a key, do we?"

"We'll find one," says Rafael reassuringly. "In my old man's drawer is a bunch with at least twenty on it. One is bound to fit."

"Not bad at all," mumbles Siegfried. It can be clearly heard how annoyed he is, because he didn't come up with this splendid idea. Only too gladly would he put down Rafi's plan; but it is fine.

Then the yard door opens. Little Frau Bujok appears looking for her naughty son. She can't find him, but instead finds Lena crouching on the ground and grinning.

"Have you seen Siegfried?"

Lena is a bit startled. She was so preoccupied. She looks up at Frau Bujok and continues her grinning. The half-pint girl indicates that it is necessary to strike while the iron is hot and points her thumb at the shed in back of her. Frau Bujok looks threateningly at the shed, stands quietly for a moment in order to take a deep breath, then marches inside. A not too silent slap is heard and then "Oww!" and "How many times must I tell you to stay in front of the window!" One more slap is heard and "You go on home, too, you bum!"

Then silence descends upon the yard. Lena stands up and dusts off her skirt. The performance is over. Frau Bujok comes out of the shed. Her annoyance has turned her red. Siegfried is holding on to her with one hand. With the other, he is holding his cheek. At least he isn't bawling. They leave the yard quickly. Siegfried doesn't see Lena.

Lena goes to the yard door, too. She is in no hurry. In fact, she could continue to stay there. But Rafael is now by himself, so the hideout has lost is value. He might even possibly deign now to make do with her, but she doesn't give a hoot about that. She simply is not in the mood now. Let him sit there alone and rack his brains over which of the twenty keys fits. Nothing will come of it anyway.

Hence she leaves. In the doorway she turns around once again. Rafael is taking his time.

"You are really a stupid bunch!" she calls out through the yard to the shed and does not thereby make herself endearing.


And the resistance? you ask. What about the resistance? Are the heroes perhaps assembling in the shoe factory or in the freight yard? Some at least? Have dark sewers been uncovered through which weapons can be smuggled into the ghetto at the southern border, the most poorly laid out and thus the most difficult to patrol? Or are there in this wretched city merely workmen who do exactly what Hardtloff and his guards demand of them?

Condemn them! Condemn us still! There were only such workmen. Not a single, solitary shot was fired. Law and order were strictly maintained. Not a trace of resistance. I must add, I think there wasn't any resistance. I am not omniscient but I make my assertion, as they say, with probability bordering on certainty. If there had been something there, I would have surely had to notice it.

I would have joined in. That I can assure you. They would have only needed to ask me, especially if it had been for Chana's sake. Unfortunately, I am not one of the exceptional kind who inspires others to struggle. I can not sweep others along, but I would have joined in. And not only I. Why didn't that individual come forth who could cry out, "Follow me!"? The last few hundred kilometers wouldn't have had to be so long and so difficult. The worst that could have happened to us would have been a meaningful death.

I must add, I have subsequently read about Warsaw

and Buchenwald. A different world, yet comparable. I have read a great deal about heroism, probably too much. Foolish envy has overwhelmed me. But no one need believe me. In any case, we kept quiet to the last second and I can't change anything about it. I am not unaware that an oppressed people can become really free only when it participates in its own liberation, when it goes to meet the Messiah at least part way. We didn't do so. I didn't move from the spot. I memorized the regulations, strictly observed them, and asked poor Jacob only from time to time what the latest developments were. Probably I will never get over it. I haven't deserved better. My entire private matter about the trees surely has something to do with it, as well as my wretched sentimentality and the generosity of my tear ducts. Where I was, there was no resistance.

They say, what is good for your enemies is bad for you. I don't intend to argue about it. Only tangible illustrations would make sense anyway, such as one of mine. But I don't wish to argue about it. My illustration is the electricity. Jacob can easily and even gladly do without it. He gets along splendidly without it. Doing without? No one would have ever thought how good no electricity could be. Aside from the Russians and Lena's good health, Jacob desires nothing so much as no electricity. But Jacob is a single individual and we are many. We want to have electricity. We're at the helpless mercy of our own delusions. If not our saviors, then at least we should have electricity!

The Germans, to return to my illustration, also want electricity, not only because they are ruining their eyes by candlelight at police headquarters. Their elaborate plans are going awry. Not a single chair or buffet is leaving the furniture factory. Pliers, hammers, and screws from the tool factory are lacking. No shoes, no pants. The Jews are sitting around twiddling their thumbs. Two squads of electricians, hastily thrown together, spread out looking for the damage. Special allocations with doubled rations of bread and cigarettes. Day and night they test the fuses and whatever is supposed to be tested, digging up streets, uncovering cables, accompanied by our good wishes. After five fruitless days, Hardtloff has them executed. There is talk of sabotage, which is sheer nonsense. All the electricians were somehow customers of Jacob and had a personal interest in correcting the defect. They are executed on the square in front of police headquarters. Anyone who wishes can watch. Let that serve as a warning to you to do whatever is demanded of you.

Then a German technical squad arrives in a truck like men from Mars. Uniforms like divers. They are observed laughing and enjoying their importance. We'll accomplish the thing, Erika. Let's have a look at what has stumped the Jewish bunglers. Two days and the defect is revealed in all its nakedness. A swarm of rats had gnawed through a cable and perished from their greed. A new cable is laid in the ground and once again buffets, shoes, pliers, screws, and Jacob's radio.

We want to know if it's true that they intend to sell us for a ransom. If so, where is the money? We want to know if it's true that a Jewish State is to be established. If so, when? If not, who is hindering it? Above all, we want to know where the Russians are. For three weeks now you've been making our mouths water, as you had never succeeded in doing with your pancakes. Tell us how they are breaking through the battle lines, what tactics they're using, whether they're treating prisoners as prisoners or as criminals, if they're having a great deal of trouble with the Japanese in the East, whether or not the Americans can at least relieve them of that, even if they are not invading Europe. And we also want to know about Kiepura's fate and how he is getting along in America. Lots of new events must have piled up in the interim—O.K.—they won't broadcast any special summary for us. They have no idea how we have suffered during the power failure. But you do manage to find out something in addition to the very latest. Please omit nothing, do you hear, nothing!

Jacob is to be pitied. He would need a well-equipped office, a headquarters with three secretaries, even better, with five. A few liaison officers in all the important capitals who send back to headquarters punctually and reliably every piece of uncovered detail. With the secretaries dizzily sorting out the details, reading all the important newspapers, listening to all the radio stations, and making a synopsis of all of that, presenting it to Jacob as the highest responsible person, he could then answer about a third of the questions truthfully, as truthful as newspapers, radio stations, and liaison officers happen to be.

A newspaper is sticking out of "The Whistle's" pocket. "Whistle" comes out of the guardhouse, walks past the freight cars—scraping his wooden leg along—right through the midst of Jews, who don't even notice what is limping past them. What do we care about newspapers! We have Jacob. Only Jacob looks and cares. The magnifying glass in his eyes doesn't let go of the precious object in the railwayman's pocket: a little paper with true or falsified reports of actual events, in any case infinitely more valuable than a nothing from a radio. Relief for his exhausted ingenuity, if a bold exchange of owners were successful.

In back of the last tracks, "Whistle" reaches his goal, a little wooden shed "For Germans Only"—that's what is written on the door directly under the heart-shaped hole they subsequently carved, according to native custom, I imagine.

Jacob doesn't let himself get diverted by his crate-hauling with Kowalski. One eye is constantly on the shed. If the newspaper was, moreover, the complete edition, as it seemed to be, and if the railwayman is not too wasteful, some would have to be left over. If the railwayman is no miser, he would leave the rest behind. He may not be wasteful nor may he be miserly. There is no proof for or against. If an opportunity arises, Jacob will go get what's left. But whatever opportunity may arise, it's bound to be perilous, for what could a Jew have lost in a German toilet? Brothers, for you I'll risk my life! I don't intend to steal potatoes like Misha who is more practical-minded and thinks of mundane matters. If all goes well, I'll steal a few grams of news events and manufacture a ton of hope for you. Had I been born more intelligent and imaginative like Sholem Aleichem—what am I saying, even half as much would suffice—I wouldn't need such pilfering. I would be able to invent ten times more and better than those who write in their newspapers. But I am not able to; I can't; I am so inane that it frightens me. I'll do it for you, for you and for me. I'll do it for me, too, because it's certain that I can not survive alone, but only together with you. That's the reverse side of a liar. I'll go into their toilet and take whatever is still there, if only something is left over.

"Whistle" finally enters God's sun again, takes a few deep breaths, lights a cigarette whereby he uses four matches because of the wind. He takes enough time to choke. But as for that all important pocket . . . it's empty. In trying to recall the newspapers in those days, ours had mostly eight pages, four sheets. Let's assume his also had four, that would be the usual case. You tear a sheet once, then once more, then a third time. That gives you per page —just a moment!—that gives you eight pieces per page. You can also tear it four times. But the pieces get to be rather small. Well, let's stick with three times. He certainly had enough paper. Four sheets times eight make thirty-two pieces. No healthy person needs that much. You tear up just one page and put the rest down for reading. But even if he tore up all of them, something is still lying there in any case, if he didn't throw in the rest through ignorance.

"What are you constantly mumbling about?" asks Kowalski.

"I mumbling?" says Jacob.

"Constantly. Four and sixteen and that would make this much and that much. What are you figuring out?"

"Whistle" finally disappears again into the guardhouse. Jacob looks at the guards. One is standing at the gate bored; one is sitting on a freight car running board, reassuringly distant; the third is nowhere to be seen, presumably in the guardhouse hiding away, sleeping, since nothing is happening. And there are only three.

"Keep working and don't turn around to me," says Jacob.

"Why?" asks Kowalski. "What's wrong?"

"I'm going to their toilet."

Kowalski makes an astonished expression and stops working. The next thing you know this madman will go to the guardhouse for a brandy and tobacco. He'll borrow money from a guard and they'll put him against the wall for nothing more than for what he intends to do now.

"Are you crazy? Can't you wait for the break and then go behind the fence?"

"No, I can't."

Jacob crouches and runs off like someone experienced. The stacks of crates hide him almost the entire way from the glances coming from the guardhouse, except for the last few meters. But they are part of it; they, too, are conquered. Jacob closes the door to the toilet behind him. Not a word about odors, nothing about the graffiti on the walls. The rich loot is lying next to the eyeglasses. But first a glance outside through the little heart. No one noticed anything. The station through a heart! Things are taking their course. The loot consists of the expected remainder. He wasn't wasteful. A large number of torn sheets neatly shaped as if cut with a knife. Under the sheets an entire double page is left over. Jacob stuffs the sheets under his shirt as smoothly as possible so as not to rustle while working, better on his back than on his belly. The double spread isn't worthwhile; that is, it is worth something. Four times from top to bottom obituaries with black borders, satisfying, but of meager information. Killed in action, Killed in action, Killed in action, Killed in action. We'll let them lie there peacefully. We don't want to drag around any ballast. We learn that by heart easily. Four pages of deaths. Let the next visitor have his fun out of it, too. But we don't want to get comfortable, as if we were on our own toilet. We don't want to let time pass dangerously. We'll want to get to work again and impatiently put it behind us. Then we'll go to our unwatched room, unload our back, clean up, and turn on our new radio. Tomorrow you can come once again and question me as long as the supply lasts.

Jacob looks out again, whether everything is O.K. Nothing is O.K. Nothing at all. On the way back there is one obstacle after another. A soldier is approaching the shed, you might say, resolutely, his fingers already unbuckling his belt. In his mind he is sitting already and is feeling better. With him there, nobody could leave the shed unnoticed. What do you do now? Jacob's knees remind him emphatically that he is no longer so young. As easy as the way here was, you don't notice it until later. The door can not be bolted. Some idiot has torn off the eye for the hook. Just try holding it closed! One shove with the shoulder and he'll be inside, eye you thoroughly, and do whatever else he wants to. Theoretically, that is, keep cool, unruffled.

The advantage of surprise is on our side. He still has eight steps. The planks on the back wall would take at least five minutes and more than enough noise. He still has five steps. You have no choice but the small oval hole into their dung. Why can't you bring yourself to it? You'd be thin enough.

The soldier opens the door that offers no resistance. To his dismay he sees before him an opened double page spread of a newspaper, inordinately trembling, which doesn't attract attention in such an embarrassing moment.

"Oh, pardon me!" he says and closes the door quickly not noticing the decrepit Jewish shoes under the newspaper nor the fact that no lowered pants were showing that would have completed the picture, and for which Jacob was not quick enough and the time too short. Maybe it was quite fortunate. Too much disguising can also be harmful. The important thing is that he closes the door, free of suspicion. He counts on a short wait. His belt is already hanging over his forearm while he walks to and fro since that is easier to tolerate than standing.

How long of a waiting period should Jacob count on? Beyond the edge of the newspaper and through the heart-shaped hole that soldier in gray is walking to and fro. Only a miracle can help now, so act upon your first impulse! You don't need to rack your brains, because genuine miracles aren't predictable. There are still two minutes left, hardly more, for the unexpected, and if it doesn't happen, which would be only fair and proper, the aforementioned last hours would look so ridiculous.

"Hurry up, pal, I have diarrhea," the soldier is heard pleading.

The little sheets on Jacob's back are beginning to stick together. They will have to be dried out before use, if everything turns out well in a fairy-tale manner. And Jacob tells me, suddenly he gets tired, suddenly fear and hope disappear, everything gets strangely heavy and light simultaneously—his legs, eyelids, and hands from which the four pages of those killed in action for their country gently slip away.

"Did you hear about Marotzke? He got another home furlough. If that doesn't seem fishy! He must know some people high up, don't you think? He goes very frequently and we all just wait and wait and have to hang around among these garlic eaters."

My heavens . . . garlic. If we only had a single clove, spread extremely thin on warm bread, you idiot. He thinks he's talking to a Schulz or a Müller on the toilet. A Marotzke—the name couldn't be more apropos—whoever that Marotzke may be. Jacob leans against the back wall and closes his eyes; you could wait a long time for a heroic rebellion; his is finished. It's his friend's move outside. It's he who has to keep the thing moving. Should he leave or stay. Tormented by stomach cramps, should he push the door open and stare and shoot, he would not hit a startled person. Whatever follows is his problem.

Who would guess that the needed miracle is already being processed? In broad details, it is already being drawn up. There is still Kowalski. Kowalski with his two horrified eyes in his head. He knows what's up. He sees the situation. He sees the poor soldier and the door that is still shut. He knows who is inside and who won't get out without his help—if he hasn't in the meantime already died of fright. Deliverance means distracting the German, not by throwing a pebble against the wall so that he would turn around and shout, "Who threw that?" Something must happen that demands his immediate intervention. The first thing to occur to him is the pile of crates, two meters high and rather shaky. If two of the bottom ones are pulled away, it won't stand there so proudly and ready for shipment anymore, for then its equilibrium is gone, and that would provide a nice diversion. However, what happens to a blockhead who is so inept, what happens to Jacob if no clumsy person can be found far and wide? What good is a forty-year-old friendship? Logic problems for Kowalski!

Jacob hears a quiet rumble in the distance. You can't close your ears as you can your eyes. Then he hears a soldier's boots quickly running off. Reason enough to open your eyes again. In this way and not otherwise can a miracle be understood. His arms and legs take on their former reliable feeling. And things proceed. The air seems clear your glance through the heart tells you. The Jews, who can be seen through the cutout, have interrupted their work and are all staring in a certain direction, to there where, supposedly, the miracle is taking place.

Kowalski has successfully toppled the mountain of crates. His strength was just barely sufficient. One crate fell on his head. The soldier storms over blindly from the shed into the trap and falls upon the decoy, Kowalski. It may be stated that seldom has a sleight-of-hand artist's trick succeeded so well. Although the blows take their toll —the crate on his head was nothing in comparison— Kowalski moans quietly, protects his face with his hands, and regrets profusely his unpardonable mistake.

The rest of us are standing as if rooted to the spot and gritting our teeth. Someone beside me claims to have observed that Kowalski purposely toppled the stack. The soldier beats him and beats him. Marotzke is getting a home furlough and not he. Maybe he is really enraged over so much clumsiness, but he ceases his duty quite abruptly. Something is stirring inside of him, not sympathy and not exhaustion, for the diarrhea demands its right. Everyone can clearly see it. He grimaces and runs in long strides to the shed that in the meantime had been made available just for him. That is, he calls out still: "Be sure all that is piled back in order by the time I come back, you hear!" Not until then does he exhibit his long sprints that, despite everything, look funny. The matter will brook no postponement for him. He would now implore every newspaper reader to clear out immediately, right away, because otherwise a little accident would happen. But he can save himself the trouble. He tears open the door to an empty toilet. The little accident was just barely avoided at the last second.

None of us bystanders dares help Kowalski or console him. Here you work and don't console. He wipes the blood from his face, tests his teeth to see that are all there, except one. All things taken into consideration, it might have turned out much worse. The aches will pass. Jacob will remain alive. After the war we'll give him a fancy W.C. on which he will be able to sit for hours to his heart's content and think of his good friend Kowalski who is still examining himself. Jacob gathers courage to appear in front of him because Kowalski must not discover the real reason for his bold excursion. He especially not. He has deserved not to be informed of the real reason. For him, it will have to remain an incomprehensible whim of Jacob that could have—by a hair—cost him his life.

"Thank you," says Jacob moved. "Moved" is the proper expression, moved for the first time in forty years. It isn't every day that your life is saved. In addition, by someone whom you have known for such a long time and from whom you, to tell the truth, wouldn't have expected it.

Kowalski doesn't give him as much as a nod. He gets up groaning, goes over to the crates that had better be piled up before the soldier comes back from his emergency, and tests what his word means here. They would all still be nicely arranged in rows just like the few teeth in his mouth if Jacob were a normal person, if he hadn't irresponsibly pursued strange longings and now others have to pay bitterly for them.

Jacob exerts himself. For each crate Kowalski stacks, Jacob manages three. Kowalski is gripped by the question of guilt, by rage, and certainly by his aches, too.

"Did you at least have a good shit?" inquires Kowalski and has difficulty keeping from screaming. "Look at my face; take a good look! It must look nice! It wasn't him; it was you! But what am I getting excited about! The main thing is that you shit in grand style. Everything else is unimportant. One thing I can swear to you, Heym, just try it again! Go ahead and try it, then you'll see who'll help you!"

Jacob entrenches himself behind his work. Kowalski is right from his point of view. What mitigates all that can not be revealed by Jacob. And anything said would only add to the anger. Someday, Kowalski, when all this is past, when the two of us are sitting quietly somewhere with our brandies, when the pancakes are crackling in the pan, I'll explain everything to you. Very calmly, Kowalski, you'll hear the whole truth. We will laugh and shake our heads over the crazy times these were. You will ask me why I didn't tell it right away, at least to you, my best friend, and I will answer that I couldn't because you would have then told everyone and they would have taken me for one of the thousand liars and rumor-mongers and would have been without hope again. And then you'll lay your hand on my arm because you'll understand, perhaps, and you'll say: "Come, dear Jacob, let's drink another vodka."

When the door to the toilet is opened again after an ample period of time, the pile of crates is jutting into the air, as if no one had ever worked at toppling it. The soldier approaches unhurriedly, his hands on his back, his uniform properly buttoned. He has already been expected, not really ardently, but merely that the matter is finally executed. But the way he comes and stops and holds his head —his entire manner can make you feel ill at ease, because he looks more friendly than critical. Somehow he looks at the world with different eyes. How a few good minutes can transform a person! The crates? He has completely forgotten the crates. He is looking only at Kowalski's swollen face—which is, for the time being, red, but which shows already blue, green, and purple—and seems concerned. To Jacob he seems concerned and Jacob ought to know! He turns around silently and goes away. Jacob thinks, it's lucky he discovered his sympathetic feelings afterward rather than being a good person from the start, otherwise he would have never run away from the door. He would have remained there and a bit later his kindness would have been put to too severe a test.

In passing by, our pal loses two cigarettes, *Juno* brand without filter tips. He loses them or drops them, a question that will never be clarified, just as little as his motives, to the extent that it was intentional. In any case, the cigarettes belong to Kowalski. In the final analysis, he paid for them.

Minutes later, "Whistle" comes out of the guardhouse and whistles for the noon break. The railwayman whom up to an hour ago none of us ever heard speak but who, however, is the most talkative among our Germans because a halfway useful radio set fell out of his pocket. Everything began today with "Whistle," and he knows nothing about it. He whistles as always for soup and can not know how shamelessly his negligence, or whatever it was, was exploited. Only Jacob knows. He thinks again of the sheets under his shirt and of the double-page spread that in the meantime has undergone an unknown fate and which should not really be forgotten so unused.

"Did I tell you, by the way, that the Germans are having tremendous losses?" says Jacob.

They are already in line. Kowalski turns around to him and amidst his black and blue marks is blossoming the tender bloom of a grateful smile, despite everything.

The radio turns out to be not very informative. Jacob lays one little sheet of paper next to the other on his table, a total of nine pieces, while Piwowa and Rosenblatt refrain from any disturbance. Today they are what they have already been for some time, that is to say, dead, because of cat meat and a supervisor. Today they are not meddling in Jacob's affairs because he has to concentrate upon his piecing game.

The name of the newspaper is not to be found nor the date. For that, sheer chance was to blame. The nine little sheets produce no single coherent page because "Whistle" grabbed quite indiscriminately instead of keeping to any sort of sequence. Jacob has overtime work. He tests and turns and changes and hardly finds any two pieces that fit together. At the end of all his troubles what he has are two extremely fragmentary pages with tablecloth-colored holes, two pages that look as if a prudent censor had excised anything worth knowing and thereby insured that only insignificant material reached incompetent hands. The sports section, for example—just his luck!—is perfectly complete. How happy the Jews will be to find out that the air force boxing team beat a navy group ten to six. Or that the Berlin soccer team once again didn't have a chance against the Hamburg team, as so often in the past. Then, too, the discreet page reveals something of world impact: a Gauleiter, whose name is torn off, made some positive observations on some art exhibition or other; His Excellency, the Spanish ambassador would like to see mutual friendly relations extended; and before the People's Court a trial came to its just termination against two paid agents in the service of international Jewish finance.

Here you are, sitting with a disappointed expression. You didn't expect much to begin with, merely a little push for your poor reason, just this and that hidden tip from which, with a little skill, a public banquet could be cooked up—but such a dearth you didn't expect. Not a word about Bezanika, which the Russians must surely have captured long ago! Not a single word about German difficulties! Instead, these dopes are playing soccer, having exhibits, and cultivating righteousness!

Let's at least be fair about it. Let's leave open the possibility that the newspaper is old or that the best part of it was used up by "Whistle." But either way, you would have to be a fool to have fostered so many hopes. You should have realized what to expect, if you had only taken five seconds to think about it. It's also sufficiently well known what kind of newspapers they can publish. Years ago, there was a German newspaper in our region: *Der Völkische Landbote* [*The National Courier*], and don't ask me what that was good for! People never bought it. To throw away money is a sin, but now and then you managed to get hold of it whether you wanted to or not. They used to wrap fish in it in the marketplace. At the dentist's there was a copy in the waiting room, and, of course, at the insurance company, and at times even in Kowalski's barbershop, because he wanted to give the impression of a cosmopolitan. They said to him, Kowalski, they said to him, if you keep letting that junk lying around here, you'll simply louse up your business. Or do you think a German customer will stray into your shop and let you mess with your Jewish fingers in his Kaiser Wilhelm beard? Kowalski answered, insulted, you just leave that to me; I don't make any rules for you, as to how much sawdust you should mix in your potato pancakes. That's the way Kowalski was! Moreover, my hands should fall off right on the spot if that slander is true! In any case, one glance into the paper was enough to know what was what. They constantly felt themselves threatened and humiliated and wronged by God and the world. It was not they who humiliated us, but rather we them. The question as to how long Germany should suffer from the humiliating consequences of the last war gave them no peace in any edition, three times a week. And on the last page, next to the rebus, were such incomprehensible poems that you felt they had forgotten their language.

Except for the want ad section. That wasn't the worst. They had a knack for that. Every other Wednesday or Tuesday the two middle pages were filled with little ads, and if you needed something that was rarely in the marketplace or couldn't be gotten at all, like maybe a few pretty wicker chairs, or a modern floor lamp, or a larger supply of plates because dishes didn't last long in your café, why then it couldn't do any harm to look in the *Courier*. Of course, you were guided by the names of those who had their merchandise for sale. If they were named Hagedorn or Leineweber, you didn't bother going there. If they were Skrzypczak or Bartosiewicz, then, highly unlikely. And if they were named Silberstreif, you went. Because when it came to want ads, the people from the *Courier* were not choosy; they allowed everybody, as long as he could pay. But, as mentioned, that went only for the ads every other Wednesday or Tuesday and the rest was pure and simple junk.

You should have reminded yourself about all that before you put your head so needlessly in the noose and got it out again only by a friendly miracle. That's the way newspapers were in those days and that's the way newspapers still are. Nobody has shown them since then any better method. Only their gift for successful want ad sections seems to have remained. The four pages left behind, full of announcements of those killed in action, show that there are still men at work who understand their business.

Jacob turns over to the other side sheet after sheet exactly in place. Things aren't completely hopeless. There is still an unread reverse side as fragmentary as the other side, but maybe not quite so taciturn. There is a write-up there about a hero as only our people can produce, a pilot with a French name, who is shooting enemy airplanes like

**103**

sparrows out of Africa's sky. The *Führer* replied to a message from *Il Duce,* and in Munich a truck collided with a streetcar resulting in a traffic tieup for several hours. A cartoon: a tall man is holding a burning match over the head of a small man. Question: "What does that signify?" Answer: "Dover * under fire." And a thick headline that asserts: Victories on all fronts! You can believe it or not. We'd rather not. Its lower part is missing. It is, so to say, up in the air and we know that they claim to have been near Moscow. They claimed that, not we. But we heard ourselves that there is fighting near Bezanika. There's quite a distance between the two. If a victory looks like that, we don't begrudge you hundreds of that kind.

Fine! Jacob can figure out that they are fibbing a bit. But how to answer the questions that will rain down upon him first thing tomorrow morning? He tells me, sighing, he conceived all that much too simply. You read their propaganda dispatches, he thought, and you see through them without, or with, a little bit of effort; simply twist everything around and the news items crowd into your mouth. You can release them at your leisure. But, go ahead and simply twist them around! The air force boxers didn't beat the navy, but lost; the Gauleiter with the torn off name found the art exhibition miserable; the German hero doesn't hit a single enemy airplane; the streetcar in Munich adroitly eluded the truck; and the *Führer* didn't reply to *Il Duce's* message because he never received any. I'm telling you, all trash! Maybe the cartoon will reveal something, I guess. "Dover under fire" means Dover is being shelled. Dover is located, if I'm not mistaken, in England, and if they're shelling England, England will be shelling them—that's apparent. Excellent, they'll tell me tomorrow morning, England is resisting, but England is

* Dover, or Doofer, properly speaking, also means a stupid man.

**104**

far away and what will happen to us? At most, you could interpret losses on all fronts from those victories, but what do I know about fronts, where they're located, how many there are? Losses have to be proved by particulars. I don't know any. What would you have done in my position?

Jacob makes an important decision. The power failure was a divine respite with the sole disadvantage that you had no control over its duration. We'll create another such respite, but without a disadvantage because the respite we have in mind has no end. When they ask us, What's new, Jacob? we'll let our shoulders droop and make our saddest face and whisper to them in a despairing tone: Just imagine, my fellow Jews, last evening I sat down in front of my radio, all ears, and turned the knob as always, but not a sound came out. Not a one. You understand, yesterday it was still singing like a bird, and today it's completely quiet. No amount of lamentation will help, my fellow Jews, you know what a capricious thing a radio can be. Now it won't work.

The radio won't work. Jacob crumples up the little sheets—all nine of them—into a small pile. His annoyance that he hadn't thought of this splendid idea sooner is kept under control. Much greater is the joy of discovery that even if his toilet paper served no other function than enlightening him, it was worthwhile despite everything, and the price that Kowalski paid was not too high. Now it will no longer be necessary to lie awake night after night and torment yourself thinking up stories for them the following day. Instead, you can now lie awake night after night listening, as all the others do, whether the yearned-for thunder of cannon in the distance will finally cease. The radio is out of commission; the sheets are thrown in the stove; Jacob will ignite them when heating is necessary. The damper is closed.

In the nick of time, because Jacob forgot earlier in his

haste, to lock the door; it opens. Smiling, Lena comes in without knocking.

"Did you forget me today?" she asks.

"Certainly not," says Jacob and gives her her kiss, while he, at least, locks the door now. "I was just about to come visit you upstairs. I had something to do first."

"What?"

"Nothing that you absolutely have to know. Did you eat your supper already?"

"Yes, everything you gave me."

Lena takes a look around the room. She is not looking for anything in particular, only whether everything is neat and dust-free. Her finger is rubbed over the cupboard and evaluated. The result is nothing to write home about.

"Tomorrow I'm going to tidy up your place," she says. "I'm no longer in the mood today."

"Oh, no, you won't," says Jacob sternly. "The professor said you're not yet supposed to run around so much."

Lena doesn't say anything. She sits down at the table smiling. Jacob knows as well as she that she will clean up. For some time now, there is clarity as to who is in charge. That is no longer a disputed matter. Jacob is in charge of providing meals and clothing and, in winter, the fuel. She is responsible for everything else, even if he at times pretends something else. She had dropped in not in order to argue about questions long since decided nor from fear that he could have forgotten her—he couldn't have. The reason for her appearance is because of something a few days ago when she heard much and understood little, when one thing was rather puzzling to her.

"Have you heard what they are all talking about?" asks Lena.

"What about?"

"That the Russians will soon be coming."

"You don't say!"

106

Jacob goes to the cupboard, takes his week's bread ration, breaks off his supper ration, and chews.

"Who is saying all that?"

"Well, Siegfried and Rafael and Frau Sonschein and Frau London—everybody. Don't you know anything yet?"

"No."

Jacob sits down opposite her and looks at her disappointed face. He has promised himself clarity and he knows about nothing. He divides up his bread and gives half of it to Lena as compensation. She takes it and chews too, but not by far is the bread as good as his ignorance is bad.

"That is, I have heard something," says Jacob. "But nothing precise. What's so important about it?"

Her eyes are slowly getting annoyed. How stupid they take you to be! As if she were a baby, and here she is running a household by herself. There is talk about colossal matters and he comes up with "What's so important about it?"

"What'll happen when the Russkis get here?"

"How should I know?" says Jacob.

"Better or worse?"

Jacob can merely groan. For today you have fortunately escaped from the hyenas at the railway station and, if the brainstorm about the broken radio holds up, even forever. But now you have to look around for another path of escape, because within your very own four walls a new tormentor is sprouting, a darling one, to be sure, but she can ask more questions than you have hair on your head. Or you don't look around; you accommodate yourself to your fate; a child not even nine years old—you can surely handle that situation! You'll tell her, as best you can, something about the world of tomorrow. You're interested in that, too. And even if she knows roughly what to expect, it won't do her any harm anyway.

"Will it be better or worse?"

"Better, of course," says Jacob.

"But how will it be better? What will be different?"

"We won't have to wear any more stars. Lena will be able to dress anyway she pleases, and no one on the street will ask her where she left her star."

"That's all?"

"Oh, no. You'll get plenty to eat. . . ."

"As much as I want?"

"As much as you want. Just imagine, everything possible is on the table. You take whatever you're in the mood for, and when you are full, the table will be cleared. For the next meal everything will be there again."

"You're lying," she says, because it would not be bad if he affirmed it once more.

"That's the simple truth. And you'll have pretty clothes; we'll go together to the store and . . ."

"Wait a moment. What things will be on the table?"

"Whatever you like to eat. Meat pie with butter and *challah* and hard-boiled eggs and fish. You can take your choice."

"Will you also fry potato pancakes again?"

"I will."

"In the café?"

"In the café."

"Do you still remember what you promised me? That I'll be allowed to help you in the café?"

"Sure."

"You'll stand behind the counter and fry the pancakes and I'll be allowed to bring them to the customers in my white apron. And in the summer I'll bring them ice cream."

"That's the way it'll be."

"I'm looking forward to that."

Lena is already happy. Whenever she's happy, she raises her shoulders up to her ears. Jacob finally gets to his meal, for the time being, his stale bread. Until she wrinkles her forehead after reflecting a bit because a hindrance has suddenly occurred to her.

"But what about school? You said, too, I'd have to go to school later? And if that's true, will there be any time for the café?"

"School is more important," decides Jacob. "I'll be able to serve the customers alone during schooltime. When you are finished with school, you'll still be able to help me, if you still feel like."

"But I'd rather do so right away."

"What do you have against school? Did some blockhead or other tell you anything bad about it?"

She shakes her head.

"Well, then. School is something wonderfully nice. Totally stupid children enter and come out again totally smart. And if you think I like you better stupid . . ."

"Do Siegfried and Rafael also have to go to school?"

"Of course."

After this reassurance, there is a knock. Lena jumps up and wants to go to the door to unlock it. But Jacob holds her back and puts his finger on his mouth. Knocking is always suspicious. Not every suspicion is confirmed. It could be Kirschbaum, for example, who would like to talk about Lena's recovery, or the neighbor, Horowitz, who, on his word of honor, wants to borrow a spoonful of malt coffee until the next allocation. It can be a quite ordinary knocking —we'll see in a moment—but, nonetheless, Lena doesn't need to be seen. That's nobody's business. Jacob puts his arm around her shoulder, pulls her to the window, and points behind the bed.

"You crouch down here," he whispers. "Don't move until I call. Understand?"

Understood. Lena crouches and doesn't move and Jacob opens the door. Outside none other than Kowalski with his swollen face is standing in the doorway and tries to smile.

"Well, you're plagued with me again!"

Jacob would be glad to cut it short right there in the doorway, tell me fast what's up and then good-by. But Kowalski gives the impression that he has all the time in the world. He walks right past Jacob who is holding the doorknob, sits down at the table, and says: "Don't you want to close the door?"

Locking the door proves to be somewhat noisy. Lena is quiet as commanded. Jacob sits down for better or worse on the second chair and makes an effort to give the impression of having little time.

"You're just having supper," Kowalski ascertains. "I'm not disturbing you, am I?"

"Won't you come to the point as to why you're here?"

"Is that the way you welcome a guest?" asks Kowalski friendly.

"No, I'll go get some wine from the cellar right now!"

"Why so annoyed? That's always been your whole trouble, Jacob; you didn't treat your customers friendly enough. They often told me that during their haircuts. That's why fewer and fewer came to your place."

"Thanks for the advice. But are you here to tell me that?"

Behind the bed there is silent giggling, audible only to someone who knows that somebody else is there.

"You'll laugh, Jacob, but I have nothing definite in mind. At home my ceiling is closing in on me. You can't stay in the same room evening after evening, so you go to Jacob to chat a bit, I thought. He'll feel the same way, I thought. He'll be glad. In the old days we used to get together after work and used to consider that perfectly normal. Shouldn't we begin again gradually getting accustomed to normal times?"

Before Jacob can reply that the old days were the old days and today is today and that he wants to be left in peace and go to sleep because his work at the railroad station is too much for him, Kowalski reaches into his pocket, takes out the two cigarettes, lays them on the table, one in front of himself and one in front of Jacob, thereby shutting him up for the time being.

"That's nice of you," says Jacob. Kowalski thinks maybe Jacob means the visit. Jacob looks at the cigarettes. Perhaps he means both.

"Besides, you haven't told me very much today," says Kowalski after an appropriate pause. "That information about their losses was very gratifying, but as you can imagine, other things don't interest me any less. And not a single word about them today!"

"For heaven's sake, Kowalski, why do you torment me so? Isn't it difficult enough; must you bring it up every time? I don't want to hear about it anymore! Whenever I know anything, I'll tell you. But you can at least leave me in peace in my own room!"

Kowalski nods his head a few times pensively. He revolves his cigarette in his fingers, puckers his lower lip, the swollen one. He has come with a suspicion in which there seems to be truth. He says: "Do you know, Jacob, it occurred to me that you always get unfriendly, even annoyed, whenever I ask you about what's new. On your own you never tell me anything, so I have to ask. No sooner do I ask than you get enraged. I can't get that through my head. I don't understand where the logic is. Imagine it the other way around, Jacob. If I had the radio and you didn't have one, wouldn't you then ask me?"

"Are you crazy? In front of the child!"

Jacob jumps up and turns to the window. Lena has crouched and overheard enough. As arranged, she comes out of her hiding place. To a certain degree he has called her. Her entire face is beaming.

"Good God!" stammers Kowalski frightened and claps his hands, but no one pays him any attention. It's a matter between Jacob and Lena. They exchange glances. Lena winks. Now you've let the cat out of the bag. You didn't reckon on that. Jacob divests himself of the dim thought that she could not have heard anything since children are frequently who knows where with their thoughts or at least don't understand. She is an alert rascal. She winks and everything is already self-evident. It will require a whole lot of thinking about until this new misfortune can be overcome. Everyday a new one! Once again nothing has come of listening for the thunder of cannon at night. But it's not yet night and Lena is still standing opposite you enjoying her little triumph which that fool Kowalski so carelessly handed her. You can't sink roots and continue sweating blood and water. You have to show some sign of life.

"Go upstairs now, Lena. I'll come up to you in a while," says Jacob faintly.

But first she goes over to him and yanks his head down. Jacob thinks it's for the kiss that belongs to every departure no matter for how long. But let him think what he will, Lena has no intention of kissing him, not right now. She is reaching for his head because his ears are attached to it. Into one of them she whispers: "Everybody knows it about you. You have lied!"

Then she is gone. Jacob and Kowalski are sitting again at the table, Kowalski in expectation of a stream of reproaches and feeling perfectly innocent. Because nothing would have happened if Jacob had not hidden his child from him, his best friend. And having already hidden her because he couldn't know who was knocking at the door, he should have let her come out when he saw who it was. But no, he leaves her in her corner, apparently forgotten. I ask you, how can you forget a child? You don't have to be clairvoyant, for Jacob is angry now and will commence immediately with his accusations.

"You brought that off splendidly! It's not enough that

the whole ghetto is already gossiping about it, now she, too, knows about it!" Jacob does in fact say.

"Excuse me. Even at best I couldn't see her. With my eye . . ."

Kowalski points to his eyes. Jacob can take his choice. Both are narrow as Chinese eyes; a powerful blue strikingly surrounds them. Yes, Kowalski points to his eyes, a modest momento of a lifesaving that morning. You needn't be more specific than that. If reproaches are to be made here, it's a question of who to whom. Or else, let's both of us be a little generous and forget old grudges that can't be changed anyway. The proposal is successful. The eyes take on a happy look. The mood at the table suddenly changes, warms up a few degrees, and Jacob's sympathy is immediately enticed. He moves a bit closer and with exchanged glances observes what he has been the cause of.

"Doesn't look good."

Kowalski nods it off. It'll get better. If Jacob is conciliatory then he, too, won't be petty. He is in a generous mood. The unsmoked cigarettes are still lying there. Kowalski has simply thought of everything, even matches. He produces them from his pocket as a final surprise and lights one on the worn striking surface. Brother, now we'll smoke. Come, lean back and close your eyes. Let's not ruin our pleasure with talk. Let's dream for a few drags back to the old times that will soon begin again. Come, let's recall Chaim Balabusne with his thick nickel-plated glasses and his small store where we always used to buy our cigarettes, or, rather, the tobacco to roll our own. His store was closer to yours than to mine and closer to mine than to yours. It was situated exactly between ours and despite that we never got close to him. But that was his fault. Because he had no use for pancakes and ice cream nor for haircuts and shaves. Many people said he let his red hair grow so long out of piety, but I know better. It was out of stinginess, nothing else. Well, no matter, you shouldn't think evil thoughts about dead people. Balabusne always had a good selection: cigars, pipes, boxes with little flowers, cigarettes with gold filters for the rich. He always wanted to persuade us to buy a more expensive brand, but we stayed with *Excelsior*. And the stand with the little gas flame and the cigarcutter on his counter. The stand made of brass which he was polishing no matter when you came into his store. You recall this stupid stand everytime you think of the old days, although you bought his tobacco, at most, once a week and never used his stand.

"Are you also thinking about Chaim Balabusne?"

"What brings you to Chaim Balabusne?"

"Oh, just because. Maybe because of smoking."

"I'm not thinking of anything."

The last drag; one more and you'll burn your lips. The smoke has superbly irritated your lungs and made your head giddy like after a few plentiful drinks. The world is revolving in a circle around you slowly, but you're sitting comfortably with your hands on the table. A little sighing, a little groaning. The smoke is still hanging in the room. Kowalski says: "And now down to business, Jacob. How does it look out there? What do you hear about the Russians?"

Jacob remains calm. It was anyway only a question of time that Kowalski would come to talk about the real reason for his visit. The cigarettes couldn't fool anyone. No Lena is crouching any longer now in the background. Now you can speak openly. We have already figured out the answer for you and your kind, so prepare yourself for it. So, go ahead with your despairing face and with your sadly drooping shoulders. Now for the last act in our question-and-answer play, Kowalski. You won't like it. But we can't show any consideration for that, Kowalski. That's been done long enough. We ourselves are also tormented.

"I didn't want to tell you . . ."

"They'll drive them back!" screams Kowalski.

"No, no, not that bad."

"Well, then, what else? Out with it!"

"Imagine," says Jacob quietly and perfectly saddened, "a short time ago I sat down by my radio and turned the knob, as I always do, but not a single sound came out. You understand, yesterday it played—superbly—and today it's completely silent. Nothing can be done, my friend. A radio is an incomprehensible thing and now it's out of order."

"Good God!" Kowalski shouts horrified. For the second time this evening Kowalski shouts "Good God!" and even claps his hands again, apparently because he doesn't do one without the other.

"If I only had something to smoke," says Jacob yearningly, for it's the following day and the cigarette, *Juno* without filter tip, is just a memory. He is standing on a freight car, a kind of *yontef* work, as it may be confidently called; he is receiving the sacks that we Jews are hauling, a task which has been imposed upon us today. We're bringing him the very heavy sacks over a stretch of fifty or even more meters. He merely has to get them to the sides of the car and stack them neatly there. Hence, recreational work, even more so because two of them are doing it: Jacob and Leonard Schmidt.

The day, incidentally, began with amazement on our part. When they showed us what would have to be done today, we looked at each other in amazement and thought they didn't know themselves what they wanted. Because a good two weeks ago an entire train arrived with sacks of cement, as if they wanted to build houses. We took them off one by one and covered them with tarpaulins, and today, suddenly, comes the order to load the sacks on the cars again. Their business. We're reloading the sacks obediently, just as they wish. We're dragging them to the cars. On one of them Jacob is standing amidst his *yontef* work and saying, "If I only had something to smoke"; and Schmidt answers him, almost amused, "If that's the worst of your troubles, Herr Heym."

Leonard Schmidt. He came to this ghetto like the Virgin to her Child. It befell him by means he wouldn't have dreamed were his. Because Schmidt has a past that really should have earned its continuation on the other side of the fence. His stay in our midst belongs for him among the few incomprehensible matters in this world. Born in 1895 in Brandenburg-on-the-Havel of a wealthy father and a mother who was a loyal subject of the Kaiser, he attended a first-class gymnasium in Berlin where his father had moved for business reasons (acquisition of a textile factory) two years after Leonard's birth. He became a soldier immediately after his graduation. Flanders campaign, Verdun, occupation of the Crimea and, later, Champagne; when worst came to worst, Schmidt fought hard. He was discharged from the defeated army in all honor as a proud lieutenant, and was decorated for bravery in the face of the enemy or whatever, and turned to his career. University studies were in order, as befits upperclass sons—the study of law at Heidelberg, and the final semesters in Berlin. His success could not have been better. All exams were passed with flying colors, most of them with honors. Three obligatory years of apprenticeship passed and then his visiting card "Assessor Leonard Schmidt," and finally the awaited moment, the opening of his own law practice in the most elegant neighborhood. Good clients were not long in coming; his father's connections, in fact, drove them to him. Soon he had to take on two young lawyers for the less important cases and made a name for himself ten times faster than many another. Love match, two medium-blond, beautiful daughters, the whole world tipped its hat in respect to

**116**

him every day, until an envious person from the Bar Association came upon the fatal idea of tracing his family tree, sawing away at it, and letting everything take its fatal course. His wife, two daughters, and bank account could still be saved in Switzerland because good friends warned Schmidt. He, himself, didn't manage to get out. He was still preoccupied with the settlement of the most important matters when the emphatic knocking on his door came. In Schmidt's head, the entire matter seems an idiotic joke. Perhaps he'll wake up some morning and his clients will once again be sitting in his waiting room. He was well on the way to becoming a German nationalist. But they didn't let him. They knocked at the door and commanded him to make no fuss. Horrified servant-girl face between the plush chairs covered with white sheets. They brought him here because his great grandfather attended the synagogue and his parents were stupid enough to have him circumsized, they themselves no longer knew why. Joke or not, he had been suffering doubly and threefold the first days he was new here, and having just finished his life history, he asked me unhappily: "Do you understand that?"

And a short time later—you could think, to the extent you had anything to do with him, that he was getting accustomed gradually to ghetto life—he comes to the railroad station dressed in an outfit that makes your heart stop beating from surprise. On the left side of his chest is a military decoration on which is hanging a little thing, black and white, that upon close examination proves to be an Iron Cross. "Be smart!" someone tells him. "Take off the Cross and hide it! They'll shoot you down for that like a mad dog!" But Schmidt turns away from him and starts to work, as if nothing were said. We all go out of our way to avoid him. No one wants to be drawn into the matter. There is nothing to be done for him. We don't let him out of our sight from a safe distance. Not until after a good hour does a guard notice the monstrosity, gulps a few times, stands speechless in front of Schmidt, and Schmidt stands pale in front of him. After an eternity, the guard makes an about-face, pivoting on his heel, looking as if his speech had failed him. He enters the guardhouse and immediately thereafter returns with his superior and points to Schmidt who, in the meantime, is the only one working. With his finger, the superior beckons Schmidt to him. No one holds out any hope for Schmidt's crazy head. The superior bends over to the decoration, examines the thing carefully, as a watchmaker scrutinizes a damaged little part.

"Where did you get that?" he asks.

"Verdun," says Schmidt, in a trembling voice.

"That won't do here. That is forbidden here," says the superior. He takes the decoration from Schmidt's chest, puts it in his pocket, writes down no name, shoots no wrong-doer. Treats the incident like a nice amusement that would give rise to general gaiety in the pub in the evening. He returns satisfied to the guardhouse; the guard is attentive once more to other things, not a word more about it. Schmidt has had his joke and we our drama. That's how he obtained his unique fame soon after his arrival. So much for Leonard Schmidt's personal life.

"In my entire life, I have never yet had any dealings with law courts," says Jacob.

"Aha," says Schmidt.

They are taking it easy; the two of them take a good hold of one of the sacks that we carriers have been laying in the freight car opening and lifting with an "Up she goes!" to the proper spot. Even the rain doesn't bother them because their freight car has a roof. During the little breaks that arise now and then, they lean against the side, from their brows wipe the sweat that has inexplicably accumulated there, and chat like in peacetime. When Kowalski or the Shtamms or Misha unload their sacks panting and eyeing them enviously, telling them maliciously they should take care of themselves otherwise they would yet work themselves to death, they smile, "Just don't worry about us."

"That is to say, once I was a witness," says Jacob.

"Aha."

"But not in court. Only in the district attorney's office. The one who handled the case."

"Which case?"

"It was a question as to whether Kowalski owed Porfir, the money-lender, money. Porfir had miraculously lost the IOU, and I had to testify merely that Kowalski had given him back the money."

"Were you present at the time?" asks Schmidt.

"Not at all. But Kowalski had previously explained everything to me in detail."

"But if you weren't present and knew the circumstances only from hearsay, you shouldn't have been allowed to appear at all as a witness. How would you know with certainty that Kowalski had, in fact, given this gentleman his money back? He might have—I don't want to insinuate anything—but, nonetheless, it would be conceivable that Kowalski could have lied to you, so that you would testify in his behalf."

"That I don't believe," says Jacob without reflecting long. "He has many bad qualities that no one knows as well as I, but a liar he is not. He told me right away that he hadn't given Porfir his money back. Where could he have got it?"

"And although you knew that, you testified to the public prosecutor that he had paid it back in your presence?"

"Yes, obviously."

"It's not at all so obvious, Herr Heym," says Schmidt amused. It's dead certain he has misgivings about the remarkable conception of justice of this peculiar people which supposedly is his.

"In any case, it helped quite a bit," Jacob says at the end of his story. "That cutthroat Porfir didn't succeed in his suit. He lost his money—but what am I saying—*his* money! He skinned, ultimately, almost every one of us small business people. Thirty-percent interest! Can you imagine that? The entire neighborhood shouted for joy when Porfir and Kowalski came out of the courthouse after the verdict—Porfir boiling with anger and Kowalski beaming like the sun."

At the freight car ledge Kowalski with his motley-colored eyes drops his sack on the floor. With half an ear he had overheard "Kowalski beaming like the sun," and asks: "What kind of stories are you telling about me?"

"The business that time about Porfir's lost IOU."

"Don't believe a word of it," says Kowalski to Schmidt. "He says bad things about me everywhere."

Kowalski trots back for the next sack, wet as a poodle, after throwing a what's-that-for look at Jacob. The non-sweaty Schmidt and Jacob exert themselves a little, too, without chatting for a change, to see how many sacks fit into a single freight car. Up to the next little interruption, until something important comes to Schmidt's mind, until he asks: "Please don't be offended by my curiosity, Herr Heym, but what is Sir Winston saying about the present situation?"

"Who?"

"Churchill. The British prime minister."

"No idea what he is saying. Haven't you heard yet? My radio is out of order."

"Don't make jokes!"

"What do you take me for?" says Jacob seriously.

Schmidt seems taken aback, Jacob notes, exactly like the others today from whom you couldn't keep it back first thing in the morning, with drooping shoulders and a desperate voice—the only news of the day. The somewhat arrogant Schmidt, whom a wit had dubbed Leonard Assimilinski, this Schmidt seems to feel touched to the core, like all of us. Suddenly he is exactly like the others.

"What happened?" he asks quietly.

The answer to that was rattled off in the morning. There wasn't time enough to present it to every individual person like to Kowalski, wrapped in crepe paper. Jacob had to decide upon substantive deletions. How it happened? "Well how? Like a radio goes on the bum. Yesterday it was still working, and today it doesn't any more."

The reactions were mixed. Some cursed an unjust God; others prayed to him; they consoled themselves with the fact that radio and Russians were two basically different things. One man wept like a child. His tears ran down his cheeks unnoticed among the raindrops. One man said, "I hope that isn't a bad omen."

Jacob couldn't say yes or no. He had to abandon them to their little griefs. Better to that than to the whole truth. Neither can he speak any consoling words into Schmidt's droopy ears. His supply of consolation is exhausted. Let's please remind ourselves now and then that Jacob is just as much in need of consolation as all the poor wretches around him, just as cut off from all supply of news, and that the same hopes torment him. Only a crazy accident had made a special person out of an equal and even until today has prevented him from opening up his cards on the table. But only till today. Today I have let you take a peek into my sleeve. You have seen how empty it is. No more ace of trumps is there. Now we're all equally clever. Nothing differentiates us any longer. Nothing except your faith that I would have been a special person someday.

"Nothing at all will help, Herr Schmidt. We have to go on. And now!"

Through the railroad station an unfamiliar voice booms into the rain, which has let up, "Hands off, there!"

Jacob and Schmidt run to the door to see what's going on

outside. The twin Hershel Shtamm is standing on the siding at a quite ordinary-looking freight car that is still bolted. He probably thought it was the next in turn to be loaded, when he hears the unfamiliar voice that can only mean him and quickly pulls his hand away from the bolt lever. He was just about to push it up. The only thing noteworthy up to now about the incident is the voice, which, by the way, is very remarkable, for it belongs to "Whistle" and is therefore unfamiliar. "Whistle" in his railwayman's uniform is walking as fast as his wooden leg permits toward Hershel Shtamm, who backs away frightened. "Whistle" stops at the freight car and tests the bolt, which is still in place.

"Didn't you listen before? This car is not to be touched, damn it!"

"Yes, sir," says Hershel Shtamm.

Then "Whistle" turns to all the Jews who have stopped working and are enjoying the charm of what has never been heard. In a shouting voice he turns around: "Have you all understood it now, you shitheads? This here car is not to be touched! The next time there will be shooting!"

So that's how his voice sounds. I would say a not very successful debut. I would say a weak baritone. A more pleasant timbre would have been desirable. "Whistle" strides with dignity back into the guardhouse. Hershel Shtamm gets to work again as quickly as possible, in order to get out of the limelight. We, too. The incident that never quite developed into one has come to a temporary conclusion.

"What sort of a freight car was that?" asks Schmidt.

"How should I know," says Jacob.

"Herr Shtamm can consider himself lucky that he got away unharmed. The guard did, in fact, order us this morning not to have anything to do with that freight car. No doubt you heard it, too?"

"Yes, yes."

"Then why does he go over there?"

"My heavens, how should I know?"

Schmidt has no feel for when a conversation is finished. He expresses several views on the practicality of strict adherence to orders, on the increase of the chances for survival that follow from such an attitude. He formulates a short lecture on the factual legal situation that prevails now because of the momentary power relationships. Jacob listens with only half an ear. Frankly, Schmidt is not particularly sympathetic. He considers himself, without ever stating it explicitly, better and more intelligent and more cultured. He probably would have had no complaint against the entire ghetto, if they had not thrown him, of all people, in with us. Whenever he takes pains to eradicate the differences, which he does most of the time, we can not help feeling that he is feigning: "You see how nice it is of me, I am acting as if we were the same." The differences are there; he cannot overcome them—even the way he looks at or speaks to us or eats or talks about the Germans or about the old days, and especially the way he thinks. You have no choice in your fellow sufferers. He is without question a companion in misfortune. He trembles no differently than we over his bit of life—that is to say, a bit differently to be sure, in his own special way, which is not so agreeable to ours.

Soon Hershel Shtamm comes by dragging a sack, his fur cap, under which he hides his piety, drenched.

Jacob asks him: "What was the matter, Hershel?"

"You won't believe it, but I heard voices in the freight car," says Hershel.

"Voices?"

"Voices," says Hershel. "As true as I'm standing here. Human voices."

He can feel cold terror on his back, especially he who is always much too hot under his fur cap. He puffs up his cheeks and nods a few times, worried. You can imagine what that means. Jacob can. He accompanies Hershel's recital with helpless sighing, with closing of eyes and raising of eyebrows. They have a small, inaudible conversation as Schmidt stands there and doesn't understand a single word.

Misha comes by. He unloads his cement sack and says quietly: "You have to get to work. The guard is already looking over at you."

Jacob suddenly has two left hands. The sack slips from his grip. Schmidt says, annoyed, "Hey, be careful!"

Jacob must be more careful. He feels, he recalls later, like someone who had been dreaming of happiness and quiet places when somebody comes along and pulls off the warm blanket and you're lying there naked and trembling from disenchantment.

"You've become so quiet?" says Schmidt, after a while.

Jacob continues to be quiet. Unspeakably saddened, he takes in the sacks, from time to time only a stolen glance to the insignificant freight car on the siding behind whose wall human voices have been heard. Air holes right under the roof. No one is tall enough to be able to look out and no one is shouting, neither from the inside nor from the outside. Why isn't anyone shouting? The sacks must be stacked neatly. Standing reddish brown on the siding, as if forgotten. But they won't forget it. In many respects, you can depend on them. Yesterday it hadn't been here yet. Tomorrow it will have left. Only a short stop-over on the way to somewhere. Such a car has already been loaded and unloaded and loaded a hundred times—crates, coal, potatoes, under strict surveillance, machines, stones. Exactly such kinds of cars. But this one here is not to be touched, otherwise there will be shooting.

"Do you believe that it's true?" asks Schmidt.

"That what's true?"

"About the voices?"

"Don't ask such questions. Do you think Hershel Shtamm is putting on airs?"

"But who could it be in the car?"

"Who do you think?"

Schmidt's mouth gapes. Not until now does a terrifying suspicion occur to him.

He exhales. "You mean . . ."

"Yes, I mean!"

"You mean, they are now sending some more to the camps?"

That's the way it is, unfortunately. Schmidt doesn't understand the game of allusions, that certain things are not mentioned and are nonetheless stated. He'll never understand. Deep down, he'll remain a stranger. Everything must be clearly and bluntly spelled out for him.

"No, they're not sending any more! The war has been over for a long time. We could all go home, if we wanted to. But we don't want to because we're having so much fun here!" says Jacob with his eyes distorted. "Whether they're still sending more! Do you think, there aren't any more here? I'm still here. You're still here. All of us here are still around. Don't think for a moment it's as good as over!"

Schmidt interrupts the necessary lecture with a quick hand movement. Horrified, he points outside and calls out. "Take a look! Shtamm!"

Hershel had never attracted attention until that time of praying, which led to the power failure, according to his conviction. Now he is making up for it. He is standing on the siding next to the freight car. The guards still haven't noticed him. Hershel is pressing his ear to the car side and is talking. I see him, pious Hershel, clearly moving his lips, listening, then speaking again. His brother, Roman, happens to be standing beside me, his eyes big as mill wheels. He is about to run over to Hershel to bring him back before it's too late. Two men have to hold him back by force and one has to whisper, "Stay quiet, you idiot, you yourself will draw their attention to him."

I can't hear what Hershel is saying and what those inside

are telling him. The distance is much too great for that. But I can well imagine it and that has nothing to do with vague guesses. The more I think about it, the clearer do I know his words, although he never confirmed them.

"Hullo! Do you hear me?" says Hershel first off.

"We hear you," a voice from inside the car must have replied. "Who are you?"

"I'm from the ghetto," says Hershel then. "You have to hold on; only for a short while longer do you have to hold on. The Russians have already advanced past Bezanika!"

"How do you know that?" they ask from inside—everything quite logical and inevitable.

"You can believe me. We have a hidden radio. I have to leave now."

The confined express their gratitude unrestrainedly. A white dove has strayed over to them into the darkness. Their words are irrelevant. Perhaps they wish him good luck and riches and long life to a hundred and twenty before they hear his footsteps departing.

Stupefied, all of us are looking at Hershel who is wending his way back. Crackbrained as we are, we simply stand there and gawk instead of continuing to work and to act as if everything were quite ordinary. First we keep Roman from committing a great blunder, then we commit it ourselves. Maybe Hershel wouldn't have got away with it in any case. Who can know that after the fact? At any rate, we don't do anything that might divert them from him. Only now does he seem to discover fear. Until then everything had taken its own course, as if in accordance with unfathomable laws that somnambulists obey. His cover is more than insufficient, as good as non-existant. Hershel knows well why he is frightened. A pile of crates, an empty freight car further on, otherwise nothing in his path that he could really use for accompanying cover. I see him sticking his head around the corner of the car, centimeter after centimeter. He is already with us with his glances. I can already

126

hear him tell about his trip around the world. Up to now his opposition has been quiet. The guard at the gate is standing with his back facing the railroad station area. Not a sound arouses his attention. The other two had disappeared, presumably into the house, where the rain had driven them. I see Hershel making his final preparations for his big sprint. I see him praying. Although he is still standing by the freight car and moving his lips, it is clearly evident that he isn't talking with those inside, but rather with his God. And then I turn my head to the guardhouse. It has a small attic window, which is open. On the window sill is a rifle that is being aimed in utter tranquility. I can't make out the man behind it. It's too dark in the room. I see only two hands adjusting the direction of the barrel until they are satisfied, then stopping as if modeled for a painting. What should I have done, I, who have never been a hero, what should I have done? If I were one, at best, shout. But what good would that have done? I do not shout. I close my eyes. An eternity passes. Roman says to me: "What are you closing your eyes for? Look, he'll make it, that crazy fellow!"

I don't know why at this moment I think of Chana, whom they shot to death in front of a tree, the name of which I don't know. I'm still thinking of her after the shot, until everyone around me is talking all at once. Just a single ordinary shot. The two hands had, as stated, plenty of time to prepare everything for the best possible advantage all through Hershel's prayer. It sounds strange. I've never heard a single shot, only several at once, as if a naughty child defiantly stamped its foot, or as if a balloon were blown up too violently and then burst, or even, since I'm now luxuriating in pictures, as if God had coughed. God coughed in Hershel's face.

Those locked in behind the reddish-brown sides might ask, "Say, there, what happened?"

Hershel is lying on his stomach between two rail ties

across the track. His clenched right hand has fallen into a black puddle. His face, only half of which I can see at first, seems strange to me with the open eye. We are standing around him—this small break is not begrudged us—Roman bends down over him, pulling him away from the track, and turns him on his back. Then he takes off the fur cap. His fingers have difficulty unbuttoning the flaps under the chin. He puts the cap in his pocket and goes away. For the first time in this railroad station, Hershel's earlocks are allowed to blow free in the wind. Many of us have never seen them before and know them only from hearsay. So that's how Hershel Shtamm really looks without disguise. For the last time, his face bordered black from the wet earth and much hair. Someone closed his eyes. I won't lie; why should I? He wasn't handsome. He was very pious. He wanted to promote hope and died because of it.

The guard at the gate has come up behind us unnoticed. It is just about time to turn our thoughts to other things. He says: "You've gaped enough, or haven't you ever seen a dead man before? Scram, get to work again; quick, quick!"

We'll take him along after work and bury him. That is permitted without being expressly written in any of the many regulations. That has simply become customary. I look up again to the window that in the meantime has closed—no more rifle, no hands. Nor do any of them come out of the guardhouse. They are no longer concerned about us. For them, the affair is finished.

Life goes on. Schmidt and Jacob are again busy with the sacks. Schmidt has understood enough now to keep quiet, to keep to himself why Hershel insisted on going to the freight car, although the railwayman had warned him before expressly and definitively.

In Jacob's head his self-reproaches open up lots of thoughts. He knows with horrifying preciseness what role he has played. You fabricate for yourself meager consolation. You imagine a large scale with two pans. On the one, you put Hershel; on the other, you pile up all the hope you have circulated among the people in the course of time. Which side will sink? The trouble is, you don't know how much hope weighs. No one will tell you. You have to find the formula alone and make the calculation alone. But you'll calculate in vain. The difficulties pile up; here's another: who is to tell you what harm has been prevented by your inventions? Ten catastrophes or twenty or even only a single one; what has been prevented will remain eternally hidden from you. Only what you have done is visible. It's lying there next to the track in the rain.

Even later, at noon, you haven't come any closer to the answer to the problem with the many unknown quantities. Off by himself, Jacob is spooning up his soup. Today, everyone leaves everybody else alone. He has avoided Roman Shtamm. Roman didn't look for him. Only at the wheelbarrow on which the tin bowls are placed after use they suddenly are standing opposite one another. They look each other in the eye, especially Roman. Jacob tells me: "He looked at me as if I had shot his brother."

The hours after work belong to Lena.

A while ago, Jacob had stopped in the vestibule in front of his door with her and had said: "Now pay attention, Lena, if something happens, so that you'll find the key to my room." He had said: "Here in back of the doorframe is a little hole in the wall; do you see? I'm sticking the key in now, and then the rock in front of it again. It is very easily removed. If you stand on tiptoes, you'll be tall enough. Try it." Lena tried it; she stretched, removed the rock, and with the greatest effort got the key, proudly showing it to Jacob. "Excellent," Jacob said, "note the spot well. I myself don't know why, but maybe it will be important someday. And one thing more, don't reveal the place to anyone."

In the meantime, Lena no longer had to stand on her tiptoes. For two years she had tirelessly grown up to the little hole behind the doorframe. If anything happens, Jacob said. Something is happening today. Lena gets the key, unlocks the door, and is standing breathlessly in the empty room. She does experience a little fear that will disappear. If Jacob comes in unexpectedly, she'll simply tell him she is tidying up. The motivations that impel her to it are adventurous. He would hardly approve of them, but what he doesn't know won't hurt him.

There are two obstacles in her way. She has no illusions. The first is the hiding place, unknown for the time being. The second is, she doesn't know what a radio looks like. There are not unlimited hiding places in this room. In several minutes it has been turned upside down. The second obstacle seems much more difficult. Jacob has explained all kinds of things to her. She could, for example, easily describe a bus although she had never yet seen one face to face. She could talk about bananas, airplanes, and bears that start to growl when they are turned on their backs. During the power failure that time Jacob even traversed with her the very secret path that light takes from the coal mine to the little bulb under the ceiling; but about a radio he has never mentioned a word. Several clues exist: everyone is talking about it; its possession is forbidden; it reveals things to you that you didn't previously know; it is so small that it can be well hidden.

"Will you show me your radio tomorrow?" she asked him last evening when he came to her in the attic after Kowalski's unsuccessful visit.

"No," he said.

"And the day after tomorrow?"

"Again, no."

"And the day after the day after tomorrow?"

"I said no! Don't ask me again."

Even her otherwise infallible making eyes at him remained fruitless. Jacob didn't even look at her. Thus her new attempt, after an ill-humored pause: "Will you ever show it to me sometime?"

"No."

"Why not?"

"Because."

"Will you at least tell me what it looks like?" she asked then, her scheme already halfway formed in her mind. But he refused to answer to that, too. Thus her half-a-scheme became a whole one.

In short, Lena has to find a thing about which she knows nothing except that Jacob keeps it hidden, a thing devoid of color, form, and weight. Fortunately, Jacob can not have so many unfamiliar things in the room. The first object she finds and has not yet seen must bear the name "radio" as far as can be judged.

Lena begins with the hiding places that are obvious: under the bed, on the cupboard, in the table drawer. Possibly a radio is so big that it won't fit at all in a table drawer. Maybe everyone who sees that would laugh aloud because Lena is looking for a radio there. But it's not her fault that Jacob is so stubbornly mum about it. And, besides, no one is watching. It's not in the drawer. Nothing is there. Under the bed and on the cupboard there is only dust. Only the inside of the cupboard is left, otherwise there is no hiding place. It has two doors, one on top and one underneath. Basically, you could save yourself the trouble about the upper one. Behind that door are the four plates, two deep ones and two flat ones; the two cups, one of which Lena dropped on the floor while washing and broke off its ear; in addition, a knife and two spoons; the ever-empty sugar bowl, in back of which is the food to the extent there is any. In back of this door Lena is at home. She often sets the table, serves, and clears away. That examination can be avoided, except for the fact that the enterprise should not fail because of a superficial error. She looks in: the four plates, two cups, sugar bowl, knife, and spoons; in addition, a piece of bread and a bag of beans. No surprises.

To the door underneath. Lena hesitates. Her fingers are already holding the key and can't decide. If the thing looked for isn't there, then it is nowhere. Down below in the cupboard; she had till now lost nothing. "My things are in there," Jacob said, and that sounded thoroughly harmless. His things. Now she understood for the first time what was hidden behind two such innocent words.

Her hesitation has its limits. Lena finally opens it. Outside the vestibule, footsteps run past. No use locking the room door. If Jacob arrived, he wouldn't ask what she was doing here. He would ask why she locked herself in, and there is no answer to that. Lena clears things out. Trousers and shirt, needle and thread, a pot—why isn't it up top?—boxes with nails and screws, an empty picture frame, the book on Africa. She takes a little break. The book has more to offer than merely the letters of the alphabet which Jacob has been strangely stressing so very much lately. The pictures merit several moments attention, despite everything.

The woman with the tremendously long breasts that are so flat and look dried out and with the ring drawn slanted through her nose, the meaning of which Jacob intends to explain later on. The naked men with their faces completely painted, holding long spears in their hands, and on their heads huge shapes of feathers, hair, and ribbons. Or the skinny children with bellies round as balls; also animals with horns and stripes and endless noses and even longer necks. All that can keep you occupied but not so much that you would forget your real goal.

Lena crawls into the cupboard up to her belly, a final obstacle is overcome, a moderate pile of laundry with a green towel on top. And then the path is cleared to this never seen object. Proud victory grin! It is standing unpretentiously in the corner in the back, secretive and forbiddingly. She takes it out: a little, fragile grid, a small screw, glass, and round. She stands it on the table respectfully and sits down in front of it. Now you can have yourself a ball! His "thing," Jacob said. The minutes pass in staring. What will you find out that you didn't previously know? Does this thing talk like an ordinary person or does it reveal its secrets in another way, such as by magic? After some experimental silence Lena concludes that it won't reveal anything by itself. It has to be brought to speak. Perhaps it must simply be asked something. If it does, then hopefully not by a particular magic incantation like Ali Baba at Sesame.

"What's my name?" Lena begins with the simplest, but the request appears to have been too complicated for the thing. Lena gives it ample time—in vain. Her disappointment turns to the thought that the unfamiliar must be requested of it, something you yourself hadn't previously known. After all, she does know her own name. She asks: "How much is thirty times two million?"

Since the answer is still not forthcoming she undertakes new measures. She thinks of the light that can be opened and closed at will. Possibly the thing can be started up exactly the same way. Let's try it with the little screw. It's rusty and can hardly be turned, only a quiet squeak after much effort, and her fingers are hurting already. Jacob is standing there in the doorway and, as anticipated, asks: "What are you doing here?"

"I," says Lena, "I was about to," she says—you have to recover from the fright—"I was about to tidy up here. Did you forget?"

Jacob remembers. He looks at the Sodom and Gomorrha in front of the cupboard and back to Lena who was about to tidy up. Before he opens his mouth she knows it won't be so terrible. "But I hope you're not yet finished," says Jacob.

Of course, she isn't finished yet. Why, she has just begun! She jumps up and stuffs pot and book and laundry back into the cupboard so quickly that his eyes can keep up only with difficulty. Then the picture frame follows. In her haste she spills the nails from the box and quickly gathers them up. Needle and thread now. Where are the needle and thread? They'll be found the next time. The door bangs shut and the disorder is already forgotten. Only the thing remains on the table. He saw it anyway. There stands his only secret and he is still biding his time getting angry.

"You're not angry with me, are you?"

"No, no."

Jacob takes off his jacket and washes his hands from the railroad station. Lena is gradually getting restless and the thing is standing there unheeded.

"And what did you really want here?"

"Nothing at all. I have tidied up," she says, and knows that it's foolish.

"What were you looking for?"

Now his voice is gradually getting louder, but the question strikes her as very stupid. There he is already sitting in front of the thing and asking hypocritically what was being looked for. That's why we're refusing the obvious reply.

"What is the lantern doing here?"

"What lantern?"

"This one here. Do you see any other?"

As Lena becomes silent and her eyes grow bigger from surprise and stare at the alleged lantern, while her big eyes gradually fill with tears, Jacob draws her close to him and asks very quietly: "What's the matter?"

"Nothing."

He puts her on his knee. She weeps quite rarely. Who can know what goes on in the mind of such a little girl who broods alone all day? "Come on, tell me what's the matter. Does it have anything to do with the lantern?"

"No."

"Should I tell you how it works?"

Lena stops her tears. After all, Jacob isn't at fault for her mistake; and besides, tomorrow is another day. Somehow the hiding place will be discovered that she missed today. She attends to her eyes and nose with her sleeve, which is not sufficient. Jacob's handkerchief rushes to her aid.

"Should I explain it to you?"

"Yes."

"Look. This object is a kerosene lantern. In the old days there were only such kinds of lanterns, before electric light was known. The kerosene is poured in here into this small trough. This here is the wick. It absorbs the kerosene. Only its tip sticks out. It can be made longer or shorter by means of this screw here. The wick is lit and then the room gets brighter."

"Can't you try it?"

"Unfortunately, I have no kerosene."

Lena slips off Jacob's knee. She takes the lantern in both her hands and examines it from all sides. So that's why you waited in vain for an answer. At home in those days at the Nuriels, there was no kerosene lantern and no radio. Mistakes occur because of lack of experience. After a final glance she puts it back into the cupboard. Order is perfectly restored again even with Lena. In her unsuccessful voyage of discovery she even discovers a humorous side.

"Do you know what I thought?"

"Well?"

"But you musn't laugh at me."

"Why should I?"

"I thought that was your radio."

Jacob smiles. He recalls that as a small lad he took a hunchbacked old neighbor for a witch, a similar fallacy. But now his smile gets weaker and weaker. Lena had admittedly looked for the radio. It would have been very good if she had been left with her belief. What difference does it make to a lantern to be taken for a radio? He could have sworn her to a sacred silence: now you have finally found it; now you know what it looks like; not a word more about it now, especially to strangers. And for weeks there would have been peace, at least at home. But the opportunity has been missed. Lena didn't reveal her secret until it was too late and you didn't have the presence of mind to size up the situation properly in the room with the lantern on the table and the meaning of her tears. She will immediately ask, fine, that was a lantern, but where is the radio? Immediately, or in an hour, tomorrow the latest. She's already restlessly shuffling from one foot to the other. That it's out of order will not satisfy her. Then show me the broken one. And unfortunately, you are not one of those who can answer bothersome questions with a slap in the face even once, by way of exception. To be sure, there would be an excuse, a very simple one. Jacob could claim he had burned it, since a broken radio, if found, is not any less dangerous than one in good repair.

He could say that, then he would happily be rid of the radio for Lena and the whole world. But yesterday at the railroad station also plays a certain role. The dead Hershel Shtamm, his brother Roman with his tormented looks, the imprisoned, unknown people on the siding, all of them also have something to say about it, before the radio is finally destroyed. And the individual Jews who arrived with questions in the morning full of expectation and left again dismayed without the news to which they have a right. In the meantime, they will have arrived home; relatives and friends are knocking on their doors to hear what was new at the railroad station. Nothing, they will learn; the radio doesn't tell anything any more; it is broken; it was still working yesterday; and today not a sound comes from it. The relatives and friends will leave and spread the latest news in all the homes and streets that soon will look as wretched as before the evening when a spotlight caught Jacob about 7:30 P.M. on the Kurländischendamm. Much must be thought about before frivolous conclusions are drawn, before peace that is no peace is bought.

"Will you show me the radio now?"

"I've already told you no yesterday. Has anything, perhaps, changed in the meantime?"

"I'll find it then," says Lena.

"Then keep looking!"

"Do you want to bet that I'll find it?"

She switches to an open offensive. Let her rather look than ask questions. Jacob will not talk her out of the next radio she finds. And the radio she'll never find will, for the time being, be spared from the fire. Many reasons are responsible for that, foremost, Hershel with the earlocks. He had as good as repaired it in the morning when he was lying in the rain between the railroad ties.

Jacob is going to work in high spirits. Whoever notices his attitude and his jaunty stride and makes comparison to yesterday or to recent days will note striking changes. There strides a well-adjusted person. In high spirits because his hours in bed were rich in important resolutions. His connection to the outside world has been reestablished. The radio has played half the night, right after Lena had been shaken off. It came on and played until his sleep arrived unrequested. But this and that piece of news stayed with him, nothing to be sneezed at! In high spirits because the little flame of expectation must not be extinguished. That was Jacob's decision. For half the night he sought twigs, wood, and tinder for it. He succeeded in making a substantial leap forward—he and the Russians. Quietly he had them win a big battle because of superior equipment, at the Rudna, a little river which doesn't exactly splash by your front door but is, however, gratifyingly closer than the city of Bezanika.

In reviewing the dispatches he had set into circulation up to now, it struck Jacob that, on the whole, it was a question solely of long-drawn-out futilities, even including the very first one about Bezanika, nothing substantial. He had made a colossal story out of each of his brainstorms, often unbelievable and transparent. Up to now doubts have not been forthcoming only because hope had made them blind and stupid. However, during the night before the battle at the Rudna, Jacob finally recognized the source of his difficulties. In other words, hardly had the light gone out when it came to him in a flash why his inventions came to him with so much difficulty, and lately almost not at all. He was too modest, he suspected. He had always attempted in his dispatches to move in realms that would not be verifiable later when life once again was normal. With every piece of news he had been constrained by a bad conscience. The lies came clumsily and reluctantly from his lips, as if they were seeking a hiding place to crawl away to with all due speed before anyone examined them closer. But this procedure was totally wrong, as he figured out last night. A liar with pangs of conscience will remain a bungler all his life. In this line, caution and false modesty are not apropos. You have to be unstinting. Conviction must be written all over your face. You must act like someone who looks like he already knows what others will find out from you a moment later. Numbers and names and dates must be bandied about. The battle at the Rudna must be only a modest beginning. It will never be important in history, but in our story it will hold a place of honor. And after everything has been endured and everyone who is interested can read about the true course of the war in books, then let them come and ask: "Say, you, what sort of nonsense did you tell in those days? When was there ever a battle at the Rudna?" "Wasn't there?" can be then the amazed reply. "Show me the book . . . Really, there wasn't any. It's not mentioned here. Well, then I guess I heard it incorrectly in those days, pardon me." They'll go away with a shrug; perhaps there will even be some among them who will be grateful for the error.

As for the progress of the battle events, Jacob had done a little preparation in which his knowledge of geography came in handy. For the next three days the battle at the Rudna along with all its aftereffects should suffice. There is a limit to everything. Because the crossing of the river is not entirely devoid of problems. We're not making it that easy for the Russians. The Germans have blown up the only bridge, Jacob thought. Before the advance can be continued a makeshift pontoon bridge must be built and on that the Russians spend three or four days. Then that's finished, too, and the Russians are advancing to the town of Tobolin of which the Germans have made a kind of fortress. It, too, will hold out for three days. It is being surrounded, heavily shelled by artillery and stormed by the infantry. In a hopeless situation Major Karthäuser, a splendid name with matching rank, signs the capitulation document. Tobolin is liberated. Quite incidentally, Misha will be happy about that. An aunt of his lives there, who hopefully has survived this victory. His aunt Leah Malamut owned a costume jewelry shop and, when Misha was still a boy, used to send him a little box with colored buttons and beads on every birthday. But let's not stay any longer than necessary in Tobolin. From there to the county seat, Pry, the next town in our direction, is a long way. About seventy kilometers have already been outlined in broad features, but not yet finished in all details. That will be Jacob's nightwork for awhile. Up to Tobolin everything is clear for the time being, and today at the railroad station the result of the glorious battle at the Rudna will be announced.

In high spirits Jacob goes to work. A neat, brilliant,

little idea illuminates his mind and could be tacked on to the event at the Rudna. Maybe secret German plans could have fallen into Russian hands, in which case all the opponent's activities on this front are known for weeks in advance and therefore made ineffective. That would be like the frosting to Jacob's cake; but immediately there are doubts concerning the probability, since secret plans would hardly be kept in such an insecure place. The Germans are certainly not idiots. Nor are the Russians idiots, either. Even if they captured such plans, they wouldn't trumpet them out into the world via radio. They would surely keep them to themselves and, in all secrecy, take proper measures. Thus, we'll forego this brilliant little idea. Even the extant one is sufficient to give the Jews a bit of the morale with which Jacob is still going to work: high spirits.

On the corner of Tismenizer Street he sees Kowalski waiting; nothing special in itself. Kowalski often waits here for him. He lives there. In approaching, Jacob sees, however, that Kowalski has a companion. Beside him is a young man; that is rather unusual. Above all, that young man hasn't been seen here before.

Even from afar Kowalski is pointing his finger at Jacob. The stranger lets his glances follow the finger as if Kowalski were explaining to him, it's that one there, the one in the dark gray jacket.

Jacob reaches them. They shake hands and all three continue on their way. The formal introduction still hasn't been made. Kowalski says, "You're late today. We have been waiting a long time for you."

"Did we perhaps make an appointment?" asks Jacob. He looks at the young man, who is silent, from the side. He seems a bit clumsy and embarrassed and is rigidly staring straight ahead. A blind man would recognize that it had something to do with his presence there. Kowalski had said, "*We* have been waiting," thus, the young man is not coincidentally here. Kowalski's fingers are involved in the matter. He must have sent for him.

"Don't you want to introduce us?" says Jacob.

"You don't know each other?" Kowalski acts amazed. "This is Josef Najdorf."

"I'm Jacob Heym."

"I know," says the shy young man who is named Najdorf. His first words that as yet allow no conclusions.

"Don't you work at the railroad station?" asks Jacob.

"No."

"Then where?"

"In the tool factory."

"But then you are walking in the wrong direction. You have to walk in the exact opposite direction."

"We begin later than you," says Najdorf, and it is clear he is uncomfortable with his explanation.

"Aha. And because you still have a little time, you happen to be accompanying us to the railroad station. Very clear."

Najdorf stops suddenly as people stop before they run away. He gives the impression of being disturbed. He says quietly to Kowalski, "Can't you do without me? Do understand, I don't want to have anything to do with this entire business. You see, I'm afraid."

"Don't start that again. Haven't I explained everything to you from beginning to end?" says Kowalski nervously and takes him by the arm before he can desert him. "Do get it through your head! He'll be quiet; I'll be quiet; and you'll be quiet, too. Besides us three nobody will find out about it. What can happen?"

Najdorf still looks very unhappy, but he stays when Kowalski releases him cautiously.

"What will I be quiet about?" asks Jacob, who would now like to find out more. Kowalski motions him with a gesture to wait. The gesture means many things. It means, you see what condition the young man is in. He must be given a moment's peace. He must be given a moment's peace so that he may control himself and his fear. Kowalski can make such meaningful gestures. He winks encouragingly to Najdorf, which is not so simple with swollen eyes. He says, "Now you can tell him what you are."

Najdorf still hesitates. Jacob is more than a bit curious. Early in the morning a surprise about which a young man is afraid and about which you have to keep silent although for reasons as yet unknown. Kowalski is not that successful every day.

"I'm really a radio mechanic," finally says Najdorf tormentedly.

He's a radio mechanic.

There's no chair there for Jacob. The looks fly back and forth, the happy ones as well as the dirty ones. A senseless rage toward Kowalski makes breathing difficult for Jacob. This idiot of a friend is playing God and worrying about repairs the extent of which he hasn't the vaguest notion. And surely he imagines you have to be grateful to him for his initiative and his pains. Because it is probably not easy to come up with someone in a single short evening, already over by eight o'clock, who knows something about radios —but not too difficult for a friend like Kowalski. He is standing there and beaming expectantly: "How in the world did I do it; splendidly, of course." One more bit of aid like that and I can hang myself immediately. And for him you have won the battle at the Rudna! You would be tempted to burn up the radio after all. Right after good-bys were exchanged yesterday he must have run off and made the whole ghetto crazy. He didn't know this Najdorf previously, that's for sure. Kowalski's friends are unfortunately mine, too. From one to the other he must have slunk and asked familiarly, in his penetrating voice:

"You don't happen to know anyone who can repair a

radio, do you?"—"A radio? Why, for heaven's sake, do you need someone who repairs radios?"—"Well, why do you think?"

Somebody sicked him then on this poor Najdorf who has more sense in his little finger than Kowalski has in his entire head. His fear is the best proof. He told him God knows what in order to calm him, dragged him here, and set up the most embarrassing situation imaginable. And now you're standing face to face with a real live radio mechanic.

"Well, you certainly have a good profession!" says Jacob.

"Don't I though."

Kowalski is happy as a child. His friendly favors simply do not cease. Recently the miraculous rescue from the toilet, today the second feat. And that's supposed to be emulated in a situation where there is so little room for favors! But he doesn't expect any big gratitude. Among true friends these things are taken for granted, not much talking but, instead, acting. And because the time is gradually getting late, and because up to now Jacob has not indicated any visible signs of joy or comprehension, Kowalski explains to him: "He is to fix your radio, you know. And no fear, the young man is reliable."

"That's good to know," says Jacob.

"Of course, I can't guarantee anything," says Najdorf, modestly and willingly. "If, for example, a tube is burned out, I can't do anything. I have no replacement parts. I told Kowalski that right away."

"Just go over there and take a look at it," says Kowalski.

Jacob has to find an excuse in a hurry. You would think it would become easier from one time to the next, because practice makes perfect. However, in fact, it is always equally difficult. Reluctantly he recalls last night's resolutions, easier conceived than carried out when such obstacles appear. But Jacob keeps himself under control. For happy news, happy faces are proper. Jacob is successful in neither. The sight of this help-crazy Kowalski will permit of no smile. With great effort Jacob twists his mouth into a smile and forces his eyes into a grim friendliness. He attempts to feign that he has just thought of something extraordinarily important.

"You could not have known about it," he says. "You've gone to all that trouble for nothing. The radio has been working fine since then."

"You don't say!"

"But it was nonetheless kind of you."

"How did it happen? Did you fix it yourself?" asks Kowalski, and it is not clear whether he is really happy or whether he's disappointed that his helpfulness was all in vain.

"It's working fine. Isn't that good enough for you?"

"But how?" asks Kowalski. "A radio doesn't fix itself."

If Najdorf were not present, Jacob could invent something; a tube was loose, or he banged it hard a few times with his fist and then it began to play again. Kowalski knows as little about radios as he does. But this Najdorf is unfortunately still there with his expertise. He looks relieved not only because his help is not needed now but also because he has his professional interest at stake. And now, go ahead and give them, on the spur of the moment, the proper explanation that will satisfy both blockhead and specialist equally. You surely must know how you fixed your own radio—quickly, and put on a happy expression to boot.

"It was only the lead-in wire. I simply shortened it a bit."

Well, everything fits together nicely. Jacob is proud of himself a little. The three parties are satisfied. Najdorf shakes hands good-by—once again, many thanks for his troubles. He walks in the direction of the tool factory and no longer needs to be afraid.

Kowalski and Jacob continue on their way to the railroad station. Jacob is devising revenge for his ruined morning that had begun so well. Accordingly, the battle at the

Rudna will be kept from Kowalski. Let others give him the happy news. Battles won in sleepless nights and torments are too good for friends who use every opportunity to wring your heart out. Even if what Kowalski did today happened without malicious intent, the difficulties he gets you into even without malicious intent predominate terrifyingly. This state of affairs can not be simply tolerated idly. The day before yesterday he sicked Lena on me, today Najdorf. He himself is the most tireless of all the questioners. As a countermeasure, a single battle kept from him would be appropriate.

"Were there any new developments last night?" asks Kowalski.

"Nothing."

A few friends say hello. The street is the only one leading to the railroad station and is gradually getting crowded. Jacob notices people looking inquiringly at him; Kowalski, too, apparently. He is basking a bit in Jacob's splendor and whispers to someone, "The radio is working again."

As if he had his part in it. The other man quickens his pace and whispers it to an other. Soon many are turning around to Jacob and look better than they did yesterday. Jacob nods imperceptibly that it's true, you've heard it correctly. The repaired radio will probably reach the railroad station before its owner.

"I wanted to ask you something," says Kowalski. "I've been thinking that it's really about time to start thinking about other things, too."

"For example?"

"About business, for example."

"About business? About what business?"

"I'm a merchant," says Kowalski. "Isn't now the best time to prepare at least mentally for everything later?"

"What merchant? And what do you want to prepare for? Isn't your barbershop there waiting for you?"

"That's the question. You know, I've been thinking for

a long time whether or not I should begin something else afterward?"

"Something else, at your age?"

"Why not? Between you and me, I have some money stashed away. Not a fortune, you understand, but can't it be better invested than in an old shop I've never really been fond of? You, either, to be honest about it? And if I do something like that, I want to be certain that it's not squandered."

"And what should I do about it?"

"Now and then business reports are announced over the radio, aren't they?"

"Yes."

"Hasn't there been anything by which you could be guided? Any tip?"

"I'm not interested in such things."

"You're not interested in such things!" says Kowalski. "You've probably heard something."

"What do you really want to know? I haven't understood a word up to now."

"I simply want to know what line of business has the best prospects."

"Sometimes you really get childish, Kowalski. Do you seriously think they announce over the radio: We recommend that you invest your money after the war in such and such a business?"

Kowalski comprehends that. He says, "O.K. then, I'm asking you as a friend. If you had money, where would you choose to invest it?"

Jacob thinks awhile, too. Such an investment requires thinking about. Where would he choose to invest it? "Maybe in luxury businesses? If you recall, after the previous war everybody was crazy about them. And David Gedalye, you know him, too, built himself a magnificent house from liquor."

"Yes, he did. Yes, he did," says Kowalski. "But how

about the raw materials? Do you think there will be enough potatoes right afterward to make liquor?"

"That's not the way to figure it. There will be raw materials for nothing. For postwar business you'll need no logic, only a good nose."

Kowalski continues his doubts. It is obvious his nose has no inclination for liquor. His money is too good for that.

"Textile goods would probably have good prospects. Clothing is always needed," he says.

"Maybe you're right. For years they have manufactured clothing only for soldiers, military trousers, socks, jackets, coats. The civilians have worn out their old clothing. And what does that mean?"

"So?"

"There will be a demand."

"That's only half the truth, Jacob. Don't forget that in the same period many things lay unused in the closet, the clothes of all the soldiers. And today they're still like new."

"Hm," says Jacob thoughtfully.

And so on. They consider two or three other possibilities. Kowalski even toys with the idea of a partnership with Jacob in order to finance a large-scale inn with all the frills. But for Jacob such an undertaking is too risky. Besides, Kowalski is surely not very serious about that. Jacob returns to his first proposal, namely, Kowalski should stay in his old shop and if he doesn't know where to invest his stashed away money, he should then modernize; go ahead and buy new chairs. Because regardless of demand, hair and beards will always continue to grow. By the time they arrive at the railroad station, Kowalski is, once more, almost a barber.

Lena wins her bet, because in the long run Jacob is no match in the unequal struggle. He shows her his radio.

After several days' fruitless search nothing else was there

that she didn't already know. She switched over to pleading. She can plead like no one else. She especially knows how to implore Jacob with flattery, tears, feeling insulted in a very special manner, more tears, and all of that with an unbelievable persistance. For a few days Jacob held out. Then his strength gives out. One evening—predictable in advance—Lena wins her bet.

For me, probably the only one still alive and capable of having misgivings, that evening is the most incomprehensible in the entire story. Even when Jacob had explained it to me as well as he could, I didn't completely understand him. I asked Jacob, "Didn't you carry it too far? She could have betrayed you and everything would have been done for." "Oh, no," Jacob answered smiling, "Lena would never betray me." I said, "I mean completely unintentionally. A heedless word will slip out of a child's mouth. Somebody picks it up and builds an entire story out of it." "Lena weighs precisely what she says," Jacob answered, and I had to believe him. But there was something else that seemed hardly comprehensible to me. "There is something else, Jacob. You couldn't be certain that she didn't see through everything. How easily she could have noticed what was really happening. She is a clever girl, as you yourself say. Wasn't it fantastic luck that she didn't see through it?" "She saw through it," Jacob said, and his eyes became quite proud. "You know, I really didn't care whether she noticed anything or not. I simply wanted to give her some pleasure without regard for the consequences. That's why I went into the cellar with her." And after a pause that was much too short for me to comprehend that evening, he added, "Well, no, I did care. I think I wanted her to find out everything then. I finally had to show somebody my radio and Lena was my most preferable choice of all. With her, it was like a game. All the others would have been horrified over the truth. She was happy about it afterward. That's why I said to her that evening, come along now to the cellar. Let's listen to the radio together." And now I suddenly smiled. Now I said: "If I had known then, what you were capable of doing, I would have come to you and asked you to show me a tree." Which Jacob, in turn, was not able to comprehend.

Let's listen to that evening.

A great deal of excitement. Lena is hanging on to Jacob's coat. The cellar corridor is long and gloomy. The metal doors they pass by on tiptoe are all locked, as if they had inestimable riches to hide. The air is damp and cold despite the month of August outside. In concerned anticipation Jacob insisted upon a winter dress, stockings, and scarf for Lena. On the ceiling and walls droplets are hanging and glistening like weak light bulbs.

"Are you afraid?"

"No," she whispers decisively, and that's not too much of a lie. Her curiosity will let her forget everything else. Nonetheless, at the end of the corridor the object is waiting which had been looked for for days and had nearly been given up for lost. Would she say now, I'm afraid, let's turn back?

Finally Jacob stops. Almost the last compartment in the long row. He takes the key out of his pocket, unlocks it, and opens the light which is only a bit brighter than no light at all.

The cellar must be described. Four meters square and no windows. Most striking, a wall cut diagonally across the room, making almost two rooms out of it, leaving only a narrow passage free. The builders intended it for coal storage. The inventory can be quickly enumerated: an iron bedstead with red rusted springs, a little pile of oven debris with tile pieces, green and brown, and several stovepipes with elbows. And in the corner beside the door, the only valuable object: a carefully stacked little pile of wood in which the immodest poacher Piwowa slept months ago when the logs still provided an opportunity for sleeping. Then a glance behind the partition: more oven debris, bricks, a spade, a pail riddled with holes, and an ax. That's all. I'm so exact, not because the objects enumerated were of any significance, but because I was there later in my search for witnesses and traces and non-existent trees. Just as I measured the distance between the police station and the nearest corner with my tape measure, and went to Jacob's room in which since then a single old woman had been living who knew nothing about the fate of any prior tenants (the lodgings office had assigned the room to her for the present), I was in this cellar, too. The cellar room belonged, just as before, to the room upstairs. Frau Domnik handed me the key without any questions. She only said she had never yet gone down. She owned nothing that had to be put in the cellar and therefore I shouldn't be surprised at the dust and possible disorder. She wasn't to blame for it. It was dusty and spider webs were everywhere, that's true. But I saw nothing in disorder. I found everything exactly as Jacob had described it to me.

The bedstead, oven debris, ax, and pail, even the pile of logs was still lying near the door.

Jacob locks the door from the inside. He says, "That's so no one will disturb us." Then: "And now sit down here," and points to the iron bedstead.

Lena has already looked around a bit, until now in vain. Nonetheless, she sits down without objecting. He would be able to demand even more manifestations of obedience under these circumstances.

"Where do you have the radio?"

"You'll endure it a bit longer."

He squats in front of her, takes her chin in one hand, turns her face to himself so that no glance goes astray and begins with the most necessary preparations: "Listen exactly to what I tell you. First, you must promise me that you'll be good and do everything I now ask of you. Sacred word of honor?"

The sacred word of honor, used only at quite important occasions, is given impatiently. Her eyes demand him not to dwell so long upon preliminaries.

"You'll remain sitting here very quietly. The radio is behind that wall there. I'm going there now to turn it on, then it'll play and we'll both hear it. But if I see you stand up, I'll turn it off again immediately."

"Can't I see it?"

"By no means!" says Jacob decisively. "You're not even allowed to hear it either when you're so little. That's strictly forbidden. But I'll make an exception in your case. Agreed?"

What can she do? She is being blackmailed and has to give in. Listening is better than nothing, even though she had promised herself the direct view. Besides, she could, she could . . . we'll find out.

"What's your radio playing?"

"I don't know that ahead of time. I have to turn it on first."

The preparations are concluded. No more can be done for your own security. Jacob stands up, goes to the wall, stops at the opening, and looks at Lena once more with looks that should bind her as far as possible to the bedstead. Then he disappears finally.

Jacob's eyes must first get accustomed to the new light. It hardly extends behind the partition. His foot stumbles against the pail full of holes.

"Was that the radio?"

"No, not yet. It'll take another moment."

Something to sit on will be necessary because the fun can be drawn out once it starts. Jacob turns the pail upside down and makes himself comfortable on it. Quite late he runs into the problem as to what type of program the radio has to offer. Lena had already touched upon it in passing and the time is ripe for an answer. That should have been thought about earlier—among all the other things that should have been. Maybe even have practiced a bit. However, the radio must play just as it comes. It makes music; there is talking from it. Jacob recalls that ages ago his father could imitate an entire brass band with tuba, trumpets, trombone, and bass drum. You could laugh yourself sick. After supper, if the day had passed without great annoyance, he could sometimes be persuaded. But would such an orchestra hit it off at the very first try? His father had polished it over a long period. Lena is quietly waiting in her winter dress and Jacob is already perspiring although the performance hasn't even started.

"It's starting," says Jacob, prepared for the first thing that comes out.

A fingernail plunks against the pail; that's how radios are turned on. Then the air is full of humming and whistling. The warming-up time is skipped; that particular is reserved for connoisseurs. Jacob's radio has right from the start the proper temperature. The choice of station is also quickly accomplished. An announcer in a high-pitched voice, as stated, the first thing that comes out, proclaims: "Good evening, ladies and gentlemen, near and far. You will now hear an interview with the English prime minister, Sir Winston Churchill." The speaker then hands over the microphone. A man in a middle voice-range can be heard. The reporter: "Good evening, Sir Winston."

Then Sir Winston himself, in a very deep voice and clearly foreign intonation: "Good evening, everyone."

Reporter: "I very heartily welcome you to our broadcast studio. And now for the first question: Would you kindly tell our listeners how you assess the present situation from your viewpoint?"

Sir Winston: "That's not too difficult. I'm firmly convinced that the entire mess will soon be over, at the very most a few more weeks."

Reporter: "And may we ask where you get this nice certainty?"

Sir Winston (somewhat embarrassed): "Well, on all fronts there is good progress. It seems quite likely that the Germans will not be able to hold out very much longer."

Reporter: "Wonderful! And how is it particularly in the region of Bezanika?"

A little incident occurs. The perspiring and the cold air in the cellar, or else something or other gets into Jacob's nose. At any rate, the reporter, announcer, and Sir Winston all sneeze together in confusion.

Reporter (the first to recover): "Bless you, Mr. Prime Minister!"

Sir Winston (after blowing his nose): "Thank you. But, back to your question. In the region of Bezanika it is particularly bad for the Germans. The Russians are routing them at will. Bezanika has long since been captured. It so happens that they won an important battle yesterday at the Rudna River, in case you know where that is."

Reporter: "Yes, I know that river."

Sir Winston: "Then you also know where the front is already. It will certainly not last much longer."

Reporter (rejoicing): "Our listeners, then, will be very happy, if they do not happen to be Germans. Sir Winston, thank you very much for the informative talk."

Sir Winston: "You're welcome, I'm sure."

Announcer (after a short pause): "That, ladies and gentlemen, was the scheduled interview with the English prime minister, Sir Winston Churchill. Good-by."

A fingernail plunks against the pail. That's how radios are turned off. Jacob wipes the perspiration from his forehead. A bit weak that interview, he thinks, and also a bit

153

over Lena's head. But you're not—unfortunately, that will never change—a Sholem Aleichem in inventiveness. Don't demand too much from a tormented man. I hope it will suffice for today. Jacob appears again. It turns out that things are going splendidly not only in the region of Bezanika but also not any worse here in the cellar. Lena has finally heard a radio with her own ears, strictly forbidden for children, and is fascinated. It could have happened differently, too. To mask your voice was an innovation, moreover, three different kinds at once. Lena could have also coldly demanded that he stop the nonsense now and finally turn on the radio. That would have been a blow to Jacob, even the thought of it, but she wouldn't even dream of such words. Everything is as nice as could be. He sees that immediately.

"Did you like it?"

"Yes."

Mutual satisfaction. Jacob is standing in front of her and is about to talk of leaving: we've all had our fun; your bed is waiting; but Lena says: "It isn't over yet, is it?"

"Why, of course."

"I'd like to hear more."

"No, no, enough for now," he says, but he says it only feebly. A short dispute: it's late already; Lena would like to hear more; perhaps another time; just a little bit; never satisfied; just turn the radio on again; she'll be happy with everything. Jacob sneezes again. On this evening the whole world has the sneezes. While wiping his nose he examines her expression and finds no suspicion. That is the deciding factor.

"What do you want to hear?"

Well, Jacob is once again sitting on the pail completely silent, gradually overcome by ambition. By ambition concerning the brass band. That thought gives him no peace although it has been silent for a good forty years and covered with dust and the instruments rusty. Jacob wants to try it, resolved as he is today.

In the beginning is the plunk, then humming and whistling. The second time around it sounds more skilled. Then it starts full blast, the music, with drum and cymbals to which the first measure belongs. Drum and cymbals are followed by a solitary trombone that needs several notes to get on the right track. The melody is uncertain, Jacob says. An improvised melodic line, interspersed with diverse familiar themes, but devoid of any regular tempo. What is clear is that it's some sort of march. His feet timidly take over the percussion, supported by his fingers which make use of the pail, thereby freeing his mouth for the rest of the instruments. A single trombone does not yet produce a brass band. It must be alternated with the trumpet and that, in turn, with the falsetto clarinet, and every now and then a tuba blast from the bottom of your throat. Jacob loses, as they say, all his inhibitions. The only constraint he submits to—despite his haste he does have a certain standard in mind, strictly adhered to in those days by his father—to be sure, is that vowels are to be used sparingly and, if possible, completely to be avoided. Because instruments are expressed only in consonants or, more exactly, only in sounds that can be described in a pinch as consonants, but are only distantly related and not the same thing. Since no simple "da de dum" or "la li la" pass his lips, it is necessary to formulate sounds that exist in no alphabet. The cellar resounds with sounds never yet heard. Perhaps, too much effort for a child like Lena who would be satisfied even with less elaborate material. But let me remind you, ambition is at stake, a voluntary test, and mastery thrives best without constraint. Soon the proper tone is achieved without difficulty. Trumpets and trombones throw each other phrases back and forth, practice variations, and almost always bring it off successfully. The clarinet is necessarily pushed to the background more and more, too unnatural a register, while the tuba can be heard more and more often, from time to time even undertaking a little showpiece of its own, a succession of notes in the lower registers, and when the breath gives out, taking refuge in drumming on the pail for two or three measures.

In a phrase, a piece of music history is being written. Jacob is a clamoring success. Lena is brought to her feet from the bedstead. She stands up inaudibly, forgotten are all the sacred words of honor. Her legs slink unopposed to the partition. She has to see the thing that sounds so much like Jacob and yet very differently, that can speak in various voices, sneeze as he does, and make such peculiar noises. Just a look—even at the price of a discovered breach of promise. For legs that have their own strong will, there is nothing to be done. However, so much caution would not be necessary. The din that the object makes drowns out everything. Nonetheless, she slinks up to the narrow opening. The trombone is just finishing a skillful solo and is letting the trumpet take over. Lena carefully stretches her head around the corner invisible to Jacob who is sitting not only sideways, but also keeping his eyes tightly shut, a sign of the greatest mental and physical effort. Oblivious to the world, he is making noises in accordance with rules known only to him. No, Jacob doesn't notice that he has been sitting naked and unguarded for several moments. Later he will become keen of hearing by means of Lena's hidden allusions, and not until much later will she tell him to his face what really happened there in that cellar. For now, a few seconds of staring and amazement are sufficient for her. Lena has voyaged to India and discovered America. Her trip concerned the viewing of this thing and now it can be determined with certainty that it looks precisely like Jacob. Afterward, only one question remains. She will inquire as to whether he has another radio besides this one. Presumably he doesn't; otherwise, where would he keep it hidden if not here? Lena knows what no one knows. She sits down again quietly on her spot. Her pleasure in listening has not diminished, just mixed with a few thoughts that are nobody's business.

Then the march is over, but not yet the performance. When Jacob reappears exhausted and delighted and with a withered mouth, Lena tempestuously demands an encore—all good things come in threes and now truly so! That proves to him she has not suspected anything. That was also proof enough, he thinks; if this march went well, then nothing more can happen to him.

"But this is the very last one!" says Jacob.

He sets out again for his broadcasting room, his next program already in mind, and plunks. Lena is quite lucky. Jacob soon finds the radio station where fairy tales are told by a kind fellow who says, "For all the children who are listening to us, the storyteller will tell the tale about the sick princess."

He has a voice similar to that of Sir Winston Churchill, just as deep but somewhat softer, and yet without a foreign intonation.

"Do you know that one?" asks Jacob as Jacob.

"No. But how come there is a storyteller on the radio?"

"What do you mean, how come? There just is."

"But you said the radio is forbidden for children. And aren't fairy tales only for children?"

"That's correct. But I meant it's forbidden for us in the ghetto. Where there is no ghetto, children are allowed to listen. And there are radios everywhere. Clear?"

"Clear."

The storyteller, upset a bit over the interruption, but justified enough in looking for the reasons in himself, takes off his jacket, lays it underneath him because the pail is hard and edged and the tale one of the longer kind, if it can be told in its entirety. Heavens, how long it's been, occurs to him now of all times. His father was not available for fairy tales. They were his mother's concern. You lay in bed and waited and waited for her to finish the housework and come to you. Almost always you fell asleep waiting. But sometimes she did sit down beside you and slipped her warm hand under the cover upon your chest and told stories. About the robber Yaromir with the three eyes who always had to sleep upon the cold ground because there was no bed big enough for him; about the cat, Rashka, who didn't want to catch any mice, only birds, until he saw a bat; about Lake Shapun into which Dvoire, the witch, forced all the children to weep until it swelled up and overflowed wretchedly drowning Dvoire; and sometimes about the sick princess.

"When is it going to start?" asks Lena.

"The Tale of the Sick Princess," begins the fairy-tale man.

About how the good old king who ruled over a big country and had a first-class beautiful palace as well as a daughter; the old story about how he was quite terribly frightened. Because he loved her tremendously, you know. Whenever his princess had fallen and had tears in her eyes, he had to weep himself, so much did he love her. And he is frightened because she didn't want to get out of bed one morning and looked very sick. Then the most expensive physician from far and wide was sent for to make her quickly healthy and happy again. But the physician examined and tested her from top to bottom and said, perplexed, "I'm terribly sorry, Mr. King, I can find nothing wrong. Your daughter must be suffering from a disease that I have not yet encountered in my whole life." Then the good old king was even more frightened. He himself went to the princess and asked her what for heaven's sake was wrong.

And then she said to him she wanted to have a cloud; when she got it, she would get better immediately. "But a real one!" she added. Wasn't that a scare! For everybody can imagine that it is not at all simple to procure a real cloud, even for a king. From sheer worry he was unable to rule the entire day. In the evening he had letters sent to all the intelligent men of his country in which were written they should drop everything and come to his royal palace at once. The next morning they were already all gathered there, the doctors and the ministers, the astrologers and the soothsayers. And the king stood on his throne so that everyone in the hall could hear him well, and he called out, "Qu i et!" It became very quiet then, and the king announced: "To that wise man among you who can get a cloud from the sky for my daughter, I will give as much gold and silver as will fill the biggest wagon in the whole country." When the intelligent men heard that, they began right away to explain and speculate and aspire and calculate. Because everybody wanted to have all that gold and silver, why not? A particularly shrewd man even began to build a tower that was to reach the clouds. He thought to himself, when the tower is done you'll climb up, grab a cloud, and collect the reward. But before the tower was even half so high, it toppled. Nor did the others have any luck. Not one of the wise men was able to procure for the princess one cloud she wanted so badly. She grew thinner and thinner and sicker and sicker, because from sadness she didn't take a bite any more, not even *matzos* with butter.

One fine day the gardner boy, with whom the princess sometimes played outside when she was still a healthy girl, dropped into the palace to see whether flowers were missing in any vases. And thus he saw her lying in her bed under her blanket of silk, looking pale as the snow. He had already racked his brains for the last few days as to why she no longer came into the garden, but he didn't know the reason why. And that's why he asked her, "What's the matter with you, dear princess? Why don't you come out into the sun anymore?" And then she told him that she was sick and would not get better until someone brought her a cloud. The gardner boy thought about it a bit, then he exclaimed, "But that's quite simple, dear princess!" "Really? Quite simple?" the princess asked amazed. "All the wise men in the country are racking their brains in vain and you claim that it's quite simple?" "Yes," the gardner boy said, "you must just tell me what a cloud is made of." The princess would have almost had to laugh, if she hadn't been so weak. She replied, "What a stupid question you're asking! Every child knows that clouds are made of cotton." "Aha, and will you tell me also how big a cloud is?" "You don't even know that?" she was astonished. "A cloud is as big as my pillow. You can see that yourself if you only push the curtain aside and look up at the sky." Then the gardner boy went to the window, looked up at the sky, and exclaimed, "Really! Just as big as your pillow!" Then he left and soon brought the princess back a piece of cotton that was as big as her pillow.

I'll forego the rest. Everyone can easily imagine that the princess regained her bright eyes and red lips and recovered her health, and that the good old king was happy, that the gardner boy didn't want the promised reward but, instead, preferred to marry the princess, and if they haven't died . . . That is Jacob's story.

It was probably the same evening, at most the previous one or the one following. Tender, beautiful Rosa is lying with Misha and listening to the battle at the Rudna. Misha is telling it quietly, but he isn't whispering. Between speaking quietly and whispering there is a big difference. You will ask, quite properly so, why isn't he whispering? And you will ask why the closet is no longer in the middle of the room, but is instead in its normal position against the wall, and why the curtain is covering the window again instead of dividing the room into two halves? Where was the folding screen now kept, you will wonder, and especially why Rosa is suddenly lying naked although the light is still on, and how come she is no longer embarrassed? Then, you will kindly take a look at the second bed and you will find it empty and all the questions will be resolved into one: Where is the deaf and dumb Isaak Fajngold with his keen ears?

I know the answer just as little as Misha does, not to speak at all of Rosa. A week ago he left for work early in the morning, just as he did every day and has since disappeared. It wasn't taken so tragically the first evening. Misha thought maybe he went to visit a friend and chatted away the time and then noticed it was past eight P.M. and thus too late to go home, so he lay down on the floor and slept there. "What do you mean 'chatted away the time'?" Rosa asked distrustfully. "Isn't he deaf and dumb?" "Oh, do you think deaf and dumb people are incapable of talking?" Misha answered in a flash. "Maybe you think they are condemned to keep everything that goes through their minds to themselves? They can communicate just as you and I, but in sign language."

But, on the second evening Fajngold didn't return either, nor on the third. That's why on the fourth day Misha went to the only friend of Fajngold he knew, to Hersh Prashker. He works together with Fajngold in the sanitation squad, clearing the streets of rubbish and those who have starved to death. But Prashker didn't know, either. He said, "I wanted to come to his apartment tomorrow to find out why he doesn't show up at work. They'll come get him. He's already on their list." "When was he there the last time?" "Tuesday." "And Wednesday morning he left his house as usual."

**161**

He never arrived, nor did he come home. Maybe he escaped or died or had an accident or was arrested right on the street. What makes death or an accident unlikely is that he was never found. We asked around. What makes a planned escape unlikely is that all his things are in his closet, not even the photo of his grandson is missing. He would never have parted from that. He guarded it like a treasure. Which leaves only the arrest on the street. Why is a mystery because Fajngold had always been an able and law-abiding man. But you know the saying, Where there's a will, there's a way. And from all that, it follows logically why Misha is quietly telling about the battle at the Rudna rather than whispering it.

It's already the second evening in a row that Rosa is lying next to him and that hasn't happened before. Old man Frankfurter, a man of the theater and no inherent friend of all too strict morals, gave some food for thought: "Well, fine, children, you love each other; that's understandable. But don't overdo it right away." That's why, and also because of Rosa's reserve, the number of their nights together was kept within modest limits. Misha had to talk her into each one almost as if it were her first, with very few exceptions. And now already the second in a row. Rosa imagines that's about what it must be like when you're married, but, to tell the truth, she doesn't feel at ease with it. It's not because Misha had suddenly changed from before, say, less inhibited or more impudent. His worth had not diminished one iota. She looked at him with no less love than she did on the first day. Or, let's say, on the fifth day. No matter how mysterious it may sound to some, it's because of Isaak Fajngold. She had in a strange way grown accustomed to him. But how can you grow accustomed to someone who only inconveniences, no matter how deaf and dumb he may be? To such a situation, in which being alone is self-evident, how can you grow

162

accustomed? You can and you can not; let's examine it. In this room Rosa first began to make love in Fajngold's presence. He was there right from the very first second. Her privacy from him was a firm component of all the caresses. Then second, Fajngold's bed is not simply empty now. No, Fajngold is not lying in it any more. That's a distinct difference. Every look behind the folding screen, superfluous and therefore folded away, recalls his gloomy fate, uncertain to be sure, but the longer you rack your brains, what is really uncertain is only the kind of death he met. And third and last, when Misha told her Fajngold had disappeared, her eyes grew terrified, as expected; but after a while her eyes were not at all so terrified anymore; she caught herself thinking, at last. That wasn't meant to harm Fajngold. Him she wished only good luck. It concerned only her and Misha and was meant to indicate, at last, alone; at last, no inconvenience; at last, a free nook for the two of us. She caught herself thinking it and she felt quite uncomfortable. She found such thoughts shameful and was compelled to think repeatedly, nonetheless, at last. Then she thought, in addition, it's good Misha doesn't know what selfish things are going through my mind. And she also thought, whatever happened to Fajngold happened thus and so. Thoughts kept to yourself can not interfere with you.

But they did interfere. It wasn't quite so simple. For several days she gave Misha excuses why she couldn't come along to his room and he left disappointed. Until yesterday, until she couldn't or wouldn't find any more excuses. He asked her, "And why aren't you coming by today?" She replied "I am," and then he said it: "At last!"

They went to the room. Misha had previously switched things around, since Fajngold's absence could be considered as final. The closet was, as mentioned, against the wall. The curtain hung on the window. Rosa remained standing in the middle of the room and had to get used to it, because she had never yet seen it this way. Fajngold's made-up bed, of course, attracted her attention. She felt right away that it would yet be a matter of contention. She asked, "What sort of box is that?"

"His belongings. In case someone takes them away," Misha said. And immediately the proper mood was set.

At some point they lay down together, but were silent for a long time and motionless and devoid of joy. How different everything was on this evening. The light was still on. Misha lay on his side and she on her back since the bed was too narrow for two on their backs. With a look at Fajngold's smoothed-out bed, he asked, "Don't you think we could . . ."

"No, please!" she anxiously interrupted him.

"O.K., then."

He turned out the light and shoved his arm under her head, that's the way it usually starts, and wanted to kiss her; but she turned away. Until he asked her, "What's the matter with you?"

"Nothing."

He thought for a while, which probably means nothing, then said, "But you hardly even got to know him. And even if you did, what can we do about it?"

He wanted to kiss her again. She even let him now, but just barely. He soon noticed that there was no further use, closed his eyes, tomorrow is another day, and fell asleep. That was the only thing that was the same. He was always first to fall asleep.

In the middle of the night she woke him. He wasn't angry. He hoped she would at last have considered matters differently. For that you like to be awakened.

"I must tell you something, Misha," she whispered.

"Yes?"

The fact that she was silent he interpreted completely

wrong. He pulled her over to him and wanted to touch her face all over with his lips when he noticed that it was wet and salty from the eyes down. Fright penetrated to all his limbs since he was accustomed to her laughing rarely, but never weeping. Even when her only girl friend had to board the train half a year ago, she couldn't weep, although for days not a word was heard from her. And now suddenly her face wet, enough to frighten you, but she didn't sob or wail. It must have happened very quietly, to herself. He wouldn't even have awakened if she hadn't awakened him. And besides, it was as good as over with, in judging by her voice.

"I have a request that will sound strange to you."

"Speak."

"I would like the room to be as it was before."

"What do you mean like before?"

"The closet in the middle again. And the curtain."

"But what for? Fajngold isn't here any longer, is he?"

"I would just like it that way," she said.

It really struck him as strange, at first strange, then childish, then foolish, and then simply ridiculous. Then he recalled having once heard or read something about the unfathomable moods of women and that it was advisable to nip them in the bud. The entire change she wanted would have taken him no more than ten minutes. But he said, "Only if you can give me a sensible reason."

"I would like it that way," she said.

And that was not a sensible reason, not by a long shot. He resolutely refused. He told her that it did her honor that Fajngold's disappearance affected her so, although she didn't know him at all, only his breathing and snoring. But after all, in the ghetto lots of people are lost each day who are just as little known, and if each one caused such a to-do, it wouldn't be bearable. And she accused him of being an insensitive, crude boor—their first argument had come up—and if it hadn't been for the eight o'clock curfew, she would have certainly got up and dressed and good-by. But instead she just turned her back to him, so that he would see how very much she detested him.

The following day, that is, today, he picked her up right at the factory, because at her house, in the presence of her parents, reconciliation would have been much more difficult. As it was, it was difficult enough, not because there was a lack of good will, but rather because they were so inexperienced in terminating quarrels. In the end they both admitted they hadn't acted completely properly. A kiss in a front door and they were able to breathe freer once more. They dropped by her house in order to tell where she would spend the coming evening. Frankfurter didn't look enthusiastic. He couldn't know that last night was a big flop for all purposes. Misha heard Frau Frankfurter telling her husband quietly, "Go ahead, let her."

Then to his room. They were both friendly to one another to the best of their abilities and showed each other their good sides after their spat. But it was evident that more time would have to pass until everything would be as before.

Misha told her about the battle at the Rudna, or better, because we're once again abreast of things, Misha is quietly telling her about the battle at the Rudna, finishing at last, what he heard today from Jacob, so to speak the latest from the air waves. Rosa is melting for joy. She knows where the Rudna flows and what progress the battle signifies since Bezanika and would even be in the mood to begin with new planning. But Misha is not inclined to plans, not at the moment. They won't run away as this second evening in a row would. He closes the light. In order to devote himself to Rosa, he won't talk any more about victories. Last night was for practical purposes a big fiasco. The Rudna and Fajngold and words said in anger are forgotten. They get closer to each other in more intimate ways, as far as your own will can control it. But the will does not reign unlimited. Comparisons are misleading. That's the way it is now. Really, no different from before. They lie a bit next to and look at one another. Maybe they even hear no strange breathing interrupting them from the other half of the room. Let's state it frankly, making up for a missed night turns out quite wretchedly even if they would never admit it; even if they act happy like young lovers.

With slight regrets, let's leave them in the hope that easier times will come again. That hope is permitted us. Let's still hear Misha smilingly ask in the wave of compatibility, what he shouldn't have asked, "Would you still like me to divide the room again with the closet and curtain?"

He says that, and above all, smilingly, because for him there is no doubt that Rosa now sees things differently, that she will speak of the stupid mood that came over her yesterday, and that the nasty incident would be best forgotten.

And still, let's overhear Rosa saying, "Yes, please."

Jacob is forced to hear with his own ears how distorted his information is passed on.

Jacob wants to go to Lena in the attic—not yet time for bed, but more is necessary than simply seeing to it that she washes herself thoroughly, brushes her teeth, and goes to bed on time. At the railroad station they let us go two hours earlier. There was simply nothing else to be loaded there. The guards were not in the mood to watch idlers hanging around. They invited us to disappear. A few especially bold speculators suspect that there is far more than laziness behind this invitation. Maybe these guards are trying to become chummy, they reason. They could have had us wait two hours, you know. We lined up, but they sent us home. Maybe new times are knocking at the door unpretentiously.

In any case, the two hours are well spent with Lena, Jacob thinks. As he is putting his hand on the door handle, he hears that she is not alone. He hears Rafael's voice asking, "Well, what's it about anyway?"

"About a princess," says Lena.

"Is she kidnapped?"

"How do you get that idea?"

"Of course, she's kidnapped. I know that one. She's kidnapped by a robber. He wants to have a pile of ransom for her but the prince kills him and frees her. And afterward they get married."

"What nonsense you're talking," says Lena annoyed. "That's an entirely different story. Do you think there is only one tale about a princess?"

"Then tell it already!"

"Shouldn't we wait for Siegfried?"

"He won't come."

Jacob hears them waiting. The attic window reverberates. Rafael shouts, "Siegfried!"

Then he says Siegfried is nowhere to be seen, and soon thereafter Lena screechingly demands that Rafael stop the nonsense. Which kind is not known, but he no doubt doesn't stop right away. Then he asks, "From whom did you hear the story?"

"From Uncle Jacob."

That's significant when you're secretly standing in front of the door. Jacob never told her a tale about a princess. He above all should recall that it was the storyteller, and she without even a tremor in her voice is making one man out of two different people. That's significant. Jacob also played march music and asked questions and gave answers. Or else in her haste Lena made a mistake, or, what would be best, she's resorting to a white lie so as not to reveal the radio. That's still a question. That will yet have to be discussed.

"He won't come any more. Begin now," says Rafael.

That's how it happens. Lena clears her throat. Jacob perks his ears. He hasn't ever heard his information being passed on.

"Once upon a time there was a king, a good old man, and he had a daughter, who was the princess," begins Lena.

"What was the king's name?"

Lena appears to be thinking if names were mentioned at all. Too long for Rafael; he says, "You must at least know what his name was."

"His name was Benjamin," Lena recalls. "And the princess was named Magdalena."

"What was his name? Benjamin? Do you know who is named Benjamin? My uncle in Tarnopol. His name is Benjamin. But not a king!"

"You can believe it or not. The king in this tale at least was named Benjamin."

"Well, O.K.," says Rafi magnanimously. The story won't be ruined because of the name. Jacob is almost certain that his arms are folded across his chest in a patronizing manner.

Lena continues, but more hurried than at the start, as if disconcerted, as if in expectation of further objections. "One day the princess became ill. The physician couldn't find anything wrong because he didn't know her disease; but she didn't want to eat any more bread nor drink any more. Then the king himself went to her. He was terribly fond of her, you see. I almost forgot to mention that. And he asked her what was wrong. Then she told him she wouldn't get better until someone brought her a piece of cotton that had to be as big as her pillow. And then the old king . . ."

**169**

She gets no further. Rafael has had it now. He has made a real effort and patiently listened. But too much is too much. His credulity has broad limits but there are limits.

"What sort of disease did your Magdalena have?"

"You heard it."

"And I'm telling you there isn't any such disease! Not in the whole world!"

"You don't know that!"

"If she at least had the measles, or whooping cough, or typhoid," says Rafael, shaking angrily. "Do you know what the princess really had? A fart in her head!"

He laughs, much louder than Jacob, but Lena can find nothing humorous in his explanation. She asks, "Do you want to hear more of the story or not?"

"I don't want to," says Rafael, still amused. The best jokes are your own. "Because she had a fart in her head, you see. Because the whole story is total nonsense, you know, starting with the king. In the whole world you won't find a king named Benjamin. And then princesses don't ever eat bread but only cake instead. And the biggest nonsense is this disease. Have you ever seriously heard of people getting sick if they don't have any cotton?"

Lena seems impressed by Rafael's reasoning. At least she's quiet. Hopefully without tears, thinks Jacob. And he insists upon it. She is a clever girl. Anyone can make mistakes. The excitement in the basement may have been at fault in causing the misunderstanding. Or at Lena's age such transitions of thought are simply beyond her. Jacob's hand is once again on the door handle. You should step in, console, and explain or else, God forbid, they could resort to their fists. It would be quite innocent to walk in and say hello Lena, hello Rafael, nice of you to visit her, how is your mother? Then the conversation will of itself come to the disputed case and will be told by both sides—quiet, children, be polite, first one, then the other. Then, no doubt, pacifying words will be found that will put unclear matters in a new light. No need at all, children, to be so angry with each other. The reality seems to be so and so, and in the end, good will and understanding. He is about to plunge into the fray when he hears Rafael's peace-loving voice, "Whenever your uncle tells you a fairy tale again, tell him to come up with something better than such nonsense. The princess, you know, had a great big fart in her head."

Hostilities do not ensue. The door opens. Jacob's old accustomed luck with doors. It opens outward and grants him a hiding place. Rafael is leaving for more rewarding amusement. For sure, he wants to look for Siegfried and report to him. He is heard running down the stairs whistling. He is whistling "Lemons and Oranges" and continues while Lena shouts after him the meager rest still necessary for completion, "And she did so have that disease! And the gardening boy got her the cotton! And she got better because of that, and they got married!"

Everything is told although to closed ears; down below a song dies away, the front door clicks shut; up above a disappointed, long tongue is stuck out and the attic door is banged shut. Jacob is still standing in front of the door as in the beginning. Doubts arise even now whether the two free hours would be well spent with Lena. He tells me it would have been quite nice with the two children, but suddenly he hadn't been in the mood; he had suddenly felt exhausted. He wanted rather to keep the two hours for himself. And he asks me if he is boring me with such details, I should tell him.

I tell him, "No."

Jacob goes for a walk for his two hours. Rest is obtainable not only in small rooms and with children grown dear to you. His inclination to go walking stayed with him, despite searchlight and police station, walking in a town you never had left for more than a week in your entire life. The sun is shining friendly on your way, as friendly as are the memories in pursuit of which you have left your house and toward which every other street builds a bridge. You knew it beforehand. Twice around corners and you're standing, to be sure, in front of the house in which often enough it was determined how good your next winter would be. None other than Aaron Ehrlicher, the potato merchant, lived there. Upon the prices he set much depended: the pancake price and, therefore, your turnover. He never allowed haggling, this amount and not a penny cheaper. If that is too expensive, Herr Heym, you can gladly shop around for potatoes that are cheaper elsewhere. And when you have found the place then kindly give me the news; I'd like to buy there, too. Not once did he allow haggling with him. Jacob told him once, "Herr Ehrlicher, you're not a potato merchant, you're a potato salesman." Of course, only as a joke, but Ehrlicher did not laugh resoundingly. People were never certain whether he was a poor wretch, small tradesman like yourself, or a businessman of greater importance. His wife wore a beautiful brown fur coat and his children were fat and round and conceited. On the other hand, his office smelled of mildew, tiny, shabby, only a table and chair and bare wall. Sighing, he displayed it and asked, "How should I lower prices with this?"

Unfamiliar people live there now. You turn over the page with Aaron Ehrlicher and walk on. Two free hours are a long time. You go to Libauer Lane, precisely to Number 38. You go to no house as often as to this one whenever you go walking and stand in front of none as long. There are good reasons. You even enter the gloomy courtyard. Everything has reasons. Suspicious eyes examine you through the windows as to what a stranger is doing in their courtyard. But you're not such a stranger here.

On the fourth floor, behind the last door left in the corridor, you have, to express it pompously, gambled away or won your life's fortune. You weren't able to make up your mind when it came down to it and still don't know today how good or bad it was. Josefa Litwin asked you to your face what your intentions were and nothing more intelligent occurred to you than dropping your head and stammering you needed some more time to think it over.

She was a beauty, if your eyes were the judge. You saw her on the train for the first time and immediately thought, boy, oh boy! She was wearing a dress of green velvet with a white lace collar, and a hat no smaller than an opened umbrella. At the very most she was in her mid-thirties, thus exactly right for you at forty then; right as far as age went. But you didn't consider in your train compartment in your wildest dream that there opposite you was sitting your biggest problem of the following years. You just stared at her, you told me, like a young idiot. Maybe she didn't even notice it. A coincidence or not, when both of you got off together, no porter in the vicinity. She asked you whether you could carry her heavy suitcase, she lived only a few streets away, Libauer Lane, Number 38. But she didn't ask you as a man of lower rank, although you wouldn't have refused even then. She was helpless and friendly and asked you for a favor in her position as a weak woman. In your position as a gentleman. Full of joy you said, "What a question!" You tore her suitcase to you as if you feared a porter might appear and walked behind her to Number 38, to her apartment door. You put down the suitcase there. For a few seconds you smiled to each other embarrassed; then she thanked you nicely and said good-by. And you stood there and thought, Too bad.

A few weeks later, and that was certainly a coincidence, she came into your café one afternoon in the company of a man. You recognized her immediately, without any right annoyed at the man, but then you were happy because she recognized you, too. You two said nothing. The other two drank soda pop and had raspberry ice cream. You observed them and couldn't determine what their relationship was. And why should you?

But when she came in the next day, this time alone, you knew that was no coincidence. For the first time you were happy that your café was empty. Besides her, no customer was in the room and on the very next day. You sat down with her and chatted and got acquainted. She had been the widow of a clockmaker for four years. The ice cream she had you, of course, didn't let her pay for. She could consider herself invited out. For today and as often as she liked. The man from yesterday was called a casual acquaintance. No reason not to get together more often. No reason, even if it were different. Well, for tomorrow in the café, once more in the café, then in another restaurant, in a neutral place so to speak, a little dance in due respect. Then, soon, in your apartment, you were informed about her modest, but by no means paltry, financial condition, and that she was childless, and finally, also, in Number 38. A cup of tea and tarts baked herself, perfume delicate and sweet lay in the air. The conversation was about fondness from the very first moment on, really, and have some more tea, and there's more cake in the pantry.

That was an evening that no poet ever described, my God, and a night, my God . . . oh, well. What should I say? The story is not about Jacob and Josefa. Soon this page, too, must be turned. But this much more: four whole years came of that; four years living together as husband and wife, although they never finally moved in together, although one subject was always avoided—rabbi or civil marriage. Most thoroughly by Jacob. They had the chance to explore each other thoroughly. Josefa was "all that glitters is not gold"; less precious metals were also mixed in.

Sometimes Jacob found her tyrannical, sometimes too garrulous, at times not thrifty enough. And she, too, found this and that fault in him without it having to come to a breakup immediately. Quite the contrary. Despite everything, they got along well with one another and Jacob was thinking already, it won't be over so quickly. But when she suddenly proposed to him—how suddenly could it be? —they should perhaps move into a common apartment and that she could help in the business, he was afraid he would become his own employee and said, "We'll talk about that later."

All right, later then. Josefa was in no rush, so it seemed, at any rate. Until, as mentioned, that certain evening came to Number 38, Libauer Lane, in which Jacob gambled away or won the fortune of his life. Who can know? He dropped by as always, took off his shoes, and laid his feet on the sofa as always. Josefa was standing at the window with her back to him.

"What's the matter with you today?" Jacob asked her. "Isn't there any tea?"

Josefa didn't turn around immediately, but in a few moments. She had an uneasy look and sat down not beside him on the sofa, but instead in the armchair opposite him.

"Jacob Heym, I must talk with you."

"Please do," he said, prepared for all kinds of things, but not for what now occurred.

"Do you know Avrom Minsh?"

"Should I know him?"

"Avrom Minsh is the man with whom I came to your café the very first time, in case you recall."

"I recall exactly. You said at that time he was a casual acquaintance."

"This morning Avrom Minsh asked me if I would be his wife."

"And what did you tell him?"

"Jacob, it is serious! You must finally make up your mind!"

"I?"

"Stop your jokes, Jacob. I'm thirty-eight now. I can not always continue to live this way. He wants to go to his brother in America. He asked me if I wanted to come along as his wife."

What was Jacob to answer then? The pistol at his chest didn't please him, especially since Avrom Minsh had been kept a secret from him up to now. A marriage proposal is not made to a casual acquaintance. She has to be somewhat acquainted for that purpose and for four years you had illusions that you knew one another most intimately. The state of affairs whereby Josefa gave him to a certain extent the first option could not dissipate Jacob's disillusion, not by a long shot. He silently put on his shoes again and carefully avoided meeting her eyes up to the door. At the open door he said, embarrassed, "I must first think the matter over calmly."

You think and think and even till this day you're undecided. The two hours freely bestowed aren't all that long. A sympathetic person opens his window and calls out quietly through the courtyard, "Say, you there!"

Jacob is startled and sees the moon at the roof. He asks, "What is the matter?"

"You don't live in this house, do you?"

"No."

"It's long past seven already."

"Thank you."

Jacob pulls himself together. Homeward without stopping, so that other houses suspected of memories will remain unheeded; it's long past seven already.

Lena is already in bed. It must be explained to her why you've returned so uncommonly late from work; because today there was especially much to be loaded. As a result of that she doesn't talk about private worries with fairy tales or about all-too-suspicious sons of neighbors, nor can Jacob hardly ask about them. She knows how fatiguing the days at the railroad station are and the additional hours. He mustn't stay long; give her a kiss quickly and go to his room; the love is completely mutual.

Jacob leaves her with a conscience that could be purer. On the stairway he plans to make amends to Lena, for tomorrow or real soon. At his table he is in the meantime not unhappy with the past day, all in all, at his supper of bread and malt coffee. At the railroad station the Jews were contented and reserved; the battle at the Rudna had taken effect; then two dreamy hours as a gift; a pleasant tale at the attic door; less pleasant, Aaron Ehrlicher; and then Josefa. Josefa still, between the few bites, between his gulps. He simply can't get the woman out of his mind. What would have come of us two good-looking ones, if I, at that time in Number 38 . . . ? I don't know and yet the question posed for the thousandth time is answered almost by itself: a life between heaven and hell, that is quite the usual one. How could it have turned out otherwise, and by what means, than those four experienced years? Filled with variety, strife, and misunderstanding, with moods, fun, and with a bit of coziness. And with concealment of secrets, as you discovered on the last day. You simply can't stop thinking of the woman, until someone is knocking at the door.

There is knocking. Jacob would immediately be inclined to call out, "Come in, Kowalski!" That is, not really inclined, it's simply that he suspects, but then he doesn't suspect any more, because it was past seven more than an hour ago, so that now it's been long past eight, and even Kowalski isn't that crazy. Jacob calls, "Come in!"

Professor Kirschbaum honors Jacob at supper; is it an inconvenience; no, of course not; would he like to sit down; to what do we owe the rare pleasure.

Kirschbaum sits down, delays the start of the conversa-

**177**

tion with various glances, until he gets the proper attention which Jacob doesn't understand what for.

"Can't you imagine why I'm visiting you, Herr Heym?"

The first thought: "Is it because of Lena? Has her health deteriorated?"

"I haven't come because of Lena. I've come, to get immediately *in medias res,* because I would like to speak with you about your radio."

You're disappointed and disconcerted. For a few hours you had happily forgotten the monstrosity. Now the battle at the Rudna will have to be dragged out again. You're no longer a human being to your fellow citizens. You're an owner of a radio, incompatible with one another, as it has seemed for a long time. Furthermore, the right to normal conversations of former times has been forfeited. About the weather, or pains in your lower back for which Kirschbaum would be an ideal partner, gossip about mutual friends, or important little things are not discussed in your presence—you and your treasure are too good for all of that.

"You, too, want to hear news," says Jacob and concludes that he now, in addition, has Kirschbaum on his neck, O.K., fine, one more or less doesn't matter.

"I don't want to hear any news," says Kirschbaum, however. "I've come here to reproach you. I should have done it long ago."

"Reproach?"

"I don't know, my dear Herr Heym, by what motives you've been guided, when you were spreading around the information known. But I can hardly imagine that you have carefully weighed the danger you have exposed all of us to."

Not news, but reproaches instead! Brainstorms I need! That won't change: Kirschbaum is quite a peculiar fellow. Must you, professor, spit into my leisure time, my hard-

**178**

earned time; must you preach to me right away about a sense of responsibility, about matters I've known a long time ago, when my radio was still a completely hidden thing to you; you're preaching to me? Instead of patting me on my shoulder and saying, Bravo Herr Heym, keep up your good work, people need no medicine as much as hope; or if not that, instead of at least staying away—for I've long ago learned to do without pats on my shoulder— you come knocking at my door, may the devil take you, meddle in my business and want to teach me to survive! And, in addition to all that, I must keep an attentive expression, because his misgivings are nonetheless completely honorable, because he may some day yet be needed for Lena; and he must also be shown good reasons for his actions, although none occur to you, which are none of his business. Only so that his learned mouth, after long explanations, may be in the position to say, "Oh, yes, yes, now I understand."

"I don't need to tell you where we are living, my dear Herr Heym," says Kirschbaum.

"No, you don't need to," says Jacob.

"And yet it seems urgent to me. What would happen, for example, if the Gestapo got wind of this information? Have you thought about it?"

"Yes."

"I find that impossible to believe. Because otherwise you would have acted differently."

"Yes," says Jacob. "I would have."

Jacob gets up for a stroll for the $n^{th}$ time today, past table and bed and closet and Kirschbaum. Although not embodied in words, his anger goes to his legs. But not his entire anger. The room is too small for that. An unmistakable remnant is left for his voice, which annoys Kirschbaum at first. When Jacob says, "Have you ever once seen their eyes when they ask me for the news? No? And do you know how necessary they need good news? Do you know that?"

"I can imagine it vividly. Nor do I doubt that you are motivated by the best intentions. Nevertheless, I must . . ."

"Spare me your 'nevertheless'! Isn't it enough for you that we have practically nothing to stuff in our mouths, that every fifth person among us freezes to death in the winter, that every day half a block is transported off? Isn't all that sufficient? And if I try to use my very last means to keep them from simply lying down and croaking, with words, you understand, with words I'm trying that! Because I have nothing else, you see! Then you come and tell me it's prohibited."

Strangely, Jacob thinks now of all times, of a cigarette, he tells me, of a *Juno* without filtertip. What Kirschbaum is thinking about is uncertain. In any case, he reaches into the pocket of his shabby double-breasted jacket, you won't believe it, now of all times, and takes out a little box. And matches, and asks Jacob, incongruously and politely after his shouting had barely died away, "Would you like one?"

Some question! That's the way it is among civilized people. A tactful example, perhaps, a good one; perhaps even an expression of future gentle doubts. Or neither of the two. In any case, they are silent and smoking and smoothing out their wrinkled foreheads.

The smoke avidly inhaled provides not only well being but also makes for greater reconciliation, I tell you. While smoking Jacob undergoes a transformation of feelings or something similar. Because a noble benefactor is sitting timidly in front of him. Kirschbaum is helplessly turning his cigarette in his narrow fingers, hardly even daring to venture a passing glance or even opening his mouth for anything except for his next draught. Because otherwise, uncontrolled outbursts will follow: Spare me your "nevertheless." Or: Isn't that sufficient for you? He came by in order to have a talk with his neighbor. After all, such a radio is not private property in this city like a chair and a shirt. He didn't come to accuse but rather to discuss important matters in calm assertion and reply and then this. "Then you come here and tell me it is prohibited." Kirschbaum didn't leave. That indicates good will or especially great fear. He stayed, reached into his pocket like a magician, and fulfilled secret wishes. For that alone, he can be granted a few neighborly words.

"Of course, I know myself that the Russians won't arrive any sooner," says Jacob half way through his cigarette. "And even if I tell it a thousand times, their route will be the same. But I want to draw your attention to another little detail. Since the news reports have circulated in the ghetto, I know of no incident where anyone has taken his life. Do you?" Whereupon Kirschbaum looks up amazed and says, "Really?"

"And previously there were many. No one knows that better than you. I can remember that you were often called in and most of the time it was too late."

"Why didn't I think of that?" asks Kirschbaum.

One of the following days brings the unprecedented. An auto drives through our little town, the only passenger auto in the long story. Unprecedented to be sure, but no hopes should be deduced from that, not even by the most skilled fantasists among the bold speculators. You'd be more inclined to say quite the contrary. It is traveling resolutely without a detour. The exact route must have been studied from the map before starting the trip. A black car. The streets become deserted as it pulls up. In the back seat are two men in plain clothes, a neatly pressed uniform behind the steering wheel. Only the two in back are important. That is, they, too, are not terribly important. Basically, the entire auto isn't important, despite its SS banner and where it's from and where it's going, and whom it's transporting. Or, a little important let's say, or, not entirely unimportant as far as the results are concerned.

The two men are named Preuss and Meyer. I know what they're saying. I don't know what they're thinking, although that presents no unsolvable puzzle. I know their military ranks, if need be, even their precise vitae, hence their names, too. Unfortunately, I will have to interfere later with the story in a rude and direct way when it comes to explaining, because no possible gap must remain. My explanation will patch it up in a makeshift way, but later on the gap will really become evident in its full dimension.

The auto stops in front of Siegfried and Rafael, who as always are loitering in the street, on the curb, and who, as the sole heroes far and wide, do not hide. All the other Jews, neither blind nor crippled, are standing behind their windows or in protective vestibules trembling for two foolish children and from the still uncertain trouble that the German auto can only stir up here. But many an initiated person will think the damage not so uncertain. The auto stops, in the end, not in front of *any* house. It stops in front of Jacob Heym's house.

Preuss and Meyer get out on a special mission. Preuss is quite tall, brown-haired, slender, handsome, at best somewhat delicate. Meyer, as he was described to me, a head smaller, like a bull, and at first glance wildly resolute. Apparently a carefully assembled combination. What one lacks the other has, and vice versa, hence a happy complement. They enter the house.

"Do you know which apartment?" asks Preuss.

"One flight up," says Meyer. "The names should be on the doors."

One flight up. Jacob lives two up; nevertheless, one up, up to Kirschbaum's door. There is a polite knocking on it, and patient waiting until a woman's voice, from which it can be deduced that visitors are very unwelcome, asks: "Who is there?"

"Please open up," says Preuss.

Although no very plausible reason for opening, a key is carelessly put into the lock, turned, and the door opens, at first only a crack, then without reservation. Meyer puts his foot quite unnecessarily between door and threshold. Elisa Kirschbaum is standing there, old and severe, with well-disguised fear. Her oft repaired apron can not deceive. Not just anyone is surveying them. Even the way she holds her head. A lady is surveying Preuss and Meyer. Her fear is well hidden, not her scorn, an indifferent look into the faces of two annoying visitors, then a look at Meyer's foot that is protruding there on the threshold so horribly superfluous. Meyer fidgets.

"You wish to see?"

"Hello," says Preuss politely. Perhaps these looks simply force him to. "We would like to see Professor Kirschbaum."

"He isn't home."

"Then we'll wait," says Preuss. Of course. He enters, passing her. Finally Meyer, too, can remove his resolute foot from its position. He follows him. They take a look around the room. What are they all talking about? They're not so bad off here. Buffet with knickknacks, sofa and two arm chairs, a bit threadbare, to be sure, but still. A bookcase loaded with books as in the film, on the ceiling a three-armed lamp, almost a chandelier. Why, they're living here high off the hog! Maybe only this Kirschbaum; he is supposed to have been a bigwig before; special ration or something. They have brains, these kikes, always weasel in, and everywhere feel immediately at home.

Meyer plops on to the sofa, Preuss not yet, because Elisa Kirschbaum is standing at the door and doesn't cease looking as if she were waiting for an explanation.

"Are you Professor Kirschbaum's wife?" asks Preuss.

"I am his sister."

"You'll permit me then."

Preuss sits down, too, in an armchair, crosses his legs, lots of time. Elisa Kirschbaum is standing. Nothing helps. She has to ask, "What is it all about, please?"

"That's none of your damned business," says Meyer. He can no longer remain silent. What is happening here already seems unreal anyway, a farce, pure farce, but not with him. To a shameless question he wants to give more than an answer. He wants to straighten out the world again a little, otherwise who knows what'll happen.

Well then, Elisa Kirschbaum can't simply call her maid and tell her to hand that boor his hat. Her arsenal of weapons is conceivably empty. But, at least she can punish Meyer with disdain by turning to Preuss and coldly insisting, "Would you kindly tell this gentleman that he is in a stranger's apartment and that I am not accustomed to such behavior."

This and that bristle in Meyer. He wants to jump up, flare up, shout out, but Preuss looks at him in an official way, special mission; then he says, "You're completely right. Please excuse us."

"You wanted to inform me why you're here."

"I think I would rather explain that to the professor in person. Do you know when he'll come?"

"No. Around eight at the latest."

She sits down in the unoccupied chair, very straight, laying her hands in her lap. Now only waiting. I can say for sure that Kirschbaum arrives after about a half hour. The time passes quite uneventfully. For example, Meyer lights up a cigar and throws the match on the floor. Elisa Kirschbaum picks it up, brings him an ash tray, and opens the window. Meyer is dumfounded.

Or, Preuss, after several taps on the table, stands up.

The bookcase interests him. He opens the glass panel, inclines his head on his shoulder, reads the book spines, and then selects a book, leafs through it, another, leafs through it, that goes on for a time, and puts them all back again in the proper place.

"They are exclusively books on medical subjects," says Elisa Kirschbaum.

"I see."

"We have obtained a document of authorization for that," she says. And when Preuss still continues looking at others. "Do you wish to see it?"

"No, thanks."

He finds one especially to his taste. He sits down with it and is occupied. Forensic medicine.

Or, suddenly Meyer jumps up, dashes to a door, tears it open, looks into an empty kitchen, calms down again, and sits down.

"Could have been," he explains to Preuss, who continues reading.

Or, Meyer again stands up, this time without haste, goes to the window, and looks down. He sees two women tugging two children from the auto into the adjacent house, sees a face behind almost every windowpane in that house. The man in uniform is standing beside the auto, bored.

"May be drawn out," Meyer shouts down. Then he sits down again, as stated, for half an hour.

Or, Elisa Kirschbaum goes into the kitchen; she is heard puttering around, and returns with a tray. Two dinner plates, two cups, knives, forks, teaspoons, two linen napkins. She sets the table. Preuss hardly glances up from his book; Meyer responds differently; for him things are getting increasingly out of hand.

Preuss, hardly glancing up from his book, says, "Let her."

After about half an hour, the professor arrives. They

hear his attempt to get his key into the door lock; another is on the inside. Meyer grinds out his cigar in the ash tray. Preuss lays the book on the table between the plates. Elisa Kirschbaum opens up.

The professor, terrified, remains standing in the doorway. No great attempt to hide it has been made although he is standing there not entirely unprepared. The auto below in front of the house. Indeed, rather, connections with Heym would have been anticipated, or more correctly, not anticipated but suspected. He had simply not anticipated any connection with himself. In vain. Preuss stands up.

"We have guests," says Elisa Kirschbaum. She removes the forensic medicine from the table, places it in the bookcase, and closes the panel. With a cloth that she takes out of her apron pocket she wipes over some finger marks.

"Professor Kirschbaum?" Preuss finally asks.

"Yes?"

"My name is Preuss." And then looks over to Meyer.

"Meyer," growls Meyer.

The shaking of hands is avoided. Preuss asks, "Do you know Hardtloff?"

"You mean the Gestapo boss?"

"I mean the SA battalion leader, Hardtloff. He is requesting that you come to him."

"He's requesting me to go to him?"

Elisa Kirschbaum struggles to maintain her composure. So also does Meyer, to be sure. Requesting him. The entire tone here. This farce. Preuss says, "Yes. He had a heart seizure this morning."

The professor sits down, baffled, and looks over to his sister who, meanwhile, has been standing as if carved of stone. Hardtloff had a heart attack this morning.

"I don't quite understand."

"You are to examine him," says Preuss. "Although I can imagine that the battalion leader's suffering doesn't particularly concern you. There should be no reason for any alarm on your part."

"But . . ."

"What 'but'?" asks Meyer.

Once again glances at his sister. Her whole life has been spent overcoming unpleasant situations, with her composure, with her control, and her inexorably sharp mind. She has kept everything burdensome away from him, thus a final look at her.

*"Dis leurs que tu n'en as plus l'habitude,"* she says.*

"What's she saying?" Meyer asks Preuss and now stands up, too, to his full height.

"Please listen," says the professor. "What you request of me is out of the question. As a physician I could not justify it under any circumstance since, after such a long period of time, I . . . After all, I haven't treated any patients for more than four years."

Preuss remains remarkably composed. He lays his calming hand on the shoulder of the battle-tested Meyer, special mission, then he approaches the professor with urgency. His eyes express censure, but are not unfriendly or even angered, rather sympathetic, as if they wanted to call someone who was behaving thoughtlessly to his senses before it was too late, while he says, "I fear almost you have misunderstood me, professor. We haven't come here to make a request of you. Please, do not give us any difficulty."

"But I told you that . . ."

"Do you have to take anything along?" asks Preuss resolutely.

The professor finally comprehends that he no longer needs to look for excuses. Something else impels the other two than to test their powers of persuasion. The relative friendliness of this Preuss is his personal trait and guaran-

* "Tell them that you've been out of practice."

tees nothing. Thus all "ifs" and "buts" are forgotten. His sister is emulated. To be as unapproachable and dignified as she, that at least, now at least. Her whole life long she has been admired for that, even more than feared. Some used to call her eccentric. No drama of collapse will be granted to two German vassals. Whether anything had to be taken along has been asked. No one will fall on his knees before them. How Elisa stands there! At first try, that can not be imitated. However, quite commonplace movements can be found, a Wednesday expression, as if a completely ordinary occurrence had taken place. A dignitary has fallen ill. He is to be examined, the usual small details.

"Have we understood each other well?" asks Preuss.

The professor stands up. Underneath the book shelves are doors. He opens one, looks for his leather bag, plump and brown, the doctor's bag.

"It's in the closet," says Elisa Kirschbaum.

He takes the bag out of the closet, opens it, peruses its contents, then holds it out to Preuss who doesn't bother looking in.

"Medical supplies."

"Fine."

Elisa Kirschbaum opens the closet a second time, a scarf. She hands it to her brother.

"I don't need it. It's warm outside," he says.

"You do need it," says Elisa Kirschbaum. "You don't know how chilly it is after eight."

He puts the scarf in his pocket. Meyer opens the door. The departure is at hand.

"Good-by, Elisa."

"Good-by."

That's what a parting looks like.

Then in front of the house they get into the car, certainly according to a predetermined seating arrangement, Preuss and the professor in back, Meyer up front beside the man in uniform. Elisa Kirschbaum is standing at the window. The entire street is standing at windows. But only one is open. The car turns around in a single swoop; the flat edge of the curb is mounted. A pale blue cloud hovers for seconds. At the end of the street the car turns to the left toward Hardtloff.

Preuss snaps open a silver cigarette case and asks, "Would you like a cigarette?"

"No, thanks," says Kirschbaum.

Meyer shakes his head without turning around. From the corner of his eye he looks to see how the man in the uniform finds the farce. He, in turn, is simply sneering out in the direction of the drive. Preuss stares at both of them in the rearview mirror. Not Kirschbaum. He is sitting as if every movement were to be avoided.

"Put your bag on the floor," says Preuss. "We have a good distance yet."

"About how long?"

"Oh, about thirty minutes."

Kirschbaum keeps his bag on his lap.

They come to the gates of the ghetto and stop. Meyer rolls down the window. A guard sticks his helmet inside and asks, "What sort of fellow do you have there?"

"Just say, you don't know him!" Meyer calls out. "That's the famous Professor Kirschbaum!"

Preuss hands the guard an identification paper and says very formally, "Open the gate. We are in a hurry."

"Yes, yes, no harm meant," says the guard. He gives a hand signal to a second guard who opens the barrier and pushes open the gate.

They continue riding. Now in the free part of the city the surroundings change. Passersby without yellow stars will be very evident to him, stores with merchandise, not overly well-stocked, to be sure, yet customers come and go, and especially trees bordering the streets, I imagine. The Imperial at the market is showing a German film. Now and then an auto passing by, a streetcar, soldiers in off-duty dress with two girls on their arms. Kirschbaum looks moderately interested. The scenes can not tell him much, can arouse no memories as, for example, in Jacob, since this is not his city.

"If I'm not mistaken, you should basically be happy to get hold of a new patient finally," says Preuss.

"May I find out how you hit upon me?"

"That wasn't difficult. Hardtloff's personal physician was at his wit's end. He insisted upon the consultation of a specialist. But, try to find a specialist in these times. We looked through the lists of residents and came upon you. The personal physician knows you."

"He knows me?"

"Of course, not personally. Only your name."

They are coming into the better neighborhoods. The houses become smaller, individual residences, more greenery, more trees, too. Kirschbaum opens his leather bag, takes out a little phial, unscrews it, and shakes out two tablets into the palm of his hand. Questioning glances from Preuss.

"For heartburn," explains Kirschbaum. "Would you like some, too?"

"No."

Kirschbaum swallows the tablets, screws the phial shut, and puts it back into his bag. He is sitting as before.

"Do you feel better now?" asks Preuss after a short time.

"They don't take effect so quickly."

They are leaving the city; once again a check; to a certain extent the landscape is rural. Hardtloff has himself a secret little spot. A birch tree forest on both sides. Preuss says, "You will, of course, be taken back again when everything is finished."

Kirschbaum puts his bag on the floor now. The entire trip it was on his lap, but now so close to the destination it is put on the floor. Breathing deeply he leans back.

"Would you give me a cigarette now?"

Preuss gives it to him, also a light. Let's mention once more Meyer's badly overplayed lack of composure. Kirschbaum suffers a light coughing spell, controlling himself soon, and throwing his half smoked cigarette out of the window.

"On the other hand, I can somehow understand your qualms," is the way Preuss picks up again a topic of conversation thought to have been long lost.

"I no longer have any qualms," says Kirschbaum.

"Oh, yes, you do; I can tell you do. Your position is not very enviable. I understand it well. If you succeed in saving the SA battalion leader, you won't find much favor in the eyes of your own people. And if you don't succeed . . ."

Preuss interrupted his absolutely pithy analysis. The rest would be tactless and superfluous besides. Kirschbaum, too, will have understood what value Hardtloff's survival would have. For the first time during the trip Meyer turns around toward the back; his face doesn't hide the fact that he, too, understands the continuation of Preuss' talk and especially what he thinks of this continuation. In that light, so to speak, he turns around for a moment. Kirschbaum pays no attention to him. He seems sufficiently preoccupied with himself. Preuss attempts one or two more insignificant sentences but Kirschbaum no longer participates.

Then they are at the Hardtloff villa. An approach through a luxuriant park, a flowering round circle with a dried-up fish pond, everything a bit neglected but splendidly laid out, very splendidly.

"We're here," says Preuss to Kirschbaum, who is still distracted, and gets out.

Rushing down the outside steps is the physician, a bald-headed, short man in shiny boots, unbuttoned uniform jacket, looking unkempt like the garden. His haste indicates concern or anxiety, probably anxiety. He bears the responsibility here. For Hardtloff's health and, as we have heard, for today's daring experiment. Even from the upper steps he has called down, "It has become worse again! Where were you so long?"

"We had to wait; he wasn't home," says Preuss.

"Quick, quick!"

Because there is no movement inside, Preuss opens the door on Kirschbaum's side and says once again, "We're here. Please get out."

But Kirschbaum is sitting as if he were not by a long shot finished thinking. He doesn't even turn his head to Preuss. Last minute rebelliousness or the proverbial absent-mindedness of the scholar, the most poorly chosen time imaginable for whatever. They are getting impatient. Meyer would know already what would be necessary to do.

Preuss seizes the professor's arm, saying quietly, "Don't make any trouble," propriety to the very end, pulling him out with gentle force.

Kirschbaum's exit is completed in a surprising fashion. He slides gently toward Preuss who is too taken aback to hold him. Kirschbaum falls out of the auto upon the unkempt ground.

"What's the matter?"

The physician steps between the two, stoops over his Jewish patient, and effortlessly comes to the clear result of his examination.

"Why, the man is dead!"

He tells Preuss nothing new, in the interim no longer so. Preuss takes the leather bag out of the car. Plump and brown, the usual physician's bag.

*Do you have to take anything along?*

*Medical supplies.*

*O.K.* Maybe you yourself put the idea in his head.

Preuss opens the bag and finds the phial amidst the odds and ends. He gives it to the physician.

"For heartburn," says Preuss.

"Idiot," says the physician.

Now this explanation, the one previously promised.

The explanation is really superfluous, but I imagine that some people will ask distrustfully how I claim to have got into this auto. Hardly likely through Kirschbaum. Where, then, was my informant sitting? Some people will inquire about it and not even unjustifiably so from their standpoint.

Of course, I could answer that I am not an explainer. I'm telling a story that I myself do not understand. I could say I know from eye witnesses that Kirschbaum got into the car and I've found out that he was dead at the end of the ride. The details in between could have occurred only that way or similarly. It is not conceivable any other way. But that would be a lie, because the details in between could have happened quite differently. I even think much more likely differently than they did. And these particulars, I suspect, are the real reason for my explanation.

Thus, some time after the war I took a trip to our ghetto during my first vacation. My few friends had advised me against it. The trip would only ruin my entire next year, they said. Memories were one thing and to live another thing. I told them that they were right and went. Jacob's room, the police station, the Kurländischendamm, Misha's room, the cellar—I visited everything at my leisure, measured, and checked them out or simply took a look at them. I was also in Jacob's café; a shoemaker had moved in temporarily; he told me, "Until I find something better." It seemed to me that it smelled somehow a bit burned under the leather, but it didn't seem so to the shoemaker. On the next to the last day of my vacation, I got to thinking while packing my suitcase if I could have forgotten anything. I probably would never again return to this city, and now there was still time for anything forgotten. The only thing that occurred to me was Kirschbaum's auto ride, but that seemed to me unverifiable. Besides, I thought it wouldn't be so very important for the story for the sake of which I had come. However, I went that afternoon to the Russian garrison headquarters, probably out of boredom, or because I couldn't find any restaurant open.

The officer in charge was a woman of about forty, a second lieutenant. I told her that I was in the ghetto, that my father and Kirschbaum had been close friends before the war, and that therefore Kirschbaum's fate interested me. I made a real Red Cross inquiry out of it. Then I clarified for her the connection between Kirschbaum and Hardtloff. I knew only that Kirschbaum had got into the auto, nothing more, and that was the truth. The two men who had come for him were named Preuss and Meyer or something like it. And if she might be able to tell me at least something about the two, even if she knew nothing about the whereabouts of the professor, that would perhaps be a starting point. She wrote down the names and asked me to come back in two hours.

After two hours I found out that Meyer had been shot to death a few days before the entry of the Red Army, by partisans during an ambush at night.

"And the other one?" I asked.

"I have his German address here," she said.

I was about to extend my hand toward the sheet of paper when she looked at me concerned and said, "You don't have any silly notions in mind, do you?"

"No, no, what do you take me for?" I asked.

She gave me the sheet of paper. I looked at the address and said, "That's a lucky coincidence. I also live in Berlin now."

"You stayed in Germany?" she asked amazed. "How come?"

"I don't know either," I truthfully said. "It turned out that way."

Preuss lived in Schöneberg in West Berlin. Nice wife and two children. His wife was missing an arm. I rode over there one Sunday afternoon. When I rang the bell, a tall, brown-haired, handsome man, somewhat delicate, hardly older than I, opened the door.

"You're looking for?" he asked.

"Are you Herr Preuss?"

"Yes."

I said, "Excuse my intrusion. Could I speak with you for a few minutes?"

"Certainly," he said and led me into his living room and, after some complications, sent the children out. On the wall hung a print of Dürer's "Hands" and the photo of a little girl with a mourning crape. He invited me to sit down.

I first told him my name, which made him listen attentively, although he didn't know anything concrete to make of it. But it was different when I asked whether I was properly informed that he had worked for Hardtloff. I was able to observe that he became pale before he quietly asked, "Why are you here?"

I said, "I'm here because of a story. More precisely, because of a gap in this story that you could, perhaps, close."

He stood up, went over to a chest of drawers to look through his papers, soon found what he was looking for, and laid a piece of paper on the table in front of me. It was his denazification document, with official seal and signature.

"You don't need to show me that," I said.

He left the document lying before me, nonetheless, until I had read it. Then he took it, folded it up, and again locked it away.

"Can I offer you anything?" he asked.

"No, thanks."

"A cup of tea, perhaps?"

"No, thanks."

He called out: "Ingrid!"

His wife came in. It was evident that she was still unaccustomed to having one arm. He said, "This is my wife."

I stood up and we shook hands.

"Would you please go down and get the beer keg? Sebald promised me two liters for the weekend."

After she had left, I said: "Do you recall a Professor Kirschbaum?"

"Oh, yes," he said immediately. "Very well."

"Didn't you come get him when he was to examine Hardtloff? Together with a certain Meyer?"

"That's correct. Meyer got his sometime afterward."

"I know. But what happened to Kirschbaum? Was he shot when Hardtloff died?"

"What makes you think that? The two never met each other."

I looked at Preuss amazed and asked, "Did he refuse to examine him?"

"You can call it that," he said. "He poisoned himself in the auto. During the ride, right before our eyes."

"Poisoned?" I asked, and he noticed that I didn't believe him.

"I can prove it to you," he said. "You need only ask Letzerich. He will confirm my words in every detail for you."

"Who is Letzerich?"

"He was the driver then. He was present the entire time. Unfortunately, I don't know his address. I only know that

196

he was from Cologne. But his address would certainly be obtainable somehow."

I asked him to describe this ride in more detail for me. The result is already known. It lasted rather long. Now and then his wife brought us the beer. I drank a glass. It tasted awful. I hardly interrupted him because he himself was detailed. He laid special emphasis on the fact that Kirschbaum had offered him some of his tablets. "And, in fact, I sometimes do have heartburn, not so very rarely. Just imagine if I had taken one of them!"

"That was a mass murder attempt," I said.

He told more: leaving the city, the last part of the trip, the last cigarette, Meyer's unequivocal looks, up to the villa, until the personal physician came, until Kirschbaum lay dead on the ground in front of him. That he had suddenly understood what had really happened, that he took the bag out of the car, the phial, giving it to the physician, that the physician said, "Idiot."

For a while we were silent. He must have assumed I was so shaken. But I was thinking what else I could ask him about. He had told it well, without gaps, and vividly. I saw also obvious reasons why he remembered that ride so well.

In the end, he wanted by all means to confide in me what he thought today about those wretched times and to talk, finally, with a reasonable man and unburden his heart. But I really hadn't come for that. I said I had already stayed much too long, I still had things to do, he too no doubt. I got up and thanked him for his willingness to oblige.

"And do note the name in case you want to verify it," he said. "Egon Letzerich, Cologne, Rhein."

In the hallway we met his wife who was just taking the children to the bathroom. They were already wearing pajama bottoms; up top, they were nude.

"Well, what do you say?" said Preuss to them.

They both shook my hands at the same time, bowed, and said, "Good-by, sir."

"Good-by," I said.

The three disappeared in the bathroom. Preuss insisted upon accompanying me to the outside. In case the front door might be locked already.

The front door was still open. Preuss walked in front of me into the street, took a deep breath, spread his arms out, and said, "May is in the air again."

I had the impression he was a bit tipsy; after all he had had two litres of warm beer, minus one glass.

"Oh, by the way," I said, "what about his sister then?"

"Kirschbaum's sister? We had nothing to do with her. I saw her only at that one visit. Was there more to it?"

"Of course," I said.

He hesitated a moment before he asked, "How did you get my address?"

"From the British Secret Service," I said. Then I left for good.


Hardtloff is dead, died of a weak heart. The news reached us at the railroad station. It must have happened last night. When we left the railroad station yesterday evening, the flag on the stone guardhouse was hanging limply in its usual spot. When we came to work this morning, it was fluttering gaily at half-mast. Therefore, sometime in between. In and of itself the flag is, to be sure, only a vague clue. Without mentioning names, it reveals nothing more than the fact that one of our bigwigs has departed. A guard mentioned the name, however, to another guard. In the course of the morning, Roman Shtamm overheard an informative conversation. Devoid of any objectionable intention, he came to a pile of crates. The two guards were standing behind it and talking about Hardtloff's death. It was a lucky coincidence. In lifting a crate, Roman took somewhat more time than usual. He didn't manage to do so until the two guards changed the topic.

Meanwhile, each of us knows for whom the flag is flying at half-mast. Roman saw no need to keep it to himself. It may be said that we bear the news with composure. Hardly anything will change for us. If, indeed, ever, then not through Hardtloff's death. Nevertheless, we can imagine worse things. Only Jacob regrets that it was Roman Shtamm and not he who overheard the guard's conversation. The SA battalion chief's misfortune would have made a superb radio announcement. Not only because of the content. It would have been the first dispatch that wouldn't have had to be accepted upon his honesty and good faith. Each individual would have had the possibility of convincing himself of its veracity by means of his own personal observation, and effortlessly, too. Since the morning the confirmation has been hanging on the flagpole. To tell them now that you had already heard about Hardtloff's death in the early news would be quite senseless. What's past is past. A radio is proud. It doesn't tag behind the events.

When the whistle blows exactly at noon, Jacob is finally separated from this lovely thought. The cart with the tin bowls is pulled in. We form the customary faultless line.

Someone behind Jacob asks quietly, "Did you listen again last night?"

"Yes," says Jacob.

"Did they say anything there about Hardtloff?"

"Nonsense. Do you think they are concerned about such trivial matters?"

The one in front of Jacob asks, "Which station do you listen to?"

"Whatever comes in," says Jacob. "Moscow, London, Switzerland. It depends upon the weather, too."

"Never any German stations?"

"What for?"

"Do you also listen to music sometimes?"

"Rarely," says Jacob. "Only when I'm waiting for news. I don't have the radio for pleasure, you know."

"I sure would like to hear some music again. Anything," says the one in front of the one in front of Jacob.

The soup kettles are long in coming, although the line is straight as an arrow, I swear. They still correct by themselves any irregularity, even those scarcely noticeable, but this time it does not result in the appearance of the soup kettles. Instead, the attic window in the stone guardhouse is opened; a hand signals for silence; a voice shouts from above like the annoyed God himself, "A ten-minute break! Lunch is cancelled today!"

The cart with the bowls is taken away. The hungry line disperses over the entire area. Spoons are replaced clean into pockets, sparse curses, maledictions, and dirty looks; the Russians will get even with you dogs.

Kowalski asks in my presence, "Are we not getting anything to eat because Hardtloff is dead?"

"That seems very clear," I say.

"If you ask me," says Kowalski, "it's worth it."

He doesn't exactly get a belly laugh. No lunch. That's a hard blow. To a certain extent a blow to the stomach. But Kowalski attempts it again nicely with another modest crack, "Just imagine, if every time one of us croaked, the Germans get nothing to eat. That would be a fine famine!"

*Nebich.*

Wherever Jacob goes for the ten minutes, a loyal, small throng of Jews follow him. Kowalski joins in before he is even missed. Jacob knows they are behind him. There is no meal, hence a word from him must provide replenishment. He walks over to an empty freight car. There all of them find a seat, a discretion that has long since become customary. Jacob is not completely at ease. He had intended to rest a bit on yesterday's laurels, on the liberation of the town of Tobolin. With our enthusiastic participation, Major Karthäuser had placed his signature energetically below the document of capitulation. The stronghold had fallen. But that was yesterday. No one could guess how impoverished the next day would be. Jacob is sitting amidst his congregation unprepared.

Suddenly, I am told, as they are sitting there and looking at him, for he must begin to give a report forthwith, an evil thought goes through his mind, dispersing Tobolin along with all the victories. Suddenly he realizes that two pieces of news reached the railroad station today, although only one was immediately comprehended. Hardtloff. The other, the bad news, remained unheeded, although it lay in the air clear and unmistakable. Only the effort was lacking.

"Unfortunately, the news is not at all so good," says Jacob seriously.

"Which news do you mean?"

"That Hardtloff died."

"Does his death make you feel sad?" they ask mockingly.

"Not his death," says Jacob. "But Kirschbaum's does."

Unfortunately, they must share his view. It doesn't come easy. A compelling connection. Most of them understand without any further explanation. The situation is not such that a Jewish physician could outlive his Aryan patient by very much, in this specific case especially not. "What Kirschbaum?" someone asks; not everybody is well known. It is explained to him: a great personage, a famous contemporary authority in heart disease, Jacob's neighbor here, and was called in to cure Hardtloff. Then abundant, belated, quiet mourning for the professor. The ten minutes pass without questions and reports about victories. Jacob would have wished another diversion. He detects a yearning for some kind of consolation. You can't simply leave them sitting around so hungry. The old story about the secret German plans that fall into the Russians' hands in the fortress of Tobolin passes through his mind for a second. But the whistle saves him from this stupidity by signaling in the usual way the end to lunch, so especially unappetizing today.

Despite Hardtloff's death, then, the day passes drearily. It does so anyway. In the midst of work one of the two skinny horses that pull the tanker wagon appears, then the other, then the wagon. Its sight is familiar to us, even the clattering. It can even be heard from afar. On the average it comes every third month, in the summer less rarely. In the winter when the ground is frozen, somewhat more often, but always on Monday. Its visit concerns the German little shed with the heart. It can go three months without it, not longer, or else it'll overflow.

In the driver's seat is sitting a local farmer. No one knows how he received this honor. We can't stand him. The Germans had forbidden him to talk to any of us when he came here the very first time, and he strictly observes that ban. In the beginning, long before Jacob's radio, we tried to get a word out of him. We ourselves didn't know what, but any trifle from outside. It would have even been without risk, but he just sat there in the driver's seat, his mouth grim, and kept silent, leering at the guards in the distance. Apparently he was afraid for his head or his manure. Or he is an anti-Semite or quite simply an idiot.

He stops his wagon behind the toilet. A German comes out of the stone guardhouse and mingles among the people who all act terribly busy as soon as the ugly clattering can be heard. The work for which four people are now being sought is no easier than hauling crates. Afterward you stink like a skunk and can't wash up until you get home.

"You, you, you, and you," says the German.

Schmidt, Jacob, and two unknown men, gritting their

teeth, walk to the back of the shed and start their dung work. They take the two shovels and the two buckets hanging on a side of the wagon. Jacob and the lawyer lift the lid from the pit. Then they shovel the muck into the buckets. The other two pour them out into the cauldrons. Schmidt's disgusted expression does not make matters any more agreeable. Three hours worth of work must be reckoned with. Halfway through there's a switch: shovels for buckets.

"Have you ever done this before?" asks Schmidt.

"Twice," says Jacob.

"I haven't before."

The farmer in the driver's seat is sitting with his back to them. He takes a little package out of his pocket, wax paper, and unwraps it: bread and bacon. And in addition, bright sunshine. Oblivious to the world, he is enjoying his lunch or a snack. Tears run down Jacob's cheeks.

The older one of the bucket carriers begs the farmer for a bite; quiet explanation about what happened with his lunch hour; just a little piece of bread, not to mention the bacon at all. The farmer seems to waver. While shoveling Jacob notices the farmer's simple eyes gazing around the railroad station for guards, none of whom is interested in the proceedings behind the shed house.

"Don't be afraid," says our man. "You don't have to speak with us. Just drop a piece of bread, you understand, by mistake. No one can do anything to you for that. I'll pick it up so that no one will notice. . . . Do you hear? No one, not even you yourself will notice it!"

"Would you be able to eat with this stench?" asks Schmidt.

"Yes," says Jacob.

The farmer reaches again into his pocket, takes out the wax paper, wraps up the remainder of the bread and bacon carefully, and stows it away. Either he is full or he really lost his appetite. Just one more healthy gulp from a green water flask. He wipes his mouth with his dirty sleeve.

"Asshole," someone calls him, but not even that vulgar name gets a response.

Shortly before the switch Schmidt's scooping out slows down perceptibly and finally stops completely. He insists he can't go on, that everything is spinning around in front of him, black spots. He leans back, perspiring, against the back wall of the shed.

"That's because of no lunch," says Jacob.

That's no help to Schmidt; large beads of perspiration roll down his face; he tries to vomit; nothing comes out. Jacob shovels a bucketful for him which results in a lag for the carriers. No solution in the long run.

"You must continue working," says Jacob.

"It's all very well for you to talk," says Schmidt panting, leaning against the wall, and very pale.

"Either you continue now, or you can lie down right now and die," says Jacob.

By no means does lawyer Schmidt desire that! He takes his shovel again and weakly fills his bucket that has already been waiting for a long time. He groans. It looks like a hopeless attempt and it is feared that it will come to nothing. The shovel pokes at the surface and doesn't penetrate as deep as it would have to and therefore is only half full when it comes out of the muck. Surplus work for Jacob.

"By the way, I've heard something about your Sir Winston," says Jacob, quietly enough so that the farmer, even with the best sense of hearing, would not understand anything.

"About Sir Winston?" says Schmidt, weakly to be sure, but audibly interested.

"He has a cold."

"Anything serious?"

"No, no, just a head cold or so. He was sneezing through half the interview."

"A whole interview?"

"A short one."

"And what does he say?"

Jacob intimates that this is not a good spot for a chat, the guards over there; for a while they will be concerned with other things. But in three hours one of them will come to check up, with certainty, and by then the pit must be empty. The report, thus, can be told only if it can be disguised with work. Schmidt has to understand that. His grip on the shovel becomes of necessity firmer. The drops on his forehead stay the same. What does Sir Winston say?

Jacob tells him. The conversation in the cellar between the reporter and the British premier is still in his memory, although no longer quite fresh. The situation on the Eastern front, without mentioning any cities, is desperate for the Germans everywhere—those are his very words—a big, colorful bouquet of good prospects. And Sir Winston can really afford an opinion with his overall knowledge, don't you agree? Of course, here and there difficulties still exist. I ask you, in which war does everything go smoothly?

And there are also differences between Schmidt and Lena, in the final analysis, which need to be taken into account. You are not sitting with a little girl in a cellar at night for fun, so to speak, or out of love. You're standing in the sunlight with Schmidt who has finished the university. Every word must be weighed. In three hours the pit must be free of muck.

On the morning of this day that has been chosen for the advance on the county seat Pry—the Russians will not get quite that far, but will advance very close to it, as Jacob conceives it—on the morning of this very promising day,

Misha sees on his way to work an animated little group standing around. Some are pointing in one direction and some in another. Two are talking rapidly; the others are listening in amazement. Misha does not wish to pass by without finding out more details. When the name of a street, Franziskaner Street, is mentioned, Misha grabs the arm of the man nearest him and yanks him out of the confusion to find out what, in heaven's name, is going on in Franziskaner Street.

He is told quickly. A misfortune has been inflicted upon it. Franziskaner Street is being blocked off into three parts. The Germans are searching house by house. They have reached Number 10. In a few hours nobody will be living there anymore, but will be sent to a concentration camp or somewhere else.

"And the Russians are supposed to have captured Tobolin already," says the man.

Misha dashes away. The destiny of the residents moves him not only in general, but also because Franziskaner Street is utterly special—Rosa lives there. The man said before that they were up to Number 10—that means several minutes ago. By this time Rosa would have normally long been at the factory. Misha reproaches himself for simply not having forced her to stay with him every night, especially last night. He will go to her factory. The guard at the gate will not let him in, but he can remain nearby. Until work lets out Misha himself will stand guard, for Rosa must be prevented from going home. God forbid that he should watch over an empty factory all day. If Rosa left her house on time, she should be there. There is no other hope. Misha is running. Why so fast, he himself doesn't know. Rosa's workday lasts a long time. He is running.

From the front of her factory, a textile plant made of gray brick, the world seems quite ordinary. Misha is standing on the other side of the street. Nobody besides him. He prepares for a long day, but it turns out to be much shorter than expected. A Jewish girl comes out of the factory. Misha wonders how come she is leaving during the workday. She strolls aimlessly across the avenue past him. Misha is standing indecisively until she has almost reached the next corner. Then he follows her. She is soon aware of him and turns her head flirtatiously, once and twice, a blue-eyed broad-shouldered young man is such a rarity in the ghetto, and in broad daylight yet. She immediately slows down; she doesn't even mind if he catches up with her, which ultimately occurs, too. Right after the corner he is standing beside her.

"Pardon me," says Misha. "Do you work in this textile plant?"

"Yes," she says, smiling.

"Do you happen to know if Rosa Frankfurter is still there?"

She thinks a few seconds before she says, "You are Misha, aren't you?"

"Yes," he says. "Is she there?"

"She left a few minutes ago. She was told she could go home again today."

"How long do you mean by a 'few minutes'?" he asks, his voice already shrill. "How long, exactly?"

"Maybe ten," she replies, amazed at his sudden agitation.

Again he dashes away, calculating feverishly that he will have to hurry if the ten minutes are true. From here to Franziskaner Street Rosa would need barely half an hour, more if she took a stroll, and she would not hurry. She was told she could go home, without giving her any reasons. The scoundrels, there's no need to hurry.

Suddenly Misha turns around, rushes back the same way; a slip up must be corrected, an unpardonable one. The girl comes slowly toward him and is again smiling.

"Were you also sent home?" he calls out to her even from afar.

"Yes."

"Don't go home! Hide yourself!"

He still hears her asking, "But why?"

"Because Franziskaner Street is being deported!"

"But I don't live in Franziskaner Street. I live in Zagorsk Street."

The long-winded conversation is taking up much too much of his time. Zagorsk Street then, too. He has told her everything he knows. Let her make sense out of it, save her life or not. If she is smart, she'll stand at the factory and tell everyone who is being sent home, "Don't go home, hide, no matter where you live!" That is running through his mind after he has long been running again after Rosa. He has been thinking, too, that Franziskaner and Zagorsk Streets don't even meet, between them is Blumenbinder Lane, which has few houses but several open storage areas, unused today, or at least not much. And around every new corner, he looks for Rosa. Perhaps she isn't taking the shortest route; perhaps she is taking a walk in this nice weather and wants to enjoy her free day. If she is really taking a walk, he would certainly reach Franziskaner Street before her. He could take over one end and intercept her. But only one end. Franziskaner Street has two of them. Which would you take over with so many ends, and at this time of day you won't find an accomplice at any price. A new glimmer of hope glows for moments. Misha banks on Rosa's instinct for survival. No matter at which end she appears, she will realize what is happening to her street. Maybe then she'll turn around and run to his house, hide in the yard, and wait until he returns with the key in the evening. But Misha doesn't rely on that too much. He knows her too well for that. Crazy Rosa will not be able to knock that nonsensical love for her mother and father out of her head, such useless female rubbish. At best she'll be capable of a bit of hesitation, then she will run weeping to her destruction. She'll run in there where her parents are, who can well do without her, and thereby help no one.

All this calculation of alternatives comes to an end when he finds her at last on a long street, straight as an arrow, on Argentinisch Avenue whose linden trees have been carefully sawed down close to ground level, resulting in a wide field of vision. Since the avenue is practically devoid of people, he recognizes her reddish brown dress even while it is still a dot, then her blue kerchief, her gait, as predicted, slow. Misha thinks, What luck!

Several meters behind her he stops running and quietly follows her for a few steps. Rosa is looking around at the pretty gables of the old houses in what was formerly a merchants' area. Rosa is taking a walk. His last thoughts before he approaches her, his demeanor must be innocent; he happened to be on his way to her house because he found out that her factory gave her the day off. No mention dare be made about terrible fears, not a word about the fate of the residents of Franziskaner Street, otherwise this parental love stuff might pop into her head.

He is about to cover her eyes from behind with his hands and with a disguised voice make her guess who it is; that would be a natural beginning. He notices that his hands are wet with perspiration, his face, too. He wipes it dry with his sleeve and says with a forced nonchalance, "Fancy meeting you here."

She turns around quickly, frightened at first, then she smiles. The prettiest girls smile at Misha. Rosa asks, "What are you doing here?"

"And what are you doing here?"

"I'm going home," she says. "Imagine, I wasn't in the factory one hour when I was permitted to leave."

"And why?"

"Don't ask me. They simply said I could go home. A few others, too, but not everybody."

"The same with me," says Misha.

"You have off today, too? The whole day?"

"Yes."

"Great!" says Rosa.

She takes his arm. A solitary passerby looks at the young lovebirds admiringly.

"Let's go to my place," says Misha.

"But how come you happen to be here?"

"Because I wanted to pick you up at the factory. When they let me off, I thought maybe they'd let you off today, too."

"You're a smart fellow."

"But you had just left. A girl told me, a short, pretty redhead."

"That was Larissa," she says.

They walk to his apartment, leisurely, since the direction causes him no concern. Franziskaner Street is completely avoided. Rosa tells about Larissa and that she had sometimes discussed Misha with her; he wouldn't be angry with her because of it; they do sew at the same table and the day is long. Larissa is quiet but deep; her dreamy eyes should not fool anyone. She, too, for instance, has a boy friend. Najdorf is his name. Josef; she calls him Yossele; he works in the tool factory; Misha wouldn't know him. They both live in the same house. Larissa has a mother and two grown-up brothers, too; a funny story once happened with her two brothers. They once beat up Josef Najdorf when they caught him in the attic with their sister; and can you imagine what for? For necking, of course; but Larissa really gave it to them good and proper! Since then, they're not so quarrelsome. They've realized that she is no longer a little child. Yossele is even allowed to visit her in their apartment sometimes, for a chat, of course. And suddenly, in the midst of this nice chat, Rosa stops and asks: "Say, how come they're giving us a whole day off?"

"How should I know?" says Misha.

"There must be a reason for that."

He shrugs his shoulders. He had hoped she wouldn't even bring it up. He does owe her an answer. She is right! It is strange.

"Does that have anything to do with the Russians?" she asks.

"With the Russians?"

"Well, if they feel that their situation is hopeless, won't they quickly want to act nicer to us?" says Rosa. "Don't you see? Because of later."

"Maybe," says Misha; even he doesn't have a better explanation at hand.

So to his place; strolling along, Rosa proves to be talkative in a sheer carefree manner completely unknown to Misha up to now. Misha lets her flow of words ripple along unhindered. On Larissa she hasn't finished by a long shot. Klara and Annette, and especially Nina, are also having affairs, and how! Moreover, her father has begun to foster timid hopes for the future. Two evenings ago he put a peculiar scrap of paper on the table, says Rosa. On it, divided into three groups, were theater parts, corresponding to his notions, that God willing, he would play some day. They had kept the directorship from him long enough. Rosa knows no particulars. She understands too little about the theater for that. But there were at least twenty.

At his front door something unpleasant comes to Misha's mind. No work means no lunch today. He asks Rosa whether she happens to have her food ration stamps with her. They were unfortunately at home. He thinks, that's all he needs! Should she quickly get them; oh no, no need to. He gives her the key, he'll be right back. He'll use his own stamps.

211

In the store Misha is the only customer. After work there is never less than half an hour wait.

"At this hour?" asks Rosenek the well fed. His scale, suspected of inaccuracy, is always leaning in the same direction. Only that could have helped him to his paunch. He certainly tries to hide his little monster with his much too big smock, but smock and Rosenek are transparent, and for his jowls not even such an oversized smock suffices.

"I have off today," says Misha.

"Off? What does that mean?"

"Off."

Misha puts the food stamps on the counter in front of Rosenek, all of them.

"It's only Tuesday," says Rosenek astonished; that arouses suspicions.

"Nonetheless."

"You must know."

Rosenek takes a round loaf of bread out of a drawer behind him dusty with flour; it doesn't smell at all like bread, as it once did. He lays it on the counter and slices it with the serrated knife, groaning, then upon the famous scale, which stands as true and straight as organ pipes.

"Please, weigh it accurately," says Misha.

"What do you mean? I always weigh accurately."

Misha will not get involved in hair-splitting; that leads nowhere. He says, "Weigh it especially accurately. I have a guest."

"A guest? What does that mean?"

"A guest."

Rosenek takes pity. He gives Misha the other half, supposedly, of the loaf without putting it on the scale. Two trouser pockets full of potatoes are added, since Misha has nothing with him for carrying, a bag of flour made of peas, sausage more in appearance than in essence, and a package of malt coffee.

"On the stamps there is also something about lard," says Misha.

"Yes, there is. So it is there; where should I get it from?"

"Herr Rosenek," says Misha.

Rosenek looks at him as if he were making the most difficult decision of his life; you'll kill me yet, lad. Rosenek asks, "Do you need the coffee?"

"Not so very much."

Rosenek persists a bit yet in his unhappy pose, finally takes the package of coffee from the counter, and goes into a room adjoining the store. When he comes back, he is holding a piece of wax paper in front of him. At first glance, it looks like merely a piece of folded wax paper, but then you notice something is wrapped in it. Lard. To judge by the look on his face, Rosenek cut it off his own belly.

"Because it's you," says Rosenek. "But for heaven's sake, don't tell anyone."

"Why should I?" says Misha.

Misha comes upstairs well stocked. Rosa looks in amazement at what he has brought. She had opened the window wide.

"Or else the sun will think no one is home and leave, mother says," she says.

Misha stores away Rosenek's gifts in the cupboard and cleans the potato dust from his pockets. Rosa calls him over to the window. He doesn't like her voice. He leans out beside her. A gray procession is approaching, still small and indistinct. Only the barking of dogs is heard at first, now and then and quite superfluous, since no one steps out of line.

"Which street today?" asks Rosa.

"I don't know."

He pulls her away from the window and closes it, but he can't prevent her from standing there, waiting for the procession to pass. Rosa says, "Let me. Maybe there are friends among them."

"Are you hungry?" he asks. "Should we prepare something?"

"Not now."

He spares himself further offers. He knows that she will answer everything he would propose to her now by, "Not now." Only force can separate her from the window; really silly, because she doesn't have any idea whom she will get to see in the procession; but she imagines on such occasions she must not stick her head in the sand. A kind of ground rule for Rosa. That's the way she is. It would be simplest to grab her, throw her down on the bed, and start smothering her with kisses, as if you suddenly got the urge. Misha even takes the first step toward that end, but he loses his courage at the second step, because Rosa knows him too well. She would see through the lie immediately. She must be left standing there up to the terrible sight. She will not be spared that.

He sits down on the bed trying to look composed, which makes absolutely no difference because Rosa is resolutely staring outside. Her forehead is leaning against the windowpane even more firmly so that she can view the procession that much sooner. A small spot of breath forms on the glass. She breathes with her mouth open like all excited people do.

"Come on over here," he says.

Did these idiots have to choose his particular street; aren't there enough others around? Misha has the urge to get up and go out into the corridor or at least into Fajngold's half of the room which, of course, got back its old look one day after Rosa's intervention. Just what will she do? The barking of dogs gets louder. When it ceases for a moment, steps are heard and even a single voice calling, "Step lively! Lively!"

**214**

"Misha!" says Rosa quietly.

"Misha!" she yells seconds later. "Misha, Misha, Misha. That is our street!"

Now he is standing behind her. The thought that her parents must be in the procession seems not to have occurred to her yet. She enumerates in whispers the names of neighbors whom she recognizes. Each one is holding something in his hand; an overnight bag, a suitcase, a cloth stuffed with objects worth taking along. Misha finds time to look for the Frankfurters. He discovers them even before she does. Felix Frankfurter has his customary scarf slung around his neck. His gait somehow suggests confidence. His wife, a head shorter, is walking beside him. She looks up to their window. Misha was, of course, never a secret.

Rosa is still enumerating names. Her mother's glances provide Misha his final impetus. He clutches Rosa and carries her away from the window. He wants to put her down on the bed and detain her there, but nothing comes of it. They fall down on the way because Rosa resists. He lets himself be beaten and scratched and his hair pulled. It is only her body he is clutching. They lie an eternity on the floor. She screams for him to let her go. Perhaps twenty times she screams nothing but "Let me go!" Until no more barking can be heard, no more steps. Her blows become weak and finally cease. Carefully he releases her, prepared to seize her again momentarily. But she remains lying motionless, her eyes closed, and breathing heavily like after a great exertion. There is a knocking at the door and a woman from the house asks if she can help; it seemed to her as if someone had screamed.

"No, no, everything is fine," says Misha through the closed door. "Thank you."

He gets up and opens the window, otherwise the sun will think no one is home and leave, as he had heard. The street is quiet and empty. He looks outside for a long time.

When he turns around Rosa is still lying on the floor in the same position.

"Come, get up."

She gets up, but not, as he can see, because he said it. Not a tear has yet been shed. She sits down on the bed. He dares not talk to her.

"Your neck is bleeding," she says.

He walks over to her, stoops down and tries to look at her, but she looks past him.

"That's why you picked me up," she says. "You knew about it."

He is startled when he realizes what a reproach her words imply. He would like to explain to her that no time was left to warn her parents, but at that moment she would not accept any reasons.

"Did you get to see them at all?" he asks.

"You didn't let me," she says and finally starts to weep.

He says that he didn't see them either, not even at the end of the line; maybe they sensed the danger in time and managed to save themselves. He knows how ridiculous it is. After three words he notes how uselessly he is lying, but finishes the sentences as formulated.

"You'll certainly see them again," he adds. "Jacob said . . ."

"You're lying!" she shouts. "You're all lying! You talk and talk and nothing changes!"

She jumps up and is about to flee. Misha doesn't catch her until after she has opened the door. In the corridor the woman straightens up from the height of the keyhole. She asks, "Can't I help at all?"

"No, damn it!" shouts Misha; now he is shouting, too.

The woman backs away, insulted. It may be assumed that her good will is extinguished forever, at least for this loudmouth. In any case, Rosa came to her senses through the appearance of a third party, it seems. She goes back into the room, without Misha having to compel her. He locks the door; he fears the silence. That's why he starts immediately taking over Fajngold's fallow half of the room anew, moving the closet to the wall, right in front of the large rectangle on the wallpaper, taking the curtain from its cover, and hanging it on the window again. Because Rosa will now live here. At least that much is certain.

"Have you finally heard anything about the deportations?" asks Misha.

"No," says Jacob.

"They've cleared out not only Franziskaner Street but also Zagorsk and . . ."

"I know," says Jacob.

They walk a few steps silently on the way home from the railway station. They have already got rid of Kowalski at the previous corner. In Misha's presence he had refrained from asking questions.

Five had been missing at the railway station since that day, perhaps even more. Only the five you yourself know are missing. Jacob had even thought it was six. He had included Misha because he hadn't appeared at work on that day. Fortunately, it was an error.

"How is it with Rosa?" asks Jacob.

"How should it be?"

"Do you manage with the food?"

"Superbly!"

"She can't get any more ration stamps now, can she?"

"You're telling me?"

"Couldn't someone in the house help out? With me it's similar with Lena. Kirschbaum always used to give something for her."

"I don't believe any more that things will turn out well in the end," says Misha. "They are proceeding street by street now."

It seems to Jacob as if there were a barely hidden reproach in his voice.

"Possibly," says Jacob. "But figure it out yourself. The Germans are in a panic. The deportations are the best proofs that the Russians must already be quite nearby! Seen from that angle, they are even a good sign."

"A wonderfully good sign. Try and explain that to Rosa."

On one of the afternoons when she was bored to death and weary of weeping, Rosa left the apartment although Misha had strictly forbidden her to. He would have most preferably locked her in even if she had protested. He hadn't done so because the toilet was in the yard.

She has no particular destination. She just wants to stretch her legs after an ample week of jail. The dangers Misha constantly talks about she considers exaggerated. In his room she is no more secure than anywhere else. That house can also be next at any time. And who should recognize her? There are hardly any friends left. Street checks don't start until the evening about the time of the curfew hour. Besides, all that is basically of no concern to her, and moreover, Misha needn't find out about her stroll; she doesn't intend to stay away long.

It doesn't have to be the absolute truth if she tells him later, when he happens to be home long before she is, that she had coincidentally had the key to her parents' apartment with her. And that she, without really wanting to, suddenly found herself in Franziskaner Street. Her legs took that route out of old habit, she said.

The street impresses her as unreal and empty, even avoided by passing traffic as if the plague had raged in it. Rosa peeks into abandoned ground-floor rooms, into rooms of people whom she had still greeted a few days ago. Behind one window she discovers a boy. He is about fourteen years old. He is kneeling in front of an open cupboard, stuffing into a knapsack in great haste everything he can get his hands on: dishes, bed linen, a pair of trousers, and a wooden box without even perusing its contents for usefulness. Rosa stares at him, the sole living being besides herself. The cupboard seems to be completely empty, but the knapsack is not yet full. The boy stands up and looks around the room searchingly. There he sees the big eyes behind the glass pane. At first he is frightened; then he sees the star on Rosa's chest, too, and a welcoming grin comes over his face. Apparently he anticipates a harmless competitor.

Rosa continues on quickly. She wonders whether such a person had been in her apartment in the meantime; she knows no other word, a looter. She feels no rage, but understanding alone isn't enough. She feels uncomfortable that a second, secret life exists behind the walls, a life that is not noticeable at a glance and that slowly eradicates all traces of the first.

Quietly she opens her front door and, with her heart pounding, listens. She would like to have Misha with her; maybe he could have been persuaded, but now she is here without him. You can never be certain, but after a good interval of silence she assumes that no one else is in the house. Quickly she walks up two flights. Before she unlocks the door she looks through the keyhole. Then she is standing in the room. It looks very tidy. The dust hadn't yet had much time to settle. The four chairs are standing neatly around the table upon which a yellow tablecloth is lying, at each corner a pointed tip. The faucet is dripping. Up to now, no one with a knapsack has been here. Rosa notices that right away and also that her parents must have departed without haste.

Immediately she looks for some kind of message. The thought doesn't occur to her until now. She remembers that her mother did not leave for even a minute without leaving a note. But this time she had broken her old pattern, obviously, for no written sheet of paper can be found on which would be written, at best, "I don't know where nor for how long."

Then Rosa searches once again. Now no more notes. That's it. Misha tells me, she is just a sentimental girl. She wanted to provide herself an inventory of what her parents took along. Probably she cried her eyes out while doing this. The brown and white shopping bag was missing and the black cardboard suitcase, no other containers. Since Rosa knows the entire inventory exactly, she would at the end of her search be in a position to draw up a list of what was taken along. The album of photos and reviews, too, the book of the true life of Felix Frankfurter.

Her own things lie untouched. Among many others her ration card, part of it already expired. Rosa puts it in her pocket. Otherwise there are no objects that are particularly dear to her. She forces herself to practical measures. There is a brief case. In it she lays her second dress, underclothes and stockings, and finally her coat. While doing that, she is amazed that she manages to think ahead to next winter. With her coat in it the case will not close. Rosa wants to put it on, but she would then have to take off the stars from her dress and sew them on the coat. Therefore she stuffs it into the case and ties around it her coat belt. If she were to meet the boy on the street, he would envy her her rich booty.

Rosa tightens the faucet handle. She is finished here. When she goes, she leaves the key in the door, for the boy or for another, as a kind of finality.

"You could guess ten times," Misha tells me, "and you wouldn't know where she went now."

Rosa visits Jacob whom she doesn't know except from Misha's reports, but quite well from them. Since the time of Bezanika, there had not been an evening together in which they didn't talk about him, his radio, his courage, and the

Russians' advances at the front. Rosa had asked at that time, after her initial, great joy at the novelty had passed, why this Jacob had just now begun to spread the news; for three years we had been living in the ghetto, and if he had a hidden radio, then he had it right from the start.

"Probably the Germans had been advancing the whole time up till then. Was he to report that it was getting worse from day to day?" Misha answered her, and it sounded convincing.

Thus, she is standing before his door not out of vindictiveness or personal resentment, she attempts to convince herself. Of course, he is nice and kind and wants the best, but the daily happy-sounding promises and then the empty room in Franzikaner Street, the entire quarter even; she will ask him how one is compatible with the other. She will raise qualms as to whether it is permissible to arouse such hopes in her situation. Just don't throw the radio up to me! It can say whatever it wants. You need only look around you.

Rosa knocks several times, in vain. Why didn't she think before that Jacob must come home about the same time as Misha? The waiting makes her insecure. When she does stand face to face with him, her head will feel as if it had been hollowed out. She might still leave, perhaps be in the apartment before Misha and avoid irritation which will otherwise certainly occur. The longer she waits the clearer it is she must confess that she had come with extremely foggy intentions. Jacob will always refer back to his radio no matter what she is reproaching him for: she had hoped that they would all survive unharmed the time of trial; now it has turned out differently. Faced squarely, that is her real reason. "She plays quicker than she thinks," her father once said after a card game. Her father. The thought occurs to Rosa that Jacob is perhaps spreading different news than he hears on his radio.

Now Lena is standing at the end of the corridor, freshly

arrived from the street and from Rafael. She sees a young woman with a stuffed brief case standing at the certain door and approaches curiously. They look each other over a bit. Both still foster no suspicion. Lena asks, "Do you want to see Uncle Jacob?"

"Yes."

"He should be back soon. Wouldn't you rather wait inside?"

"Do you live here?" asks Rosa.

Instead of an answer Lena takes out the key from behind the doorframe, unlocks the door, and with a little pride makes an inviting hand movement. Rosa enters the room hesitantly; a chair is immediately shoved along to her; she has fallen into the hands of a courteous hostess. Lena sits down, too; they continue to observe one another kindly.

"You are Lena, aren't you?" says Rosa.

"How do you know my name?"

"From Misha," says Rosa. "Don't you know each other well?"

"Certainly. And now I also know who you are."

"I'm all ears."

"You are Rosa. Well?"

They tell one another what they know about each other; Lena is, incidentally, still angry at Misha because he hadn't visited her even once the whole time she was sick in bed, only warm regards through Jacob. Rosa looks around unobtrusively, by no means expecting to see the radio standing around in the open, to the joy of every incidental visitor.

"What do you want from Uncle Jacob?" asks Lena, after the remaining conversational matter had soon been exhausted.

"Let's wait rather until he arrives."

"Are you carrying out an errand for Misha?"

"No."

"Don't be afraid to tell me. He doesn't keep any secrets from me."

But Rosa, nonetheless, has no intention of talking. She smiles and keeps silent. Whereupon Lena attempts to draw her out by subterfuge.

"Have you ever been here before?" she asks.

"No, never."

"You know, all kinds of people have been coming here recently. And do you know what they want?" Lena pauses, to give Rosa time to recognize the special proof of confidentiality before she reveals, "They want to hear news. Is that why you've come, too?"

Rosa's face loses its smile; she's certainly not here for that, but rather for the contrary. In the meantime, she regrets having come at all, from the first moment on increasingly more so. She feels herself to be in the wrong place with her despair; things are honest and in the best of faith here. She asks herself the question what she would do if Jacob came in now and told her that the transport with her parents on the way to so and so had met their liberators. And she doesn't dare offer an answer, not even to the second question as to whether she had deluded herself up to now on the real reason for her visit. She does not dismiss the possibility of that.

"What is it?" asks Lena. "Is that why you've come, too?"

"No," says Rosa.

"But you've heard about it, too, haven't you?"

"About what?"

"That everything will soon change?"

"Yes," says Rosa.

"Then why aren't you happy?"

Rosa straightens up. The point has been reached at which you either turn back or tell the truth. But what is the truth, aside from her misgivings? She says, "Because I don't believe it."

"You don't believe what Uncle Jacob is saying?" asks Lena in a tone of voice as if she hadn't heard it quite right.

"No."

"You think he's not telling the truth?"

Rosa likes that formulation. It's that very connection that is necessary to explore. She would be inclined to chat with this sweet girl about nice things, but by no means to continue any longer in the direction taken. How could she do that with a child! Without a declaration of conclusive reasons, she is suddenly convinced she had made a mistake which, hopefully, will have no consequences. She can not simply, just like that, get up and leave. Rosa sits lost and is waiting, no longer now for Jacob, but for a natural opportunity to end her visit, recognized by her as wrong. But that opportunity is becoming increasingly remote. Lena is getting so very excited after that frightening second that you could get scared. For her uncle is anything but a liar; Rosa hadn't said that; oh, yes, exactly what she said; how can you assert such things? Especially when she herself had heard on his radio that the Russians would soon be here, with her own ears; now what do you say to that? A man in a very deep voice told it to another man, she forgot his name, but she remembers the voice exactly; he had said literally that the rotten mess would soon be over, at most a few weeks more. Could he have been lying, too? How did Rosa ever get the idea anyway to impute a lie to her uncle; just wait till he arrives; he'll give her the right answer!

Even before everything has been uttered, indignantly and in flowing sentences, Lena stops and stares past Rosa, startled. Rosa turns her head toward the door. Jacob is standing there, his face of stone, as they say. Not a draught of air was detected.

Rosa stands up. Whether or not he had heard much or little, she believes herself detected; his eyes look so terrified. With bowed head she walks to the door. There will be no more opportunity for a pleasant farewell. She has put her foot in it! Jacob steps aside for her half a step, but once more she walks to the chair, for the brief case is lying forgotten on the floor. Rosa dares not turn around in the entire, long corridor. She does so at the stairway; Jacob is standing motionless, gazing after her; the child will tell him immediately what he already surely knows.

Let's stay with Rosa. She reaches the street at the start of dusk. There the next trouble is waiting. At first glance, wild excitement. The Jews are fleeing into their vestibules once again. At first Rosa doesn't realize why. Then she sees an auto approaching, a little dark-green truck. On the running board is a man in uniform. Rosa runs back the few meters into Jacob's house. Infected by the hysteria and without thinking, she leans against the wall, keeping her eyes closed. She opens them when she hears rapid steps. An old man, panting, stops alongside her, also from the street.

"What do they want, Miss?" he asks.

Rosa shrugs her shoulders. The car will soon drive by and be forgotten; the fuss with Misha awaits her. The man suspects that it is a matter of utmost importance, otherwise they would come by foot, as we hear about every few days. To the horror of both of them, brakes screech; the frightened old man grips Rosa's arm so tightly that it hurts her.

It so happens two men in uniform enter into their vestibule, leather straps under their chins. The old man lets go and doesn't let go of Rosa's arm. The motor is still running outside; at first the Germans think themselves alone in the semi-darkness; almost at the stairway, one of them says, "Look!"

They turn to the two figures against the wall. Rosa seems to interest them more than the man, but perhaps she just imagines it. They come several steps closer, when one of them declines with a nod and says, "No, no."

The other says, "Get out of here."

Then they climb the stairs; their loud boots startle the entire house. A door is heard banging; excited voices from everywhere in confusion where calmness would be much more appropriate. A child is crying.

"Come," the old man whispers.

Rosa runs behind him. In the doorway he hesitates because he is afraid of the car, but they must pass it if they wish to obey the German's command.

"Well then, go ahead!" says Rosa.

They rush straight across the avenue toward the opposite house on the other side. From inside, the door is already being opened for them. The old man sits down exhausted upon the lowest stairway step; he groans as if he had run around the entire block and rubs the area around his heart. Besides him Rosa sees three more men and a woman in the vestibule in which it is even darker than in the other. She knows no one. She looks over to the door made of sheet metal. A fourth man is standing at the keyhole, a rather young man, and is reporting for all of them.

"Nothing yet," he says.

"Whom are they looking for in there?" the woman asks the old man.

"Who knows?" says the old man and keeps rubbing his heart.

"Does anyone special live there?" asks a bald-headed man.

At first he receives no answer. All are on their way home from work and strangers to this street. Until Rosa says quietly, "They're after Jacob Heym."

Who is Jacob Heym? What Jacob Heym? The lookout at the keyhole straightens up and asks, "Jacob Heym? Is that the one with the radio?"

"Yes."

"Fine fix," he says without, Rosa finds, much sympathy. "It had to leak out someday."

Whereupon the old man on the steps becomes enraged, shocking Rosa; he seemed preoccupied only with his fears and his heart; now his veins swell. "Why did it have to leak out, you greenhorn? Huh, why? I can tell you why it leaked out. Because some scoundrel squealed! That's why! Or do you think it leaked itself?"

Embarrassed, the greenhorn takes the reprimand without opposition. He stoops over again to the keyhole and says after a short pause, "Still nothing."

The old man beckons Rosa to him with a head movement and when she is standing in front of him, moves over a little. Thus she sits down beside him.

"Do you know him?" he asks.

"Whom?"

"This Jacob Heym."

"No."

"How do you know then that he lives there?"

"From friends," says Rosa.

"They are still inside," reports the greenhorn.

The old man remains silent for some moments in thought. Then he says in the direction of the door, "When they take him out be sure to tell me. I'd like to know what he looks like."

For a moment it seems to Rosa a bit in bad taste, but later not.

"He has taken a big risk," says the old man, admiringly now, again to Rosa, who shakes her head and wonders what in the world she will tell Misha. Let him chastise her in their apartment about her visit; she can't hide it, even if she wanted to; the brief case and the ration card would give it away even without her own confession. But she would rather not mention Jacob; she wouldn't dare tell Misha that face to face, especially not now. And how wretched; her meeting with Jacob can be hushed up without any danger. Jacob will now be prevented from saying anything to Misha.

"Maybe he isn't even home," says the old man.

"He's home," Rosa says thoughtlessly.

The old man looks at her amazed, his question already in his look, but he doesn't get to express it for the greenhorn calls out from the door, "You're all wrong. They're taking a woman out."

Let's permit ourselves a freer view. Let's go to the street. The woman being led away is Elisa Kirschbaum. She will have to pay for the incapacity of her brother, because contrary to their expectations he was incapable of curing the SA battalion leader. They sure thought of it quite late!

Even a while back such a development had been feared in the house. Surely two and two can be added up. Someone had mentioned that concept "genealogical responsibility," which had until then been unfamiliar to us. On the very same evening of the day when the flag at the railroad station was flying at half-mast, Jacob had gone to Elisa Kirschbaum. He had raised the question with her, whether it were not better if she stayed hidden with friends whom she doubtlessly had, at least for a while, until it could be determined whether the threatened reprisals would, in fact, be carried out. For no matter how painful it may be, the worst had to be assumed with regard to her brother, and if a miracle were to occur, if he despite everything were to come back unharmed, Jacob declared himself ready to notify her immediately. But she would hear nothing of all that. She told Jacob, "That's very kind of you, dear Herr Heym. But, please, let me worry about that." As if she still had a trump card in her hand which no one knew about.

Now she is walking along in front of the two Germans, rapidly, so that no pretext be given to shove or to touch her. And rapidly, also, as Jacob surmises behind the window, in order to avoid a big scene for the street, full of hidden eyes despite its apparent emptiness. The display of concentrated power radiating from the two behind her has an exaggeratedly big effect for such a dainty prisoner. Elisa Kirschbaum stops behind the truck without looking around at her companions. One opens the tailgate; on the inside is a little ramp, she is about to walk up; whereupon the truck starts up. Elisa Kirschbaum steps into a void and falls down. The truck merely turns around and stops on the other side of the street. The driver already has his head out of the window. Jacob's vantage point is so far away that he can not make out the faces of the participants. Those who lived closer related afterward that the Germans had smirked, as if it were a matter of an oft-repeated prank. Elisa Kirschbaum gets up immediately with an agility that is astounding; she is again standing ready before the truck has finished turning around. He has to take two tries. Then she gets in; it is rather high for her; despite all her efforts she gets a push. The two climb in, also in the rear. The tailgate is pulled in. Elisa Kirschbaum has finally disappeared behind the dark green tarpaulin. The truck drives away; after a security delay, many front doors are opened. The narrow sidewalks are gradually filled again with silent and argumentative people, most of whom are on their way home from work, as we know, and strangers in this street.

Meanwhile according to the radio, the Red Army has advanced to directly outside of the county seat, Pry. Pry can not be compared to Bezanika. Everyone can conceive of Pry; with Pry you don't even have to ask where it is located. Pry is exactly one hundred forty-six kilometers from us; most of the residents hereabouts are familiar with the little town through occasional visits there. A few had even lived there and after the start of the war had been transported here, since Pry did not have its own ghetto because of its fortunate social structure.

The Russians' position becomes the subject of a dispute. Kowalski has an argument with one of his three roommates whose names are unknown to me. Now, as the good-natured Jacob and I know full well, it is the easiest thing in the world to be of a different opinion from Kowalski, but in this particular case you are inclined to agree with Kowalski. It concerns a trifling matter. It's about the fact that one of them—let's call him Abraham for the sake of simplicity—well, this Abraham maintains that the Russians had already taken Pry and were on the way to Mieloworno. In his factory, let's say in the brickworks, someone said so. Kowalski, on the other hand, swears by all that is holy that they hadn't yet captured Pry. But Abraham sees absolutely no reason to believe Kowalski more than his fellow worker.

"Who works in the railway station?" asks Kowalski in anger. "You or I? Who hears everything firsthand? You or I?"

That is no valid proof for Abraham, probably especially not, since his version sounds much more agreeable than Kowalski's. Anyone can make a mistake, he says. Then the logical objection that everything this mysterious colleague at the brickworks supposedly claims to know must in some way originate from Jacob, Abraham denies.

"Or is there, perhaps, a second radio?"

"How do I know?" says Abraham.

For all Kowalski cares, let Abraham think whatever he wants, let him be taken in by gross rumors like a credulous child. But somehow he feels himself sharing in the responsibility for the truth. For the radio is, as it were, his radio, too; a very old friendship with Jacob, not severed to this day; by a hair's breadth, and he would have even received it into his own apartment at that time during the power failure. Thus he explains patiently the long route that every piece

230

of news must traverse from Jacob's mouth to the factory, via how many people, the dangers to which they are exposed on this route, dangers of mutilation and embellishment, how everyone adds something of his own, making the good news better news, and finally the news arriving, as it turns out, in a version that its own author no longer recognizes.

"In any case, the Russians are on the way to Mieloworno," says Abraham tenaciously. "Maybe you heard wrong, or he heard wrong. You'd better ask him again tomorrow."

Kowalski doesn't ask Jacob tomorrow. The pretexts for an informal chat with Jacob are rare enough. Kowalski goes to Jacob immediately.

He finds him, as can be well imagined, in a bad state: weary, apathetic, laconic. A half hour ago they took Elisa Kirschbaum away.

"Am I disturbing you?" asks Kowalski and conjures up a smile which seems misplaced to him right after the first searching gaze into Jacob's face.

"It's you," says Jacob. He locks the door behind Kowalski and lies down fully clothed on the bed, where he had already been lying, according to all appearances, before there was a knocking. He folds his hands under his head and stares up at the ceiling. Kowalski wonders what is suddenly the matter with him. When they had returned from the railroad station before, he had seemed very happy, if you can speak at all of happiness the last few years.

"Has anything happened?" asks Kowalski.

Happened or not, Jacob detects a debility unknown up to then; frighteningly suddenly, as he was coming down from the attic before, where he had accompanied Lena, he had to hold on to the handrail. He tried to explain his new condition by his endless hunger, but that accounted only for the trembling of his knees, hardly for the origin of the other weakness, just as tormenting—his despondency. Now he is investigating that, staring up at the ceiling, and trying to talk himself out of it, to make it smaller than it in fact is, so fat and heavy. The incident with Elisa Kirschbaum was surely only a small factor. It had exhausted Jacob unquestionably, but it would be exaggerated to say it was that experience that destroyed Jacob's courage from one minute to the next. Of greater significance was Rosa's visit, to have to hear how Lena defended him with lies, with his own weapons, although the main blame of Jacob's diminishing powers should not be laid to this visit. It was a combination of a little of everything, most of it surely quite simply the situation all around him. More and more often someone takes you aside and tells you, Jacob, Jacob, I no longer believe things will turn out well, and when you have consoled him in a makeshift manner with the very latest received dispatches, then six more are standing there and want to tell you the same. According to the radio, the Russians are pressing in on Pry. God only knows whom they are in truth pressing in on, or who is pressing in on them. According to the radio, you would soon have to see the first barrage in the distance. Day after day you see the same picture, this repulsive despair. Gradually you'll have to consider battles of withdrawal, because you have been carried away in your advancing with a speed that unfortunately didn't hold up to reality.

And Kowalski is standing around idly and waiting in vain for a welcome glance.

"Should I leave then, perhaps?" he asks after an appropriate length of time and sits down.

Jacob recalls his visitor; he leaves his ceiling alone and says, "Excuse me, I don't feel particularly well."

"Anything happen?"

"Yes and no," says Jacob. "They came for Kirschbaum's sister before. But aside from that, I'm gradually getting old."

"Kirschbaum's sister? After such a long time?"

"Imagine."

Jacob stands up. In his ears suspicious sounds are ringing, combined with vertigo and nausea. The only thing lacking is for him to really get sick. He hears Kowalski saying from some distance, "What's wrong with you?"

He sits down quickly at the table; fortunately it gets better; he thinks of Lena and what is to become of her, and that he had better stay healthy. And when he finally looks at Kowalski he remembers a little plaque, a white, little plaque with the green lettering: "Temporarily closed because of illness." He got it from Leib Pachman when he bought the café from him. It belonged to the inventory along with many other things. Only once did he use it during all the twenty years that passed amidst pancakes, ice cream, and comparatively small cares. Only one time did the plaque hang in the door to the café. Even then it wasn't a real illness. Jacob had a constitution like a horse. When he wanted to repair the jammed venetian blind, he had fallen from the ladder and broken his leg, whereby the best of health doesn't help you any. That was long before Josefa Litwin's time. She would have come in handy during the recuperation. A shriveled, old witch from the rear apartment had nursed him. For payment, of course, because you had no one else. And what nursing! She pushed the table with food over to him so that he could take something himself, emptied the ash tray from time to time, and aired the room, straightened out the bed in the morning, otherwise said: "And if you still need anything, Reb Heym, call me. I'll leave my window open." Jacob tried to a few times, but she had either closed her window or was hard of hearing like an old mule. And every second or third evening, Kowalski dropped in with a small bottle, taking pity on him lying there with his leg in a cast and not being able to move. He sat there until the bottle was empty. Great conversationalists neither of them was. Jacob thanked God that the

**233**

fracture healed without complications. A few days more and the boredom would have killed him. And a short time thereafter he threw the innocent little plaque into the furnace, had his wrathful joy as it disappeared in the flames without a trace. The threat had such a lasting effect that to this day he had remained spared from any bed confinement.

"Wouldn't it be better if I left?" asks Kowalski meanwhile, at the end of his patience.

"Stay," says Jacob.

Kowalski looks at him inquiringly. It seems to him as though Jacob intended to tell him something, hardly anything good considering the past minutes along with the dragging introduction. Only a completely innocent social visit was planned, because he had made up his mind on the way not even to confirm the Pry details, since there was no possibility of an error. This Abraham must have fallen into the trap of some smart aleck. He simply wanted to drop by to say hello and to talk a little about the past and future, with whom else if not with your only old friend who, if he doesn't come to you, then you go to him!

"How much do you think, Kowalski, a human being can take?" asks Jacob finally.

So, he wants to philosophize, Kowalski must be thinking, he's waiting for a clarification to the question, for a definition toward some sort of direction; however Jacob seems to have asked it quite generally. He says, "Well, what do you think?"

"If you ask me," says Kowalski, "a lot, a hell of a lot."

"But there's a limit."

"Of course . . ."

"I'm sorry," says Jacob. "My limit has now been reached. Maybe another would have gone on. I can't any more."

"What can't you do any more?"

"I can't any more," says Jacob.

Kowalski gives him time. He doesn't know that Jacob is

preparing an unconditional surrender, the worst of all confessions. He sees only his bony face supported by his hands, maybe somewhat paler than usual, possibly somewhat wearier, but nonetheless the face of the same Jacob whom you know like no one else. Kowalski is concerned because such attacks of gloom in Jacob are quite uncommon. From time to time he is surly and quarrelsome, but that's different. He is not a complainer; all the others complain; Jacob is something of a psychiatrist. Consciously or unconsciously, people often came to him to have their own frailties exorcised. Even before the time of the radio, and even before the existence of the ghetto. Whenever a particularly crappy day was over, whenever you had stood from morning till night behind your shopwindow, waiting in vain for customers, or when some tremendous bill had arrived and you had no idea in the world how you were going to pay it, where did you go in the evening? To his café; not because his whiskey tasted particularly good. His was the same as everywhere else, and illegal too, since it was sold without a license. You went there because after such a visit the world looked a little bit rosier, because he was able to say a trifle more convincingly than others "Chin up," or "Things will get better," or something like that. Perhaps, too, because he was the only one in the sparse circle of friends who took the trouble at all to say anything like that to you. Kowalski gives him time.

Then Jacob begins talking, from all appearances to Kowalski since no one else is in the room, but according to the content to a bigger audience, thus simply out into the air, with a melancholy in his quiet voice and with this resignation never heard before, the last of a prodigious number of dispatches to everybody: that they should not, if their weak powers permit them, be angry at him; you see, he has no radio, he never did have any. Nor does he know where the Russians are; maybe they'll come tomorrow, maybe never; they are in Pry or Tobolin or Kiev or Poltava or even much further away, perhaps they have in the meantime even been completely destroyed; he doesn't even know that for certain. The only thing he can say for certain is that they fought for Bezanika at such and such a time ago; where that certainty comes from is a story in itself that would be of no interest to anyone today; in any case, that's the truth. And that he could well imagine how disconcerting this confession must sound to their ears, thus once again his plea for indulgence; his intentions were the best, but his plans came to naught.

There was then a long silence in the room. To a certain extent a king had abdicated. Jacob tries in vain to discover movement in Kowalski's face. He looks right past Jacob and is sitting like a pillar of salt. Hardly had the last word died away when pangs of conscience overwhelm Jacob, not because of the announcement itself; that was necessarily due and permitted no postponement. But rather whether it could have been delivered with more consideration, possibly embedded in a withdrawal of the Russians; not to pass the entire burden all at once to other shoulders that aren't any broader than your own. Was Kowalski the proper man in whose presence the secret had to be brought to an end, Kowalski of all people? If he had heard it from a stranger, from someone not so close to Jacob, he certainly would have believed it a mistake or an ugly slander. After a night full of doubts he would have told you, "Do you know what those idiots have been saying? That you don't have a radio!" "That's true!" would have then been the answer. That, too, would have shocked him, but perhaps not so much because he would at least have considered that possibility the night before. And that might have even been possible to arrange somehow, just that way. Kowalski's luck to have come precisely this evening!

"You have nothing to say?" says Jacob.

"What should I say?"

Kowalski manages his smile from impenetrable depths; without this smile he wouldn't be Kowalski; even looks at Jacob again, to be sure with eyes that are smiling less than his mouth, but yet give no indication of the end of all hope, instead gaze cunningly, as if they saw, as always, once again behind the surface of things.

"What should I say, Jacob? I do understand you. I understand you very well. You know, I'm rather the opposite of a hussar. You know me long enough. If I had had a radio here, no one would have heard a word from me probably. Or, even more probably, I would have simply burned it because of fear. I have no illusions at all about that. To supply an entire ghetto with news! I never would have gone that far. You don't know who might be listening in. If I have ever understood anyone in my life, I understand you now."

Jacob never expected such a soaring of thoughts. Sly Kowalski outdid himself, even applying his calculations to where there wasn't anything to calculate. How can you convince him that at least now you are telling the truth; you can at least invite him to rummage through all the nooks in the room and the cellar. But to assert, with the palms of your hands turned out, "When have I ever lied to you?" you can no longer do. And if you, in fact, challenge him to search, all the radios you find in my place, Kowalski, are yours, he will wink at you knowingly and reply something similar to, "Let's stop the kidding, Jacob; we've known each other forty years, haven't we?" He will make it clear to you that every hide-and-seek is superfluous; the impossible can not be proved by any method. Jacob says, frightened, "You don't believe me?"

"Believe, not believe, what does that mean," says Kowalski quietly and more absent-mindedly than expected, in a similar tone of voice as Jacob during his little speech to everyone. He says nothing else for the time being; his fingers drum a solemn motif upon the table and he holds his head leaned far back, deep in hidden thoughts.

Jacob considers further rationalizations. He is concerned that his condemnation be moderate, thus the reasons for his venture must be known as well as the reasons for his sudden cessation. But he himself isn't yet clear about them and because of that and because he understands that he isn't the only one involved (Kowalski is, too) he keeps quiet and postpones his plea for mitigating circumstances until a later time.

Now comes the sobering reflection that it's not at all a question of him. No one in the ghetto is so unimportant as he without a radio. Only his clientele are of importance, Kowalski in addition to many others. And they don't give a damn about rationalizations no matter how plausible they sound. They have other worries and not little ones either. They want to know, for example, how things are proceeding after Pry.

Kowalski ends his drumming and brooding; he stands up and lays his hand of friendship on Jacob's shoulder. He says, "No fear, old fellow, you can be sure of me. I won't ask you any more questions."

He walks to the door, reviving his smile anew; before he opens it, he turns around once more, and actually blinks both eyes.

"And I'm not angry at you."

And leaves.

The next morning after the most sleepless night in a long time, Jacob is on his way to work. Before he stepped outside, he surreptitiously tried Kirschbaum's door handle—he didn't know why himself—but the door was locked. Horowitz, the neighbor, caught him by surprise at the uninformative keyhole and asked, "Are you looking for anything in particular?"

Of course, Jacob wasn't looking for anything in particular, just in general; human curiosity. He explained himself quickly to Horowitz and left. Then there was the colorful spot in front of the house on the street where the small German truck had stood yesterday. A few drops of oil had dripped from it and were glittering now in all possible colors like thin threads upon the seeping remains of a reservoir that Siegfried and Rafael had created together there, at first down the legs of their trousers and then after their private source had dried up, with the help of a water pail. They had gotten to work right after Elisa Kirschbaum's departure; because of the sparse auto traffic, such an opportunity does not present itself every day. Jacob was standing by the window and watching them, along with Lena who was horrified at their filthy action.

But to return to Jacob on the way to work. Even from afar Jacob sees a large gathering of people at a street corner right in front of the house where Kowalski lives. Jacob's first thought: he assumes Kowalski is in the middle of the crowd. His best friend had gone out on the street for sure and, as is his nature, wasn't able to hold his tongue. Either he in his nocturnal musings had arrived at the conviction that he had been told the truth, or, as is more likely with Kowalski, he still doesn't believe, but rather acts outwardly as if he did, since true friendship means sticking together. Came outside and in a jiffy frightened the Jews to death with the bad news because he absolutely must be the first whether in hell or heaven, Kowalski up front! Thereby cutting off all your avenues of retreat which, after lengthy consideration, you surely didn't wish to take. But what's that to Kowalski?

Jacob is tempted to turn around, he relates, and take a little detour. Even that would be difficult enough. At the railroad station they'll torment him plenty yet. Let Kowalski stand his ground by himself here. That's his business, a convenient opportunity not to stick your own two cents in. Then Jacob notices, even at some distance from the crowd, that the people are hardly talking; apparently they had been disturbed by the presumed news. Most of them are standing around speechless and stunned, as becomes evident upon approaching. Several are looking up. To an opened window at which there is nothing special at first sight, simply empty and open. Jacob doesn't precisely know whether it is Kowalski's window or the one beside it. Upon second glance he sees what is so special: a short piece of rope on the window bar about finger length, therefore perceived so late.

Jacob rushes through the crowd into the house. He attempts two steps at a time, but only the first two are achieved in that manner. Forunately, Kowalski lives on the second floor. The door like the window is open, therefore it is draughty. Kowalski's three roommates, one of whom we have arbitrarily christened Abraham, are no longer at home. Only Kowalski is at home and two complete strangers in the room who were the first passersby to see him hanging. They had cut him down and laid him on the bed. Now they are standing around helplessly and don't know what else to do. One of them asks Jacob, "Did you know him?"

"What?" asks Jacob at the bed.

"Did you know him?"

"Yes," says Jacob.

When he turns around after a while, he is alone. They had closed the door. Jacob goes to the window and looks down upon the street. No more crowd of people, just passersby. He wants to close the window but it sticks. He must first untie the double-knotted rope from the frame. Then he draws the curtain. The muted light makes Kowalski's face more bearable. He moves a chair over; he prefers not to sit down on the bed; he sits for an indefinite amount of time. I say indefinite because he is unable to give any particulars afterward on the length of his stay.

The sight of dead people is anything but unfamiliar to Jacob. He often has to walk over someone lying on the sidewalk dead of starvation and not yet disposed of by the sanitation squad. But Kowalski is not just anyone, good God, no! Kowalski is Kowalski. A confession led to his death, moreover one that he pretended not to believe. Oh, why didn't you, madman, stay last evening? We could have talked over everything calmly and given ourselves the bit of courage to go on living. What hadn't we given each other till now, real or not; if it is successful, no one will ask later why and how. Why did you have to play the poker player on your last evening? We could have mutually helped each other, but only you knew how both of us felt; you hid yourself from your friend Jacob Heym; you showed me your false face and yet we could have lived on, Kowalski; it shouldn't happen because of us.

Barber by profession, stashed away a bit of money, as we know, intending afterward to do something else, but would have continued to remain a barber, presumably, was equipped with this and that doubtful quality, was distrustful, eccentric, gauche, garrulous, oversmart; when everything is added up in the Everafter, then, suddenly worthy: had saved Jacob once from a horrible situation, from a German toilet, subscribed to the *Völkischer Landbote* for business reasons, was capable at times of eating seven large potato pancakes in a row, but couldn't digest any ice cream, borrowed preferably to repaying, wanted to act calculatedly but wasn't so at all, with one exception.

As would be expected, self-reproaches race through Jacob's mind; he had Kowalski on his conscience; he and his trivial weariness were to blame for Kowalski's resorting to the rope; what you once start, you must then finish; you must assess your own strengths beforehand. I interrupted Jacob. I told him at this point, "You're talking nonsense. You didn't overestimate your own strengths, since you couldn't know it would last so long." And I said to him, "You are not to blame for Kowalski's death; rather, he had you to thank that he lived to that day." "Yes, yes," Jacob answered me, "but what good is all that."

Finally Jacob gets up. He opens the curtain again, leaves the door wide open when he goes away so that one of the neighbors would notice the incident whenever he returns from work and take the necessary measures. For the railroad station it is much too late. He can hardly tell the guard at the gate he had been detained on the way. His lunch is irrevocably forfeited. Jacob goes home with the single hope that Kowalski had kept his reasons to himself, that he had been discreet this one time by way of exception. Because Jacob had again found his radio.

A thousand times Jacob can find again, report, invent battles, and circulate rumors. One thing he can not prevent. The story is approaching its vile ending authentically. That is, it has two endings. Really only one, of course: the one experienced by Jacob and all of us. But for me it has yet another. In all modesty, I know an ending at which you would grow pale from envy, not a particularly happy one, a bit at Jacob's expense, however incomparably better than the real ending. I have fabricated it over the course of years. I said to myself, it's really a crying shame that such a beautiful story should come so wretchedly to nothing. Invent an ending for it that can be halfway satisfying, one that is logical. A proper ending will atone for some of its shortcomings. Besides, all of them have earned a better end, not just Jacob. That will be your justification in case you need one, I told myself, and, therefore, made the effort, successfully, I think. But then I had strong second thoughts regarding its veracity. In comparison, it sounded simply too beautiful. I wondered whether it would go if you hung the splendid peacock tail upon some sad animal just out of love. Or whether you would not thereby deform it. But then I found that the comparison was lame. However, I've never made up my mind about it. And now here I am with my two endings and don't know which one to tell: mine, or the horrible one. Until it occurs to me to reject both of them, not perhaps because of a deficient ability to make a decision, but rather because I think that in this way we will both receive our due: on the one hand, the story independent of me and, on the other hand, I and my effort that I would not want to have made in vain.

Therefore, first an ending that never happened.

Kowalski can celebrate a resurrection. Window bar and rope are not vouchsafed any look by him since Jacob forgoes his confession. They are chatting on that particular evening about unimportant trifles although Jacob's mind is somewhere else. However, Kowalski need not notice anything of that. Not until later when he is alone again does Jacob realize that it exceeds his diminishing powers to continue with his radio lies for an indefinite period of time. Nevertheless, the true state of affairs is not to become public. Jacob envisions what consequences that would have. For example, he would fear that the rash of suicides, fortunately interrupted for a time, would begin again and grow to immense proportions.

The following nights that are free because of the elimination of all self-reproaches over Kowalski's death, those nights Jacob spends searching for a final credible lie. It must explain why the radio stopped playing; he must be rid of this worst of all plagues, but he can not come up with the lie; it proves harder to find than all those up to now.

I can imagine for a moment Jacob would have hit upon

the simple idea of asserting that his radio was stolen. Lots of things are stolen in the ghetto, why not a radio too? Objects of lesser value and use have been missing. I can imagine a whole ghetto looking for the unscrupulous thief, people looking each other in the eyes checking, visits serving only as a pretext for inspection. In the evenings everyone listens at his neighbor's door; perhaps he just tuned in to London; perhaps *he* is that mean person; didn't *he* always have something peculiar in his look, which your inner voice warned you about? One thing is incomprehensible. What advantage does the thief get from his crime? None. He won't find out anything more than he would have heard anyway from Jacob or one of his followers; only the others are groping in the dark. Where's the sense? How else can his motives be explained except as those of a thoroughly low type person? I can further imagine the search for the thief taking on alarming dimensions: that a kind of illegal emergency committee is formed to comb house by house after working hours. And let's assume among the several thousand inhabitants there is another person like Felix Frankfurter, only a single one, who is also keeping a radio hidden, and, in contrast to Frankfurter, hasn't destroyed it.

I'm quite aware that this individual would be very problematic for the entire story, since either he, like Frankfurter, never listened to it because of fear, or he did listen and must therefore know that Jacob's daily reports were nothing but lies, with the exception of the battle for Bezanika. And, in addition, kept quiet about it the whole time. As improbable as each of these two possibilities may be, let us take the one of your choice just three sentences further since that man is to a certain extent only a whim, a fleeting frivolity. The radio is found in his place during the search. In anger he is beaten to death—some frivolity! Or he is not beaten to death—that doesn't change anything.

The radio is returned to Jacob, its legal owner. The mental image of the look on his face makes my entire brainstorm worthwhile. Then matters will again take their normal course. Jacob will listen and report. For days they will talk about the disgraceful incident—how could a single individual act so vilely, for no reason in the world!

But enough of that. Jacob does not hit upon the idea of the theft neither in the real ending, which amazes me, nor in my ending. In mine, he torments himself in vain. He simply can not manage to rid himself of the radio, whereupon he resolves to get rid of the Jews. He will no longer accept any visitors, doesn't open his door; at the railroad station he secludes himself; he spoons up his lunch near the German stone guardhouse, where he can not be asked anything. And immediately after work is over, he disappears like a ghost. He puts up with detours in order to avoid those impatiently waiting for him. Now and then he is intercepted, however, despite all his caution; then he is asked what is the matter with him so suddenly, why doesn't he reveal anymore.

"There is nothing new," he says then. "Whenever there is anything new, I'll be sure to tell you."

Or even more effectively, he says: "It has become too dangerous for me; I don't want to risk anything more such a short time before it's over. Please, do me a big favor and don't ask me any more."

He doesn't make himself particularly popular by that. Very few have any understanding for his situation. The great man of yesterday is rapidly sinking in their estimation. They are calling him a coward, and a shithead also, because he obstinately refuses to give the radio to anyone else who is not so lily-livered. They soon look at him in a way that is frightening. They whisper behind his back what is better not heard. But Jacob will not change his mind. Let them think him the bad guy. In their place he would think exactly the same. Let them take every occasion to convey to him what contempt means. Everything is better than telling them the truth.

However, he is not completely abandoned by those well disposed to him. I can conceive of Kowalski and Misha sticking by him. Misha continues hauling crates with him. Kowalski asks sometimes, although less often than before, "Well, what's up, old pal? At least to me you can give a little hint, can't you? No one need notice anything."

Jacob turns him down every time even risking losing his oldest friend. He doesn't lose him. Kowalski proves to be a staunch friend.

One day Misha says, "Jacob, I'm sorry, but they're talking about taking away your radio."

"Taking away?"

"Yes," says Misha seriously. "By force."

Jacob looks over at the others. This one and that one are prepared for violence. Jacob doesn't want to know who they are.

"Can't you prevent them from that?" he asks.

"How?" asks Misha. "I'd gladly do so. But can you tell me how?"

"Tell them I have hidden it so well that they will not possibly find it," says Jacob.

"I'll do so," says Misha.

At home Jacob strictly forbids Lena to enter his room while he is away. Just to be sure, he no longer leaves the key in the hole in the wall behind the doorframe, not for Lena nor for anyone else. As much as possible, she is to stay in her attic and keep quiet. To counteract her boredom upstairs, he gives her the book on Africa. She can learn to read from it; she'll get more out of that than hanging around doing nothing.

The following days will be a strenuous test for Jacob's jangled nerves. Hands in his lap, he must keep quiet and wait for liberators and burglars, uncertain with both as to whether they will come or not. Misha says he has no idea whether the other side might have changed its mind, because since his sympathy for Jacob had been noted, despite everything that has happened since he offered his services as an intermediary, he has been excluded from the deliberations. Even more, a piece of the general contempt has also fallen upon him. The same goes for Kowalski.

I myself hadn't given any thought as to my role in this matter, on which side I was, whether as friend or foe to Jacob. But knowing myself, if I consider how much the constant information meant to me, I would be his enemy, one of his worst even. Let's assume I, having made up my mind, not to be confused by all the talk, would argue for taking away his radio today rather than tomorrow. Many share my view, but Jews who think otherwise also have their say, for example, those who from the start had considered the radio a danger. Basically, they are happy about Jacob's change of mind. They say, "Don't make such a big fuss out of it. If the Russians come at all, they'll come in any case."

And then again others say, "Let's wait a bit. Maybe Heym will come to his senses on his own. We have to give him a little time."

At any rate, the burglary doesn't take place, not in my ending.

These wretched days become a challenge to Jacob's nerves in another way, too. He will have to realize some time that he has remained loyal to an almost old habit of his: he has once again overestimated his powers. He was convinced that the wave of animosity, which had to be reckoned with, would not bother him much; he would be able to survive it all right. He gave himself courage with the thought that he had practice in such things. All those years in the café had been, in the final analysis, hardly anything but a struggle of one against all. That was a frivolous fallacy. The period since Bezanika had not been taken into consideration, during which Jacob had been showered with good will, affection, and respect, with signs of absolute necessity to which you become accustomed ridiculously quickly. And now the exact opposite, after ten days at best, that afore-mentioned wave of animosity threatens to crash over his head. The cold shoulders become unbearable.

Lena notices changes in Jacob and doesn't know what to make of them. She keeps obediently to his instructions, staying in the attic and consequently hearing nothing about the entire matter. She only observes that whenever Jacob is with her he is lost in joyless thoughts, hardly speaking a word anymore, not even responding to her progress when she reads him aloud an entire sentence from her book on Africa, without help. Whenever she sits down in his lap, she is sitting there as if in a chair; just a short while ago, he used to invite her gladly to sit down on his knees. Now he seems not to notice her at all. Whenever she asks him for a story, he says he doesn't know any more and puts her off for a later time until he recalls one again. Lena asks, "Have you been bothered about anything?"

"Bothered? Why bothered?"

"Because you're so strange."

"I'm strange?" says Jacob and can not muster the energy to resist the unjust severity in his voice. "Mind your own business and leave me alone."

Lena remains alone and has very little business to mind, only Jacob to whom incomprehensible things must have happened.

On an important evening in my ending, shortly after the first of the month, because ration cards are always distributed then, Jacob knocks on Misha's door. It takes a good while until it is opened, cautiously. Amazed, Misha says, "Jacob?"

Jacob enters the room. First off he says, "If you want to

hide her, you shouldn't leave two cups standing on the table, you idiot."

"That's true," says Misha.

He goes to the clothes closet and lets Rosa out. Rosa and Jacob are standing facing each other, speechless, for such a long time that Misha feels embarrassed by the situation.

"Do you know each other?" he asks.

"We once saw each other fleetingly," says Jacob.

"Do sit down," Rosa says friendly and quickly before Misha asks about that one time. Jacob sits down and looks for a beginning, because he didn't come just like that. His concern is of weighty consequence.

"Why am I here?" he asks. "I want to ask you for a favor, and if you decline I can understand it very well. I just didn't think of anyone else to whom I could have gone with this."

"Then speak," says Misha.

"The situation is that I have been feeling wretchedly bad recently, my health, I mean. I'm no longer so young; my heart hasn't been in the best shape and my back and constant headaches, rather suddenly and too much all at once."

Misha can not yet understand what kind of favor is involved. He says, "That's bad."

"Not so very bad. It will pass. But until then, Misha, I wanted to ask you, if you couldn't take Lena in with you."

In the general helplessness there is a pause while Jacob looks at no one. He apparently expects a bit too much from the young man. Two illegal females in his apartment; but he did say right away that he wouldn't be angry at a rejection of his request.

"Well, you know," says Misha slowly, with clear intention.

"Of course, you can bring Lena to us," says Rosa and looks at Misha reproachfully.

"I would never have come to you with that, if you had been alone," says Jacob to the unhappy Misha. "But because Fräulein Frankfurter is here anyway all day, and Lena is always alone, too . . ."

"I'm already looking forward to her," says Rosa.

"And what do you say?"

"He's happy, too," says Rosa.

Misha waits yet until his face has changed its expression. That he is not particularly happy, everyone knows. He says, "O.K. Bring her here."

Relieved, Jacob puts her ration card on the table, untouched except for one coupon; Misha should no longer fear that he would request free board, too, complete room and board.

"When can I bring her over?"

"When did you want to?"

"Tomorrow evening?"

Misha accompanies him, although Jacob insists it would be absolutely unnecessary, the few steps to the outside. When Jacob extends his hand good-by, Misha holds it a moment longer than necessary and Jacob discovers in his blue eyes an important question. Misha is absolutely right, Jacob feels. One act of friendship deserves another, especially when it is sought out so modestly.

"You want to hear how things are going?" he asks.

"If you don't mind," says Misha.

Jacob lets him in on the secret that Pry has in the meantime been captured but that the Germans have dug in half way toward Mieloworno, which will result in protracted fighting, it seems; however, the first breakthroughs have taken place, giving rise for hope. He asks Misha to keep the news to himself, otherwise there would only be endless questioning at the railroad station as to why one is informed and not all the others. Misha promises, of course, in the hope of further news now and then, as I understand his tactics.

The next evening Lena moves. Jacob had given her the same reason as Misha; a separation only for several days and Lena calmly accepted it. She is, after all, fond of Misha, almost even a secret love, and he is fond of her, too, presumably. It's just that this Rosa rubs her the wrong way, because of her visit that time and the reproaches, with her there could be unpleasantness. But Jacob assures her, even on the way over, that Rosa will be a very compatible person, cooperative and kind, that she had told him just last night how much she was looking forward to Lena. It would be best not to mention a single word about that silly visit recently.

"You are a big girl already; don't be a disgrace to me."

After Jacob dropped Lena off, he immediately goes home, ostensibly to lie down. For a long while he sits in his dark room and considers whether his plan, for whose sake Lena had to leave, is defensible. He doesn't want to have to reproach himself later, in case there were to be any occasion to. Too often lately had he made the wrong decisions. To let the Russians advance almost within sight had been a mistake; his cessation of news reports had been a mistake; the radio itself had been his first and biggest mistake; it seems to him too many mistakes for a single man. The possibility still remains of undoing several of them or of falling anew into the same old rut. In three or four days he would feel better again. This kind of illness can be cured at will, then he could take Lena back; at the railroad station he could play the role of one who had mended his ways and continue providing the curious with news, both good and bad. But where would that lead to, Jacob wonders.

After about two hours, I think, Jacob had made up his mind. He drapes the blanket over the window, opens the light, takes a knife, takes off his jacket, and removes the yellow stars from front and back. He does it very carefully, also plucking out the white threads so that they do not reveal the notorious spots afterward. When that is done, Jacob puts on the jacket, seeming unaccustomedly naked now. His eyes search the room for objects that can possibly be of use for his venture; there is, of course, the pliers, which he puts in his pocket. Nothing else strikes his eye. He closes the light and looks out the window one last time on the black and deserted street. It is long past eight and curfew, probably even midnight. In the distance he could recognize his searchlight, I guess, passing aimlessly over the roof tops, bent upon its duty.

Because my caprice has no limits, I am letting it be a cool, starry night. It not only sounds pleasant, but also comes in handy for my ending, you'll see! Thus, Jacob walks along the street without his own stars and long after eight. That is, he slinks along close to the walls of the houses, trying to look like a shadow. By no means does he intend to lose his life. One street and another and another. They all have in common that they are on the shortest route to the boundary.

Finally the boundary. I have selected the most favorable spot imaginable for Jacob: the old vegetable market, a small, paved square across which barbed wire is strung. The real escape attempts succeeded or failed almost always at this spot. At the right edge of the square stands the watchtower, without a searchlight. The guard up there doesn't stir while Jacob is observing him from the entrance of a house on the furthest left side. The distance may come to 150 meters. Along the entire barbed wire encircling the ghetto without a break there is no other spot so far from a tower. Only here did they leave so much space because of economy, or because of a commanding view.

In the tower it is as quiet as in a monument so that Jacob is beginning to hope the guard had fallen asleep. Jacob looks up to the sky, bides his time until one of the sparse clouds moves in front of the obstructive moon. It finally does him a favor. Jacob takes his pliers out of his pocket and dashes out.

Let us take a short break at this intensely dramatic moment of my ending so that I may have the opportunity to confess that I can not provide the reason for Jacob's sudden flight. Or better, I won't make it so easy for myself by asserting, "He just simply wants to flee in my ending, that's all!" I'm certainly in a position to give several reasons, all of which I consider conceivable. I just don't know which particular one to decide upon. For example, Jacob had given up all hope that the ghetto would be liberated as long as Jews were still there and consequently wants to save his own hide. Or, he is fleeing from his own people, from their snares and animosity, from their curiosity, too, an attempt to find safety from his radio and its consequences. Or a third reason, the most honorable one for Jacob: he has the bold intention of returning to the ghetto during the next night. He only wants to leave to get useful information that he could then put into his radio's mouth.

Those would be the most important reasons, none of them to be rejected, as you must concede, but I don't have the courage to commit Jacob to any one of them. So I'm offering them as a selection. Let each person select the one he considers the most valid according to his own experiences. Perhaps some will even think of more evident reasons. I would only suggest that most of the important things that ever happened had more than just one reason.

Unnoticed, Jacob reaches the barbed wire under cover of the cloud. He lies down flat upon the ground. The simple plan is to crawl through under the barrier which is, of course, easier planned than done. The lowest of the many wires is located only ten centimeters above the ground, but that had been expected, hence the pliers, just in case. It is now put into action, working nimbly away at the thin wire which will not be able to resist for long and which snaps quicker than expected. But the accompanying noise—for it is tautly strung—this horrible singing Jacob imagines is capable of waking up an entire city from its sleep. He holds his breath and listens, filled with fear, but everything remains calm as the dead. Only it is getting gradually brighter, since no cloud lasts forever. The next wire is ten centimeters higher, that is, twenty above the ground. Jacob ponders: to crawl through would entail a certain amount of danger for body and clothing. He is certainly much thinner than before but nonetheless a grown man. On the other hand, he would not want to risk breaking the silence again by making the second wire ring. It would not be one jot quieter than the first and a third alternative is by no means available.

Jacob is still lying undecided, carefully plucking away at the wire to see if it might be loosened, thereby muffling its noise, when the pliers severs it, thus causing his decision to be made by a higher authority. I said right away that my ending would be a bit at Jacob's expense. A noisy burst from a machine gun disturbs the tranquility of the night. Our guard was not sleeping so very soundly. And there is nothing more to ponder; and Jacob is dead and finished with all his troubles.

But that's not sufficient, what sort of an ending would that be? Imagine further that the ghetto has been in a turmoil for a long while. Imagine the vengeance for Jacob, for according to my wishes this is the cool and starry night when the Russians arrive. The Red Army was to have succeeded in encircling the town in quick order. The sky lights up from the firing of the heavy guns. Right after the salvo that killed Jacob, a deafening thunder begins, as if it had come mistakenly from the unfortunate sharpshooter in the watchtower. The first ghostlike tanks advance in the district, the watchtowers burn, dogged Germans fighting to the last shot, or fleeing Germans finding no hole to hide in— my God, what a night that would have been! And at their windows Jews weeping, for whom everything comes so suddenly that they can only stand around incredulous, holding each other's hands, who would like so very much to rejoice for their lives and are unable to. Plenty of opportunity for that later. I can picture to myself the last battles ending at dawn. The ghetto is no longer a ghetto but only the most dilapidated section of town. Everyone may go wherever he pleases.

I picture: Misha thinking that Jacob will surely feel much better now, wanting to bring Lena back to him and not finding him home. How good the bread tastes that is handed out to us abundantly. What happens to the poor Germans whom we get our hands on. All that and more is not important enough to take up room in my ending. Only one thing is important to me.

Several Jews leave the ghetto via the old vegetable market. They see a man lying there without stars, pliers still clenched in his right hand, beneath the barbed wire with one strand snapped, obviously surprised while attempting to flee. They turn him on his back; who is this unfortunate man, they ask, and someone nearby knows Jacob. Kowalski, most preferably, or even a neighbor, or I, or it could be someone else from the railroad station; in any case, someone who knows him, except Lena. This person stares at Jacob's face in horror. Maybe the first good news from Jacob had got to him on that day when Jacob resolved to save the remainder of his life for himself. He mumbles to himself quietly words of incomprehension. They ask him, "What are you saying about 'incomprehensible'? The poor fellow wanted to flee because he didn't know it would be over so quickly. What's so incomprehensible about it?"

And the individual who chokes up undertakes the hopeless attempt to explain what to him will forever remain inexplicable.

"But that's Jacob Heym," he says. "Do you understand? That's Jacob Heym. Why did he want to flee? He must have become unhinged. He knew for certain that they were coming. He had a radio. . . ."

He says something like that and shaking his head in disbelief goes with the others to freedom. And something like that would be my ending.

But after the invented story, now at last the pale-cheeked and unpleasant one, the real and unimaginative ending whereby you are easily pushed to the silly question: What's the purpose of all that?

Kowalski is irrevocably dead and, for the time being, Jacob lives on, giving no thought to fobbing Lena off on strangers, nor does he denude his jacket of the prescribed stars. His pliers, assuming he even owns any, are left in the drawer. Nor does he induce any guard at the old vegetable market on a cool, starry night to fire upon him, setting off such a mighty echo. He missed work on that day; we know why. His hanged friend is going through his mind. But he must disappear before the next morning. Under urgent consideration, Jacob was able to convince himself with his own eyes what the closing down of the radio leads to. Maybe it doesn't take such radical forms with everyone, but certainly with some individuals and, therefore, nothing changes regarding the radio. Mourning for Kowalski, who is suddenly missed more than he had ever been sought after while he was alive, must wait patiently on the long waiting bench. Instead, the little news factory that nourished its man with so much difficulty begins working, for tomorrow like every day there will be questioning again. Life drags on in spite of everything.

Then this next morning Jacob passes Kowalski's house with lips puckered, his glance rigidly fixed upon a saving point at the end of the street. It is well known how hopeless every attempt to suppress any thought of something special must turn out. Jacob sees him lying there as vividly as if he were in the room itself, untying once again the remainder of the rope from the window frame, pulling up the chair because he didn't want to sit down on the bed. Needlessly, he still hears the conclusion, or the start, of a conversation.

"In that house there."

"Number 14?"

"No, Number 16. The corner house."

"Do they already know who?"

"Unknown. A certain Kaminski or something like it."

Even a distance from the railroad station Jacob realizes that something unusual must have happened. The able-bodied Jews are crowded around the entrance because the gate is locked. Why they are not being permitted in is at first puzzling to him, puzzling, too, why the first person who discovers him points to him, says something while the others turn their faces to him. Fifty, sixty men had waited for Jacob, I among them. We see the only person who can still stand between us and misfortune, we hope, coming toward us hesitatingly and puzzled. We make room for him, forming a narrow lane so that he can walk unobstructed to the gate and read what is posted there and then tell us that everything is only half as bad. Beside me, Schmidt, the lawyer, shuffling from one foot to the other, I hear him whispering to himself, "Well, hurry it up!" Because Jacob is walking so provokingly slowly and looking into the men's eyes instead of coming forward.

Exactly at the start of work Jacob arrives in front of the locked gate of the railroad station and reads the announcement posted there: that all of us, at exactly one P.M., are to assemble on the square in front of the precinct station, five kilograms of baggage per person, apartments are to be left unlocked and in clean condition; whoever is found in his house after the prescribed time . . . ; the same for the bed-ridden and the infirm; further information at one P.M. at the aforementioned place.

And now go and console them further; wherever you may get, it is your business; make them believe that everything is just a bad joke, that in reality it will be a mystery trip full of many nice surprises; they are really waiting for something like that impatiently, in secret. No reason for concern, brothers, they want to hear, go ahead and pay no mind to that scrap of paper; whoever is curious can even come at one o'clock to the precinct station, by all means if he has nothing better to do. Nohing can happen in any case, because—you don't even know yet; I have, stupidly, forgotten completely to tell you—the Russians are waiting behind the next corner, keeping watch that not the slightest harm will be done to you.

To us it seems as if Jacob had memorized his few lines since he has been standing motionless in front of the poster. Why is he standing so long, we wonder silently and have a presentiment of evil; what will his face look like when he shows it to us again, and what will he say; he must say something. I see, too, that the first ones are quietly leaving the ranks. I know anxiously that they are precisely right; there is nothing more to expect here; nonetheless, I continue to hope and do not move from the spot, just like most.

It isn't worth it. Jacob turns around after what seems an eternity, shows us two vacant eyes; and at that same moment even the most stupid man realizes, too, that all the potential blessedness is lost. Jacob tells me he doesn't have the time for personal horror concerning the course of things. The others' horror crowds it out. They look at him like duped believers, at someone whose day has come to redeem at last the pledges given out so loosely. He stands a long time not daring to look up, nor do they make it any easier for him, as, for example, by disappearing. For the five kilograms of baggage to be selected there remains plenty of time, the entire rest of your life, so to speak. The little lane that opened up for Jacob on his way to the gate closed up behind him. Now he is standing in a tight semicircle, like a clown who had forgotten his lines at the decisive moment, as Jacob himself later formulated it.

"Don't you have anything better to do than to stand around gaping with your mouths open?" asks a guard behind the fence.

Only then do we notice him for the first time. He is standing several meters away from the gate and he alone knows for how long. In any case, he didn't hear much, although everything important has already been said. We move at last from the spot; why provoke him unnecessarily; we disperse silently. The guard shakes his head, amused at these strange creatures. Jacob is almost grateful to him for his unintentional help.

Having arrived home, Jacob immediately goes to the attic. He expects to see Lena still in bed, but she isn't even in the room any more. Moreover, the weather is by no means the nicest; only a few blue patches are showing in the sky. Jacob may be thinking that his instructions are not being taken all too seriously. Her bed is neatly made, the piece of bread gone from the plate upon her bureau; right after he had said good-by to her in the morning, she probably got up and hurried off to some ventures that you never find out about. Jacob decides not to look for her until later; first to pack her things, then his; and when that is done, Lena will still be found. He is not concerned as to whether the notice at the gate is meant only for those who work at the railroad station or for all ghetto residents. He has no other choice but to take her along. To leave Lena behind would mean to hope for a not uncertain fate for her; that is easy to see.

The prescribed maximum amount of baggage proves to be quite liberal. Her total amount of usable things hardly comes to more than a handful. Jacob stuffs underclothing, stockings, and scarf in his pockets. While he is folding her winter dress, Lena appears. She is holding a little piece of bread. Jacob's presence surprises her very much. But his disapproving eyes immediately strike her so that she immediately interprets correctly he will be angry, because she had left the attic contrary to his wishes.

"I was only at the pump. I was thirsty," she explains.

"Fine," says Jacob.

He finishes with the dress and gives it to her to hold,

then he looks around, opens the doors to her bureau again to see if anything had been forgotten.

"Am I going to live downstairs with you now?" asks Lena.

"Come," he says.

They go to his room. On the stairway they meet their neighbor, Horowitz, who presumably is coming from the cellar, struggling with a big, leather suitcase whose locks do not hold the lid shut.

"What do you think about it?" ask Horowitz.

"Guess," says Jacob.

Only now does he know with certainty that the order on the railroad station gate includes everyone, the foolish question from Horowitz and the suitcase in his hand. At every factory entrance such a notice probably appeared overnight.

"Have you by chance heard where they're taking us?"

"No," says Jacob.

He hurries with Lena to his room before he can become involved in longer disputes. At best he would still be inclined to find out what the unattached Horowitz expected to do with the gigantic suitcase. On his notice there was surely nothing about two hundred kilograms per person.

When the door is locked behind them, Lena reveals that she can not stand Horowitz. She always makes a special effort to avoid him because he is constantly admonishing her, like: not to hang around idly, to say hello to her elders, not to look so snippy, to stop making so much noise—some remarks or other always! He had even given her arm a good shaking once because she had slid down the banister and landed at his feet. Jacob says, "He did?"

After he has taken Lena's things out of his pockets and laid them on the table, he begins packing. That is, first the choice must be made between suitcase or rucksack; there would be ample room in either. For its convenience he decides upon the rucksack, since for an uncertain long trip during which one hand must constantly be at the disposal of Lena, a suitcase could become a torture.

Lena, patient for a good while, hopes that Jacob will explain to her his strange preoccupation on his own, but he says only now and then, give me that and hold this, but nothing to satisfy her curiosity. Therefore she must ask, "Why are you packing everything?"

"Well, what do you pack things for?"

"I don't know," she says, emphasizing it by a vigorous shrugging of her shoulders, as we already know, her shoulders up to her ears.

"Then guess."

"Because we're going away?"

"Exactly that, you clever girl."

"We're going away?" Lena calls out as if to say, "And you didn't tell me till now?"

"Yes, we're taking a trip," says Jacob.

"Where to?"

"I don't know exactly."

"Far away or near?"

"I think rather far away."

"As far as America?"

"No."

"As China?"

"Neither."

"As far as Africa?"

Jacob knows from experience that she is capable of dragging out such a game for hours, so he says, "Yes, about as far as Africa."

She jumps around the room, can hardly contain her joy, while Jacob puts on a pleasant expression: the girl has, after all, never yet taken a trip. It will be especially difficult when she abruptly gives him a kiss and asks him why he, too, isn't happy.

"Because I don't like to travel."

"You'll see how nice it'll be."

He is finishing with the rucksack, two spoons on top, is about to tie it up when Lena puts her hand on his arm and says, "You forgot the book."

"What book?"

"The one on Africa."

"Oh, yes. Where is it?"

"Under my pillow. I'll get it quickly."

Lena runs out. Jacob hears her joyful voice in the corridor and up the stairs, "We're going on a trip! We're going on a trip. . . ." Only for joy, or, perhaps, even to annoy that surly Horowitz a bit, under Jacob's protection.

Then we're riding.

In the freight car it is very close and stifling. The Jews are squatting or sitting on the floor beside their five kilograms—at least thirty of them, I think. Sleeping at night, in case the trip lasts that long, will be a problem, for not everyone can stretch out at the same time. It will have to be done in shifts. It is dark, too. The few narrow peepholes right under the roof provide only meager light; besides, they are almost constantly occupied. Conversations hardly ever take place. Most look as if they were concerned about horribly important and serious matters; however, you could converse without being overheard amidst the rumbling of the rolling wheels and despite the constriction, if you desired to.

I'm sitting on a checked pillowcase containing all my things and am bored. Beside me a woman, old as the hills, is weeping, quietly, considerately. Her tears have long since run dry; nonetheless, every now and then she sniffs violently, as if entire rivers were being contained. And her husband, with whom she shares the suitcase, looks around each time apologetically, since it is embarrassing to him and he wants it understood that the matter is devoid of his influence.

To the left of me, to where my attention is of necessity directed, Jacob had obtained a peephole, but I can assure you that this proximity is purely coincidental. I didn't crowd in beside him. I do not go as far as some fools who accuse him of some sort of share in the blame for this trip; but I cannot deny that I feel an unjust resentment against him because all my hopes, built upon the bases provided by him, have collapsed. I did not crowd in beside him. I don't care whom I'm traveling with. It simply turned out that way. Looking through Jacob's legs I can spot Lena, whom I had known previously only through hearsay. She is sitting on the rucksack. Because of Lena I feel a bit more sympathetic to Jacob. I am thinking, who else would have burdened himself with a child; and I figure that carries at least as much weight as my disappointment.

I would gladly get to know her by means of eye-winking or making funny faces, but she doesn't even take any notice of me. She is gazing at the floor, daydreaming. Doubtlessly she is preoccupied with the kind of thoughts foreign to all the others, for she is smiling to herself at times. Or her lips form silent words, or she is puzzled, as if she weren't sure of her thoughts. It is fun looking at her. I find a pebble on the floor and flip it at her arm. She is startled out of her musings and looks around to see who could have done it, but not at me. Then she looks up at Jacob who, beyond any suspicion, is standing rigid at his peephole, his entire attention focused upon the passing landscape outside. She tugs at the calf of his leg.

"Do you remember the fairy tale?" asks Lena.

"Which one?"

"The one about the sick princess?"

"Yes."

"Is that true?"

It is clear from the look on his face, he finds it odd she is thinking about that now.

"Of course, it's true," he says.

"But Siegfried and Rafi didn't believe me. I told it exactly as you did. But they say there is no such thing in the whole world."

"What isn't there?"

"That you can get better if you get a wad of cotton."

Jacob bends over and lifts her up to the little window. I, too, stand up, because the wheels are making a good bit of noise and I would like to hear the rest.

"Isn't it true?" says Lena. "Didn't the princess want a wad of cotton as big as her pillow? And when she got it, didn't she get better again?"

I see Jacob's mouth getting wider. He says, "Not exactly. She wanted a cloud. The point is, she thought that clouds were made of cotton and only because of that was she happy with the cotton."

Lena stares outside a while, baffled I imagine, before she asks, "But aren't clouds made of cotton?"

Between their heads I can see a bit of the sky along with a few clouds, and I must admit, the similarity is, in fact, amazing. They do look like wads of cotton.

"Then what are clouds made of?" asks Lena.

But Jacob puts her off by promising her an answer at a later time, probably because she is getting too heavy for him. He puts her back on the rucksack and then continues watching the passing scene.

At this point, I consider the time ripe for me. I sit down, too, slide over closer to her, and ask her if she would like to hear what clouds are made of from me. Of course, she wants to and I proceed to tell her about rivers and lakes and the ocean, about the perpetual cycle of water, about the difficult-to-believe phenomenon of evaporation, how the water flows invisibly into the sky in little droplets, collecting there into clouds that later become as heavy and wet as sopping sponges until they again lose the drops in the form of rain. Nor do I omit the vapor as exemplified by trains and chimneys, all kinds of fires. She listens attentively to me, but skeptically. I know that the long complete story will not be exhausted in one lesson. I see, too, Jacob keeping his eye on me; perhaps, it is because of my instructional session that Jacob tells me several days later a much crazier story—to me, of all people! Because it is not written on my face that I will be one of the few survivors.

After my knowledge about the origin and composition of clouds is exhausted, I tell Lena not to hesitate to ask questions if she didn't understand something. But she takes no advantage of the offer. She props her head in her hands and ponders the matter once again, very calmly. After all, she has to get over a serious error: clouds are *not* made of cotton wads.

"You don't know what you're letting yourself in for," Jacob whispers in my ear.

"Why?"

"Because you have no idea what kinds of questions this child can ask."

I look at her and say, "It can't be all that bad."

His eyes answer "Just wait," then he asks me whether I'd like to stand at the peephole for a while.

"Gladly," I say.

I stand up expectantly and look out until night falls. I see villages and fields, even a little town once in the distance; at a half-overgrown pond I see a group of soldiers resting amid trucks, cannon, and cattle. And I see a few sleepy stations with their platforms and crossings and station houses with their green window boxes profuse with flowers. I wonder whether these window boxes are official regulation because they hang on every station house and are all green. And I see people who watch our train and whose faces I can not recognize. But, above all, I see trees that I had almost forgotten, although I'm still a young man, enormous numbers of trees, beech and alder and birch and willow and pine, my God, all the trees I see. The trees never end! It was because of a tree that I could never be a violinist, and under a tree I became a man for the first time, the wild boars came too late to prevent it. And at an unknown tree I lost my wife Chana and a regulation wanted to prohibit trees from me forever. Some say that trees are confusing my mind. I stand and stand; at times even today I take a ride in a train, especially in an area rich in trees; I prefer mixed woodland the most. Until I hear Jacob's voice, "Don't you want to go to sleep now?"

"Let me stand a little more yet," I say.

"But you don't see anything any more," I hear him saying.

"Yes I do."

Because I still see the shadows of trees, and I can't sleep. We're going. Wherever we go.